NOT IN
SOLITUDE

By KENNETH F. GANTZ
Lt. Colonel, United States Air Force (ret.)

I0541543

ARMCHAIR FICTION
PO Box 4369, Medford, Oregon 97504

*The original text of this novel was first
published by Ziff-Davis Publishing*

Copyright 2012 by Gregory J. Luce
All Rights Reserved

*For more information about Armchair Books and products, visit our
website at…*

www.armchairfiction.com

Or email us at…

armchairfiction@yahoo.com

MAROONED ON MARS

Young Dr. John Dane—a newspaperman and a physicist—was sure he would find plenty to report on the first trip to Mars with Colonel Cragg. But, in spite of Cragg's obvious contempt for Dane, the trip proved disappointingly dull until some of the scientists suddenly and mysteriously disappeared. From then on events rocketed to an explosive climax as it became increasingly clear that a hostile intelligence on Mars was trying to prevent the spacecraft's return to Earth.

NOT IN SOLITUDE is an exciting and plausible novel about the first Earthlings to arrive on Mars, by a man whose top-secret Air Force duties enabled him to write of outer-space travel with unusual perception. Kenneth Gantz was an editor of the Air Force's professional journal of strategy, tactics, and techniques, The Air University Quarterly Review, and was the editor of The United States Air Force Report on the Ballistic Missile.

CAST OF CHARACTERS

DR. JOHN DANE
He wasn't popular with the crew, being accused of murder—but how could he prove his innocence while locked in his quarters?

LT. BELOIT
Being stranded on Mars was surely a bad thing—but the idea of being watched by creatures unknown terrified him!

WERTZ
Volunteering for the search party was easy; returning from it proved to be more challenging than he imagined.

MAJOR NOEL
After assuming command, it was his job to ensure the safety of ship and crew—but he was losing more men every day.

COLONEL CRAGG
He was certain that five men had died because Dane ignored his direct orders, and true or not, Dane was going to pay!

DR. PEMBROKE
After being rescued, he just wasn't the same man. Something was very different—and very wrong.

LT. YUDIN
He got a phone call when they wanted a radar specialist for a tough assignment—and Mars might be his toughest yet!

CHAPTER ONE

How could you tell a man like Ames how it really was? The nothingness of it. How do you write endless sand and scrub into bulletins?

You radioed him copy about the red star and how it swelled into a blemished red moon, and then the vehicle reversed ends and the red moon vanished behind the decelerating rockets, until nearness bloated it into view again, out beyond the rim of the wide tail cone. You could have written that sitting at your typewriter in Houston. Ames could have had all that from the rewrites.

When the radio went out, you couldn't even tell him that there wasn't any story. Any Amalgamated beat of a story.

How would you make him realize it, face to face with him again in the Houston office? With the radio-typesetters and the babel wires held open all over the globe. What could you tell him about the way it actually was? He hadn't been there. Three billion people hadn't been there. How could they ever really know how different it was from their Earth-bound imaginings?

Ignoring his discarded footgear, Dane got up from the chart table and went light-bodied to the observation ports. The night already crowded black against the guard-lighted sand a hundred feet down below. Except in the east where the spark fires danced.

The last night in Houston. Luxury food. Drink spot for the nation's big-money men. "The story of the ages, you dog, you! Don't ever get to be managing editor and have to stay home and nurse the clients." The odd thing was that Ames really meant it. Like his brag that his mind differed only in skill from the millions of minds that read his client's newspapers.

What was the great story? The vastness of rusty desert? The primitive vegetation? No canals? Nothing but a flat world athirst? All those things were known with practical certainty before they left Earth. The static discharges over the lichen beds and a few confirmations and contradictions of minor scientific speculations weren't enough to show for a hundred million miles. That four men were missing and to be left behind for dead would be small change to Ames.

Maybe the real story was why they had come at all. But try to sell that one to Ames! Ames dealt in who, where, when, what, and how. You don't feed an international news service on why-stuff.

"Give me the challenge and the mystery!"

"Shock 'em and weep 'em and inspire 'em! In that order."

"A good bulletin is like a good poem. They don't read it. They feel it!"

"No journalism, please. Give me word pictures of human doings and human feelings. Readers want to see 'em doing and feel 'em feeling."

Those were the Ames' commandments. Placarded singly and in bilious combinations in Amalgamated Pressrooms all over the world.

Well, a likely space voyageur the great Amalgamated's John Dane had turned out to be. Four days on Mars, only four days of the tremendous adventure, and ready to go home. He felt his waist. Take off five or ten pounds after they got back. Ought to have done it before. Save up a little money and be shed of the Ames human-interest factory forever.

And God damn Colonel Cragg! But you couldn't talk to a man like Cragg about value as insignificant as that of human life. He was like an aging blond football player. Thick in the neck and thick in the head. With eyes that looked only straight to the front. Bull Cragg they called him in the United States Air Force. You might as well try to get him concerned about an unresolved chord as about a human matter outside his line of duty. He moved in larger orbits.

The flash bulletin out of Washington had not been unexpected at Amalgamated. WAR HERO TO COMMAND FIRST FLIGHT TO MARS! Cragg had his admirers in the Pentagon all right and his carefully tended contacts with influence even in higher places. To honor a popular figure, the War Chief had passed over not only Air General Cluett, commander of the first moon flight back in 2010, but even younger Air Force brilliants like Major Noel, the inventor of the sensational spectrum-beacon Automatic Interspatial Navigation Control. Before the rest of the make-ready was over, it was apparent that Cragg was personally committed not to a scientific expedition but to a military reconnaissance. So much for Dr. Pembroke, father of the idea and Director of Science for Expedition Mars. Director? Certainly. To the extent that suited Colonel Cragg.

Why stare out at the night? Light or dark, there was nothing to see but the crazy static discharges. Nothing anywhere but the lichens and the damned red dust the Far Venture sat on.

Dane was ready enough to go home all right. He could agree on that with the entire crew and the entire scientific party cooped up in the spacecraft. On that one thing, at least, he would agree even with Colonel Cragg—except for Dr. Pembroke. Even without the radiation.

The most Earth-like of the solar planets, a distinguished astrophysicist had pronounced it, yet structurally the opposite of Earth. A homogeneous sphere, he said, a nearly uniform mixture of silicate and metallic iron-nickel, with no core of iron like Earth. A physically alien world, more like the moon than the lush habitation that man calls home.

A monotonous sphere of reddish dust, the great astronomical observers had portrayed it, unrelieved except for eroded hills worn down by long-gone floods, flecked at the poles by a thin frost, stained widely by a green discoloration, possibly vegetative.

With an atmosphere as rare as Earth's at eleven miles high, with no detectable trace of free oxygen, a classic astrobiologist had written of it, one must concede that the vegetation apparently comprising the green areas is on the low order of the lichen or the liverwort, if indeed it should parallel in any way the growing things of Earth. But, he had summed up, life of such a disappointing level is not what men would seek when the time arrived for their first journey to their neighbors in space.

Yes and quite so. Neatly deduced and experimentally sound. But a man had to ride the decks of the Far Venture up the long slant to the splendid globe and see its particolors fade into a sky-filling dun and drab vastness, characterless and unwelcoming to man. Not till then was it completely torn from the heart that perhaps here might be a home of warm-blooded life and zest for living. Before the swooping exploratory encirclements had all been run and the spacecraft had settled on the nude red plain of Isidis Regio five miles west of the vast Syrtis Major lichen beds, Dane had known that one man, at least, doubted the adventure.

He fell into the springed fencer's squat, enjoying the limber power of his thighs as he rocked up and down. He took a couple of forward crabwise steps, then back, then forward, and scowled at his spectacled reflection in the glassite of the darkened port, before he remembered he was not alone. "Keep the legs in shape." He turned around. "In case we have to walk back." He was annoyed with himself for explaining.

Airman First Class Humphries nodded doubtfully. "Not much room to move around up here." He nodded again, demonstrating the compactness of the equipment-laden, igloo-shaped observation deck.

"You going to take some more pictures up here before we take off?" he asked.

Humphries was a small-talker. "The equipment is making them now," Dane answered shortly. "Two a minute." He went to the photo plane table and pretended to check the smoothly clicking recording camera.

Humphries said, "I don't mean them. You going to take any more newspaper pictures up here, I wish you'd be a good guy and get me in on one and get it printed in the papers when we get back."

"I'll tell you what," Dane said, "maybe tomorrow I'll get a chance to shoot you." He slid onto the high stool at the photo plane table and fiddled with his slide rule.

"I got a girl in Richmond I can use a little help with."

Dane let him ramble, the roly-poly face screwed ajar over tenuous love links. Dane was as fidgety as a shut-up cat himself. He stared distastefully at the big ashtray littered with his half-smoked butts. His hand shot out to seize it. Before he could check himself, he slammed it hard against the up-curving shell of the chamber. "Hell!" he said. "Damn-it-to-hell!"

Humphries' jaw loosened and he stared. "You mad at something, Doc?"

"Who's in command here?" Dane demanded.

"Say, Doc, you all right? I mean, what's eating on you?"

"If Colonel Cragg is in command, what can I do? Or anyone else after he makes up his mind. Like a little tin god in a big tin can!"

Humphries looked over his shoulder at the intercom. He said, "Doc, maybe you should ought to get some rest. You stayed up here all night last night. You're here when I get back. You can't keep going on two, three hours' sleep."

"You want a picture to impress your girl friend. Colonel Cragg wants a bigger picture. The Far Venture lands on Earth. All hail the great captain. So Dr. Pembroke and three men are left behind, the show goes on and all that."

"It's tough," Humphries said. "I already read them for dead ever since they don't answer no more on the radio."

"They're not dead," Dane said bitterly. "Except that Colonel Cragg says they're dead. That makes them officially dead. As good as dead."

Humphries shook his head. "You maybe ought to keep shut up. No use getting yourself in a jam with the colonel. Besides, what you going to do about it?"

"I'm not wearing a uniform myself," Dane said. "But you're right about one thing. What am I going to do about it?"

"Just take it easy," Humphries said. "Just take it easy and roll with the punches." He nodded wisely.

Dane went to his port and stared into the fitfully flaring east. After a while he went back to his plottings.

The blue-bright net patches were again the last of the spark fires to die down. After the giant bolts ceased to arc out of them and over the far-eastern horizon, the photo plane table still reported the net flashes in radiant, shattered-glass patterns for two hours past the Martian sunset. By the time their flickering crosshatches dimmed to reddish flare-ups here and there, Dane had made and developed two hundred photographic exposures of the display on the dark glass tabletop.

He began to press his calculations into the accumulated mass of discharge plottings, entering the results one by one on his master chart overlay and drafting lines to connect the like-intensity readings. Under his penciling the pattern of last night's discharges was repeating itself. Methodically he compared his partly completed plot a time or two with yesterday's chart before he noted an emerging variation. The indication was a certain dislocation of one of the major focal points of the fires.

He began now to hasten the calculations, working rapidly and getting excited but restraining his conclusions until he had done all the plotting. Then he drew a line along his straightedge, connecting the location of the spacecraft and the point of Dr. Pembroke's entry into the lichens and extending deeper into the beds. He grunted in triumph. The line ran squarely through the dislocated focus.

It could be coincidence. But why the shift of this particular focus? He pored over the chart, seeking for phenomena comparable to the shift. If any were there, they eluded him. Maybe the discharge centers of the spark fires were meaningless, like the small whirlpools that form and disappear in rapidly flowing water, vagaries of the streamlines and the urgent fluids. But again, why the shift in this particular center? Odd chance or attraction? It had to be one of the two. Unless maybe design? That, Mr. Ames, would really be it! For an instant he let himself go into wild surmise. His skin crawled before he could shake the spook away, sneering at himself. By what? Design what-in-hell by? Chance? Quite possibly chance. But assume attraction, like a steel mast drawing lightning, and you couldn't miss it. It was there to be seen. Plain on the chart, also assuming that Dr. Pembroke had chosen to follow a straight-line course. Make only those two assumptions and you couldn't miss it.

Suddenly he pushed down the commander's key on the intercom.

"Dane to Colonel Cragg."

The speaker rasped. "Cragg here."

"I'm coming down. Are you clear?"

"Not now. Let it rest."

"It can't. We have to send a search party out. Immediately."

"No. The answer is still 'no.' " The speaker clicked dead.

Dane stabbed the key. "Colonel Cragg! I'm calling a meeting at once. Of our own people. We'll make up a party ourselves. With or without your approval."

"That's what you think, *Doctor* Dane." The colonel's harsh baritone scorned the title. "Maybe you'd better come down at that."

Dane twisted away from the table and strapped on the heavy gravity footgear. He pondered the litter of photographic prints a moment, then pushed them aside and took only his master plot. For Colonel Cragg it had to be fast. With his usual feeling for the oddness of the action, he got through the hatch and climbed down the durometal ladders to the commander's quarters on 1-high deck.

The entry panel was shut. He jabbed twice at the buzzer push and bore against the latch handle until the lock hummed and he could shove through.

CHAPTER TWO

Unsmiling behind his desk, Cragg swept over Dane as if inspecting for violations of military neatness. He poked a digit at one of the plastic chairs and clipped off a phrase. "Five minutes."

Dane ignored the chair. "I have new evidence and good evidence that Dr. Pembroke is still alive. At least someone of his party is alive. I think I know where he is. I want to make up a party and go after him immediately."

Cragg pushed a thick fist impatiently at his cropped gray hair. "There's still no time. You'd never make it back by morning."

"We've got to try! We've got to stay here and try." Dane spread out his chart. "Look at this."

Cragg shoved it away. "You know I've already given the order for take-off. Give it up and face facts, man. He's dead."

Dane put the chart back. He forced himself to speak evenly. "He is alive. He moved yesterday after he signaled he was entering the lichens. Now I can show he has moved again since last night. Something's gone wrong, but at least I know where he is."

"One thing you've got right," Cragg snapped, "is that one about something being wrong. The radiation intensity is up eight percent over yesterday. At 1400 this afternoon we registered five times the penetrations we did yesterday. Or don't you know that!"

"It drops off at night," Dane said. "Way down."

"You mean it did last night," Cragg corrected him. "At 1800 tonight we still had as many penetrations as we had at the peak yesterday."

"Just the same," Dane said, "we have plenty of time to get out to Dr. Pembroke and back before it gets up to a peak tomorrow."

"Knock it off." Cragg made it an order. "I'm not taking any chance on daylight hours tomorrow. That's final. This radiation comes through the cosmic-ray shield like cheese. What chance do you think a man outside has got? I'm sorry about Pembroke, but I'm not going to risk the whole expedition for four men. If we get an increase in radiation tomorrow like the one today, we could all be sick to death by tomorrow night. Then Expedition Mars vanishes into space and they never hear of it again."

"A party could make it out and back by noon tomorrow. It's not over ten miles to go. Twenty altogether at the most."

Cragg reached for one of his stogies.

"We've got to take a chance," Dane insisted. "I'm sure Dr. Pembroke's still alive and in serious danger."

"Pembroke is in danger!" Cragg exploded. "What do you think this whole expedition is in? Where do you think we are? On a picnic in Central Park? We are all in serious danger. And with the radio dead between us and Earth ever since we landed. We take off for home at 0600 tomorrow morning."

Dane pounded a fist down on the table. "Colonel, will you be kind enough just to listen for one moment!"

Cragg sat ramrod straight. "So now we have the hard-boiled newspaperman! Power of the press and all that! How old are you, Dane? Never mind," he went on. "About thirty. I'm forty-nine. I've had time enough, maybe you haven't, to learn some things are more important than a man. One man, hell. We've got millions of men. Probably a few thousand as useful and important as even your Dr. Pembroke." His voice grated harshly. "One thing that's more important is this spacecraft and what it stands for. Even if getting off safe doesn't make as good a story for your papers as a wild-eyed rescue party charging out in the night."

Dane felt the rage to smash the arrogant scarred face. "I am not affronting your eagles, Colonel," he managed to say reasonably. "After all I'm only a civilian, but I have a duty too. To my friend. The least you can do is listen to me."

Cragg shrugged. "Okay. But your five minutes is already up." Dane smoothed out his chart. He ran a pencil along the line from the spacecraft to the boundary of the lichen beds. "At 1800 hours yesterday Dr. Pembroke radioed from here that he was about to enter the lichens. Now we prolong the line of his course another thirty-five hundred yards inside them and we are at the exact center of last night's spark fires, if we plot them by their intensity. But the night after we landed, the spark fires were irregularly distributed all along the lichen beds, as far as our equipment could record them. We recorded no concentrations like the ones I plotted last night and tonight. The first night we observed only a few of the big bolts. Last night I pointed out to you that the spark fires were more intense in the zone where Dr. Pembroke went into the lichen beds. Several extremely large bolts were recorded in that region, an obvious concentration."

"How about you coming to the point?"

At least he was listening. "The concentrations of spark fire are a lot more localized tonight," Dane went on, refusing to be hurried. "What is significant is that one of the major centers has moved four thousand yards deeper into the lichens, and it has moved exactly along a line prolonged from the course Dr. Pembroke took from the spacecraft to the edge of the lichens. I say it means that he has moved today himself. If he moved today, he was alive today. Radiation or no radiation, he's alive out there tonight. Whether he signaled us or not."

Cragg was staring at the chart. "What's this?" he demanded.

Dane followed the thick finger over a number of plottings fanning in from a broad arc.

"There are lots of concentrations. The significant one is the one I pointed out. It shows the obvious reaction of the spark fires to Dr. Pembroke's presence."

Cragg positioned a ruler on the chart to bisect the fan. He drew a pencil along the edge. The line ran like a handle for the fan, straight through the X-mark that plotted the spacecraft on the arid plain. "What about that?"

Dane said, "I hadn't checked that concentration particularly."

Cragg scowled. "It's your business to check it." He jabbed at the intercom. "This is Colonel Cragg. I want Major Noel. In my office."

"Look," Dane said, "we're wasting time. The main thing this chart shows is that Dr. Pembroke is alive and that for some reason the fires are reacting violently to his presence in the lichen beds. I propose to organize some men and start out at once to find him."

"Maybe you ought to remember this," Cragg said crisply. "You have other duties than news reporting for Amalgamated Press and giving general advice. You are also supposed to be a physicist." He gazed briefly at the door. "I'm going to be very busy. You will return to your post. Please attend to it and leave the command of the Far Venture to me."

He pushed the panel release. Major Noel's dark, compressed face came into the opening.

Cragg said, "Noel, I want to move up take-off to 2200. Can you make it?"

"Tonight, sir?" Noel's eyes flicked at Dane. "Has the Colonel heard from Dr. Pembroke?"

"No," Cragg told him shortly. "Nor likely to. You didn't answer my question."

Noel stepped farther inside. He hesitated.

"Well?"

"If the Colonel orders, the spacecraft can take off at 2200."

"Wait just one minute," Dane demanded. "If Major Noel will excuse me, I have something else you ought to know before you make your final decision."

Cragg started to refuse. Finally he said, "Stand by on the intercom, Noel."

Dane waited until the door completely closed. "I think you've had some previous experience with our Amalgamated's Mr. Ames. I guess you know he's still managing editor."

Cragg shot him a quick look. "Congratulations."

"He has a way with what he calls a 'controversial theme,' meaning something somebody doesn't like to hear about himself but a lot of people like to read about. The way he jumped on your appointment to command Expedition Mars, for example."

Cragg swore briefly. "Not to speak of your own mudslinging once upon a time. I haven't forgotten that either. I suppose you think it wasn't Amalgamated pull that got you on this flight?"

Dane said, "I doubt that anything else would have got me on after you were appointed. But that's past history. Ames has already committed himself and the biggest wire service in the world against you. What do you think he'll do with the story about how you marooned Dr. Pembroke a hundred million miles from Earth and left him to certain death? In the face of good evidence that he was still alive. He'll make a real story out of that no matter what you say. You can depend on that. It'll take care of what you've got left of your hero's halo."

He thought Cragg was going to hit him. The man was half out of his chair before he controlled himself. "Between you and me I'm not saying I think you're physically afraid. That's what Ames is going to say back on Earth. I'm not even sure what you want out of this trip. Reputation and a general's star maybe. I do think your vanity means more than your life to you. So I'm going to put you over this barrel. You can take your choice between the danger here that you might not get the Far Venture back to Earth and the certain loss of your reputation when you do get back—if you don't give a search party a chance to go after Dr. Pembroke."

Cragg smashed the straightedge down on the desk. "Look"—his voice deepened—"Dr. Pembroke and his men, I say they're dead. You've got some flimsy evidence they're not. But I am in command of this spacecraft. That includes responsibility for its safety and the safety of all the crew and passengers. It's my first duty to get the Far Venture back to Earth. That I'm going to do even if I have to leave half the personnel behind. This business is over your head. Pembroke may be the Director of Science on Expedition Mars. He can be the high priest of the almighty atom, for all I care when it comes to completing our mission. Like I told you, there are millions of men. Quite a few even as valuable as Dr. Pembroke. But this vehicle"—Cragg banged down again—"cost five years' work and three billion dollars to get it ready. Regardless of science and observations and specimens, regardless of some men's lives, the Far Venture has to get back to Earth."

"And Colonel Cragg is again the great hero. First of the Martian captains. Until Ames gets through with you!"

"You think that kind of stuff is going to work on me, you've got another thing coming. Supposing you wait until I finish. I've got no way of knowing whether you're right or wrong about Pembroke, but I don't intend to close out four men if there's some chance of saving them."

He tossed the straightedge on the scarred table. "You heard what I said about my responsibility. You said noon you could be back. Now let's see about *your* guts. I'll go you one hour better—maybe. Here's the deal I make you. First, nobody goes but volunteers. You're personally included as the first volunteer. Second, I wait no longer, regardless, than one hour past noon. If you're not back by 1300 hours, then I don't care where you are or how much you signal you're alive, or what. We take off at 1300 regardless. I will not risk the afternoon radiation peak."

Dane heard himself say, "Fair enough."

"That's not all," Cragg said grimly. "So far it's been true that both radiation and the spark fires have died down at night and haven't come back until late in the morning. But we've only been here three mornings. Tonight you plotted a spark-fire concentration obviously aimed at the Far Venture. I don't understand it and neither do you. I know I don't like it. If either the radiation or any evidence of spark fire picks up intensity in the morning faster than it has been doing, I take off without you. I take off when we register fifteen percent penetrations, no matter what time it is or where you are."

Dane thought that one over.   Fifteen hours for twenty miles. Through loose sand and vegetation. Including a search and maybe injured men to get out. Pressure suits.

He took a deep damn-fool breath. "You have a deal."

CHAPTER THREE

Dane pushed down a clumsy foot. When he felt the ground, he got free and watched the ladder retract. The thick hatch drew up flush with the hull thirty feet overhead.

He stood solid-footed in a luminescent, wine-red fog. They had already kicked up enough dust to diffuse and obscure the glaring guard lights. Every step of the heavy footgear puffed another explosion up into the dead atmosphere.

Dane's spirits sagged. The lurid scene fitted the implausible journey to which he was committed. If he let himself think about it at all, he saw very plainly how right Colonel Cragg had been.

He moved toward the rim-lit figure of Wertz, a powerful body squatting short in the grotesque pressure suit. At least in Lieutenant McDonald he was fortunate. About the chemist Wertz of large mustache he was less certain. He was assertive and something of a loudmouth, but yet his scientific reputation was solid to back him up.   And he had volunteered to come along. Abruptly and definitely he had volunteered, so firmly as to exclude any of the others at once.

From habit Dane huddled with the two of them, Earth style, in the thin nitrogenous atmosphere while they ran through their final suit, instrument, and communications check.

When McDonald gave the word to move out, it was 2120.   Fifty minutes of their time had already ticked off.

The course was 39 degrees east of the planet's magnetic pole, along the direct path across the northern reach of Isidis Regio that Dr. Pembroke had taken to the green-dark vegetation of Syrtis Major. Five miles of dust to the lichen beds.

McDonald looped the tow cord of the specimen cart over his shoulder. As soon as they left the bright narrow zone, the Martian night plunged over them. At last light the sky had been free from dust clouds and clear, but now only Earth and Jupiter and a handful of stars were picked out above them. The high frost haze was thick. Both moons were down.

To conserve battery power, they plodded along in the black dark. The air-conditioned pressure suits really worked admirably. But for the constriction of the harness and the swinging gait to accommodate the articulated joints, they were free and easy, like papier-mâché armor. Dane estimated the pace at two miles per hour.

Not much sounded off in the earphones. A halfhearted joke about sardines out for a stroll without taking off their cans. A guess about how far they had come, with a glance back at the beacon light on top of the spacecraft. Then they settled down to the work of locomotion. After an hour Phoebus rose in the west, a hazy blotch of light.

Dane thought again, as he had thought so many times in the past three days, of the pied surface of the planet swelling before the rush of the spacecraft until it was the countenance of space, only to dwindle rapidly to a narrow world of dust plains and crude plant life. A dozen times its aspect had reeled away beneath them under their sweeping orbits, revealing unlimited monotony of completely barren, orange-red flatland, vast areas of dirty green and brownish vegetation, and the roll of low hills. Occasionally long island chains of plant growth stretched out across the red terrain, linking the continent-like concentrations. From out in space they had looked like dark lines. At close range they resolved into nothing like canal banks or other relies of intelligent habitation.

Nowhere the sign of thought, past or present. No canals, no construction of ruins, no cities too small to be seen from Earth. Not even geographical diversity. No mountain or escarpment, no course of water or river pattern, wet or dry, nothing but the alternate sameness of oxidized Sahara and tundra waste. What he himself had expected to behold, Dane could not say, other than that it was the unknown. Quickly and certainly the unknown had resolved into the known. With disappointment for them all, except possibly Colonel Cragg, they had found Earth's areology devastatingly sound. Except Colonel Cragg, Dane was certain. Cragg had no other thought than to get to Mars and back to Earth.

Well, perhaps he was right. That was the primary mission. Without the spark fires and the unknown radiation Mars was like the moon. Unrewarding for the effort. As it was, Dane thought grimly, in the radiation they had now met with something, at least, that they had not bargained for.

McDonald was signaling the spacecraft on the liaison frequency. "McDonald to Baker Home," he called in the traditional jargon. They were two hours out.

A crisp reply came at once.

"How do you read me now?" McDonald queried.

"Strong and clear."

"Roger. What is our location?"

It took them a couple of minutes to plot. "You are one-zero-five yards right of course. You are approximately one-one-zero-zero yards from the intersection of course with the lichen forest. Your course to the intersection of original course and lichen forest is now three-three degrees, three-two minutes. Repeat: change course to three-three degrees, three-two minutes. Do you read? Over."

McDonald repeated the message and went out.

Wertz came in on the intercom frequency. "Did you hear that slide-rule jockey?"

McDonald said, "Yeah. That was Major Noel himself. It's a wonder he didn't give us the odd seconds. Be mighty handy. Especially with a wristwatch compass. I can hardly even see mine through this fishbowl."

"Nothing can stop the United States Air Force," Wertz said. "Precise. Daring. Glamorous."

McDonald said, "I hope nothing stops us from getting us back. I don't want to think of that take-off tomorrow."

"In front of civilians, Lieutenant?"

Under their talk Dane heard the ground bass of apprehension. The interchange quickly sputtered out and they plodded along again in silence, each so wrapped in his solitude that they came against it unaware, blundering against it in the dark with nerves jarred by a clutching around their legs before they could get their lights switched on.

The white beams danced over a thicket of waist-high plants. Dane poured his light on the things before him. "God!" he murmured, awed that John Dane, born into the clean, practical little town of New Braunfels, Texas, had come over the horizon of space to stand on another world, face to face with an alien something that lived.

They rose countless out of the soil ahead. The individual specimens looked like the spiky little cactus trees popular in a Texas florist's souvenir pots, except that these were three to four feet tall and the crisscrossing, rod-shaped branches were fibrous. They wove themselves closely into dense clumps, but they yielded readily to the pressure of wading against them.

"Looks like a big weed patch," McDonald said.

"Funny-looking weeds," Wertz said. "They look more like giant crystal lattice."

McDonald said, "We'd better get going. We've got to be back by 1300. Colonel Cragg meant that. It's be back or else. I'll get a fix."

They were sixty yards to the right of the point of Dr. Pembroke's entry. The vegetation zone met the red plain so sharply that its edge might have been laid off with a giant ruler.

McDonald said, "Dr. Pembroke couldn't pull his carts through this stuff. It's too thick. I don't see why we haven't spotted them. With these lights. We can see a hundred yards."

"Maybe he pulled them in a little way," Wertz said.

"Then they'd be hard to find when he came out, if he didn't backtrack his trail exactly."

They paced off the sixty yards, but no carts appeared. They penetrated the lichen zone ten yards and turned to look. A broad swath of depressed plants lay behind them.

"Four men couldn't come through without leaving a sign," Wertz said. "Even if it's elastic enough to spring back, they'd be bound to break a lot of it. I say they didn't come in here."

"Okay," Dane said, "but we're exactly on Dr. Pembroke's course, as nearly as instruments can tell. We could be off several feet, though, and we wouldn't see a few broken plants. Let's go on in at 39 degrees. Maybe we'll pick up their trail."

The spacecraft beacon was bright and friendly. A link with air and warmth and Earth. They lined up a bearing on it and ranged out in a front. Dane took the point. The others flanked him at fifty feet. With their lights playing about them, they pushed ahead into the lichens.

The ground lay flat, but the matted plants cut the advance to a crawl. It didn't help much to go around the denser clumps or zigzag for the small bare places that they encountered every few yards, as in open jungle.

"I don't see how the spark fires come from this kind of stuff," McDonald said.

Dane shook off the feeling of isolation. He was glad for someone to say something. "In the first place that's only the most apparent explanation," he told him. "That's just the one you would think of first, plus the fact that you don't see them anywhere except above the lichens. It's just a good guess that somehow the sunlight causes them to generate and store up static electricity until it discharges under pressure, like sheet lightning on Earth. After dark the charges don't build up any more, so they exhaust themselves. In a couple of hours the display is over."

"Personally I'm thinking about the radiation," Wertz said. "That's not static electricity. Not by a long shot. If it builds up high by noon tomorrow, the insulation in these suits won't do us much good."

Dane said, "Again we're only speculating. We don't know for sure that it's harmful. Or what exposure to it would be lethal."

"Spivak thinks it's dangerous. He's the radio physicist."

"After all we've had only three days' experience with it," Dane reminded him. "Just because it increased today over yesterday doesn't inevitably mean it's going to increase again tomorrow."

"We hope!" Wertz said.

Noise burst out like a crash of splintering timber. Dane stabbed out with his light, plunging the beam crazily into the dark night. Then he realized that it was his own earphones blasting.

He turned down the volume sharply. McDonald was overloading the microphone. Yelling for them to come.

He heard Wertz's excited "What-the-hell?" He swung around and splashed light over McDonald. The lieutenant stood motionless, the plants deep around his suited figure.

"What's the trouble?" Dane snapped into the transmitter.

"Here!"

Wertz came up rapidly.

It was prone in its bed of lichens. At first it might have been painted green. Dane bent closer and saw that the pressure suit was covered with a sprouting of tiny lichen spears, like a week's growth of mossy beard.

"Who is it?" Wertz demanded.

Fighting his clumsy armor, Dane knelt and turned it over on its back. The green scum blanked the transparent helmet. He scraped at it with the blade of his belt knife until the color came reluctantly away, leaving a frost on the glassite.

Dane put his light close to the patch he had scraped. "It's Lieutenant Houck!"

McDonald's voice was flat. "Is he dead?"

Dane thought, No, just taking a nap. A hundred million miles from his wife's bed. "I can't tell," he said. "His oxygen and his air conditioner should still be good."

Wertz got down awkwardly on one knee. "What's he doing here?"

"Look!" Dane felt the shock of revelation physically. He ran the light over the suit and poked the knife blade at the flexible corset joints. The whole side of the shell crumbled away, like acid-robbed metal in a metallurgical test.

"Exploded! Frozen like a mackerel!" Wertz gasped.

They got up and backed away, looking at their suits and the plant things all around them.

"They ate right through it, didn't they?" McDonald croaked. "They ate right through it!"

"Froze him quick. But he was damn well exploded already," Dane said.

"This stuff comes to full life under sunlight!" Wertz choked up.

Wertz was scared. Well, who wasn't? "That's what they say," Dane told him, ignoring the fact that the chemist should know better than he. "The theory is that it carries on photosynthesis in the daytime and stores enough oxygen for the night." Powerful body, powerful mind, not much guts, he thought, again revising his estimate of the man. Yet he had volunteered to come along. "After sunset they are supposed to become dormant in the cold. Eighty to ninety degrees below. Fahrenheit, that is, too. With practically no oxygen in the atmosphere, there isn't any other theory for the survival of the plants overnight. In a latent state they wouldn't need any more than the little oxygen that they could store up in the daytime."

Wertz said, "We know all that. What we've got to think about is that if they're dangerous at all, they're most dangerous in the daytime. Right now it's obvious that we haven't got a chance unless we get out of here tonight. It's plain what happened to Pembroke."

"Likely you're right about the danger in the daytime." Dane agreed. "But we've got a lot of time even after sunrise. It takes them several hours to thaw out."

Wertz said, "They must exude an acid. Like some of the Earth lichens. So you wade through them, you don't go very far."

"Even so, even after they wake up and get going, it would take it a while to eat through our suits."

"You hope!" Wertz said impatiently.

"Let's go," Dane said. "I don't like it any better than you do. We can't do anything for Houck, but we've got to find the others. Even if they're dead too, we've got to be sure. You can go on back now if you want to."

"Who said anything about going back now?" Wertz growled. "Who-in-hell you think you are anyway!" he flared up. "You follow your own nose. I'll carry my end of this little detail."

"I've got to report about Lieutenant Houck to Colonel Cragg," Lieutenant McDonald said.

"You mean just in case?" Wertz asked him.

"If there is a danger here, it must be recorded," McDonald said mildly. "We are not the last men to come to Mars."

Dane said, "Let's take a good look around here. We can start while he's calling in." He was ashamed of the undisciplined tenseness that had led him into a petty quarrel. He should have kept his mouth shut. Like McDonald.

Major Noel stood by for McDonald's briefing. Then his voice crackled sharply. "I ought to order you back now. I'm sure Colonel Cragg would do it."

"Look," Dane broke in, "Dr. Wertz and I happen to be civilians. I suppose Colonel Cragg can take off without us, but Dr. Pembroke is in charge of the scientific party. Colonel Cragg has no military command over its investigations."

"He has over you," Noel said. "You're a correspondent attached to the crew, aren't you, even if you also do happen to be holding down a slot in the Pembroke group. Or did you forget?"

McDonald said, "Sir, I'll accompany Dr. Dane and Dr. Wertz. If I may."

"I only said I *ought* to order you to return," Noel came back.

"You will go with them, and you will see that they get back. On time. Report promptly on all findings. Your power is good."

CHAPTER FOUR

They took up the 39-degree course, heading directly for Dane's co-ordinates. It was 0135, an hour and thirty-five minutes after midnight. They had less than twelve hours.

According to the last fix, they were a thousand yards into the lichens. Little more than half a mile. It was at least three miles more to the estimated location of the missing party. A mile an hour was now as much as they could expect to make through the lichen forest. Just to walk to the plotted location and return far enough to get out of the lichens would approach seven hours, with no delays. If the terrain got no worse. Sunrise being due at 0614, that made them emerge at least two hours after daylight. That was the best, any way Dane figured it.

They came into open ground, in areas forty to fifty yards across with the familiar red soil showing up in their lights. After a time a sensible downhill grade developed, but the lichens were again thicker and their speed did not improve. The haze now obscured the few stars of early night, and the beacon of the spacecraft had dipped below the crest of the descent.

Wertz said, "One thing about your theory doesn't jibe. I went along with you on your plot of the spark-fire concentrations. It made as good sense as anything that they had something to do with Pembroke's party.

But if you're right about that, how come no concentrations where we found Houck's body?"

"It doesn't fit," Dane admitted. "But if the concentrations signified anything at all about Dr. Pembroke's locations, then they proved that he moved three thousand yards farther into the lichens from one night to the next. That's what we're counting Oil."

McDonald said, "It would have helped if we could plot them in the daytime."

"A lot of things would help," Wertz said. "If we only knew about them."

Between 0130 and 0230 they made less than a mile. To maintain familiar hour relations with sun-time, their Earth watches had been synchronized at every midnight, moved back 37 minutes to accommodate the 24-hour-and-37-minute rotation of Mars. At 0255 hours by their improvised Mars time Dane estimated that they were near the place of concentration recorded for Dr. Pembroke's first night in the lichens.

He called McDonald. "How about getting us a fix?"

They were practically on it. Sixty yards short. Some to the right. They were steadily veering to the right hand.

After they had swept the location for twenty minutes, they resumed course.

Another forty minutes, at 0425 hours, and they came on a bare depression running ribbon-like and fifty yards wide diagonally across their path. It looked like an old Earth gully rounded and filled in with wind-blown red soil. It extended to left and to right as far as their lights would shine.

"Rope me," McDonald said. "I'm going into it."

He edged down the sloping bank and kicked at the loose dust. It was ten or twelve inches deep at the bottom, but he thought the footing underneath was the same clay-like stuff that had been found under the red plain.

They made their 0430 call and reported the find. The fix showed 5370 yards in and slightly left of course. They had overcorrected.

Dane said, "Anybody coming through three miles of nothing but lichen beds would be sure to explore this. It's the first different thing they would have seen."

"So we follow it," Wertz said. "It's slanting ahead pretty close to our way."

The going was slower. It was like walking in drifted snow, only the dust did not help them by packing. The minutes perversely increased their tempo.

McDonald thrust out an arm. "Something's on the ground." It could have been spread out for a sign. The shoulder strap was unbuckled. One end of the strap stretched straight forward, pointing along the channel. The other lay at right angles, indicating the bank toward the spacecraft.

"It's a specimen bag," Wertz said unnecessarily.

Dane said, "Now we know we're on the trail."

Wertz said, "Maybe Houck was coming back for help and put it down for a marker."

"We ought to see some tracks," McDonald objected. He pointed to their own passage.

"Not necessarily," Dane told him. "We had a five-mile wind early this afternoon. That's plenty to drift light dust."

They waded on. After another half-hour the dust channel bent to the left in a sharp curve.

"It's taking us back toward the 39-degree course line now," McDonald said.

The steady shuffle took them along more red channel and between more lichen-covered banks. It could be no dried-up watercourse, not on Mars, but they could not imagine a cause for it or advance any reason for the failure of the lichens to spread over it. With only minor alteration in course it was more like a wide, dusty sunken road then anything else. But who would have made a road?

"Maybe ages ago. Hundreds of thousands of years," McDonald said.

"It's pretty well agreed now that Mars is a young planet, as far as life is concerned," Dane told him. "The lichens are probably at the beginning of life here. Not the end. Between the two planets, Earth life is the old life. Besides, the lichens would have covered over a road long ago."

"It's probably a surface fault of some kind," Wertz said. "A fault could have exposed some mineral substance the lichens don't like. I'll take some samples on the way back."

"It's time for the 0530 report," McDonald said. "Maybe we ought to hold it up a few minutes. We're almost to your location."

"Better get a fix," Dane said.

"We're going to have to make speed out of here," Wertz said. "It's 0530. We left the spacecraft at 2120. That means we've been eight hours and ten minutes getting here. Eight hours and ten minutes from now is 1340 hours, and Colonel Cragg said he takes off at 1300 regardless."

"We can get back a lot faster," Dane said. "We ought to come on to them in another thirty minutes, if they're where we think they are. That's 0600. That leaves us seven hours. In a straight line it's only about eight miles and a half back to the spacecraft. With no time out for searching around on the way back and in the daylight, we ought to make it to the edge of the lichen forest in three hours and a half without any trouble and make it over the dust plain in two and a half hours more. That's six hours. We'll still have an hour for cushion."

"What do we do if we have to carry them out?"

"We take off their gravity weights, and pack them out. One each. We'll make it. We've got to."

"We can put them in the specimen cart when we get them out of the lichens," McDonald said.

The fix was 6100 yards in and 150 yards right of course. About 428 straight-line yards to go. Course 18 to 19 degrees.

According to the compass sighting, the channel ran at 21 degrees, shy. "Let's follow it." Dane said. "Pace it off. Maybe they planted another marker where they left it."

It was almost time for the brief dawn that the attenuated atmosphere afforded the planet. For the first time Dane felt real fatigue as he realized that the sun would soon be daylight around them and over the weary miles back to the spacecraft. He slogged along. Successful or unsuccessful, it would be a long hard pull.

At the far edge of his light, he vaguely saw something. A bulk in the channel ahead.

"Hold it!" he sang out. "There's something up there."

They huddled, striving to pass the fuzzy limit of vision. There was something. Something that was not naked, ocher-colored dust.

"Dr. Pembroke!" Dane called. "Dr. Pembroke. John Dane calling. Can you hear me? Can you see our lights?"

He strained for acuity below the faint hum of the earphones, but there was only the silence of the Martian night. Nothing moved.

"It's not big enough to be a man," McDonald said.

"Anyway, why doesn't it move?" Wertz said. "Our lights are plain to see."

"This is my play," McDonald decided. "I'll go have a look."

Dane said, "This safari was my idea. Whatever is out there has something to do with Dr. Pembroke. I intend to go see. Get in contact with the spacecraft and wait for me here. We don't know what it might be."

Wertz said, "Why don't we all go? Three are better than one."

Dane felt the thing brush his scalp. He had not yet put it in words. Not even to himself. Now he had to. "You're going to think I'm off my zip, but tonight, while I was plotting the spark fires, something made me think and I can't forget it. Colonel Cragg would have laughed me out of his office if I had even mentioned it. But this is it. For a minute I began to think maybe there's intelligence on Mars besides our own. I couldn't help it. You have only to look at the chart I made to see it for yourself. Some something could actually be directing the patterns of the spark fires. Something very probably hostile."

Their silence was heavy.

"I'm not cracking up. I just think you ought to know what I believe is very possible and you ought to be prepared to relay it to Colonel Cragg. If by any chance I could be right, whatever it is may have destroyed Dr. Pembroke, and it could very well be aware of our presence here now."

Wertz swore. "You pick a hell of a time to bring up an idea like that! You want to give me the shouting creeps? You know there's no life on this planet except this damn vegetation. How could there be? You going back to that idea about life based on something else than carbon? Like the silicon atom?"

"I don't know," Dane told him. "I haven't any idea. Call it a hunch, if you like."

"You bet I will," Wertz snapped. "A damn poor one. Unless you believe in ghosts. And ghost mechanics and ghost architecture. Desert ghosts," he laughed shortly.

"Nevertheless," Dane went on, "there are patterns to the spark fires that seem to be associated with our presence and with our physical location. Colonel Cragg noticed a new one. That's why he was hot to move up the take-off. Only what he was really afraid of was a step-up in the penetration rays."

He saw Wertz turn his helmet ponderously at McDonald. "Kid," he heard him say, "you're official. You stay here and report. I don't take in Dane's ghost story, but if something does pop up out there, Cragg'll believe you. He won't think you're off your base."

"Dammit!" Dane said, in spite of himself. "The sun will be up in fifteen minutes. It's getting lighter in the cast now. I'm going ahead. Lieutenant McDonald is technically in command here, I suppose. Let him—"

"I'm coming with you," McDonald said quietly. "Wertz, I have no real authority over you, but I'd like for you to stay and cover us."

"With what?" Wertz said bitterly. "A comic-strip ray gun? You want me to shoot lichens with a six-gun? Or maybe Dane's ghost men? You get up there, you'll find exactly nothing."

But when they went forward, he remained at his post. They heard him calling the spacecraft. "Wertz to Baker Home."

CHAPTER FIVE

Almost at once the feathery dust cloud of their advance obscured all sight of Wertz. A few more steps dimmed his powerful headlight to a haloed blotch of glowing red.

They stopped and told him to get out of the gully and up on the bank where he could see.

"I'm already up there," Wertz came back. "The dust is higher than I am. If I go back any farther into the lichens, I won't be able to see you over the tops anyway."

Dane was impatient to move. "We can't just stand here. Maybe it would be a good idea for him to back from the gully a couple of hundred yards and hide. We can keep in steady touch with him."

"Huh-uh," Wertz objected. "Not me. Not all alone out here I don't play any hiding games!"

"It'd be a good idea," McDonald said. "If we do come up against something, it'd be a good idea to have one of us back behind and out of range."

"Nope!" Wertz said. "You think I'm sitting out here alone not knowing what's happening, you're crazy. So something gets you, then I wait all by myself while it comes for me. We all go ahead together, I say."

His light glowed closer. Then he bulked up in the red mist and got beside them.

"We can't put out a point and be able to see him," McDonald said. "A point would kick up so much dust the rest of us would blunder into anything he ran into anyway. We go two and one," he decided. "Dane and I go ahead and Wertz as far behind as he can still see us good in his light."

"That's about ten feet," Wertz announced after they had taken a few steps. "Ready or not, here I come."

It glared at them steadily. A few seconds ago they had the only light on a pitch-dark planet. Now it was there. Steady and menacing. A tiny point of light. Low down, if not actually at the bed of the gully, and about the length of a football field ahead, it had suddenly appeared at the side of the shape they stalked.

Dane realized they had halted. "You see what I see?" He forced his voice level. He sounded flat to himself rather than calm.

To escape the rising dust, they eased forward with elaborate care. A full minute after the question McDonald said, "Yell. I see it all right. The next thing is, what is it?"

Wertz said, "A very good idea would be to wait right here for daylight. Another twenty minutes and we'll have broad daylight."

"We wait here for twenty minutes, that means we're sitting ducks for anything that's interested in us," McDonald said.

Dane snapped off his handlight. "Cut your lights a second."

"That's a bright boy," Wertz snarled. "You think darkness is going to hide you, you'd better hope your ghosts have got eyes like ours. What makes you think they see with light?"

"I don't know," Dane said. "Just cut all the lights for five seconds. While I count to five. I want to try something."

Afterwards he wondered why he couldn't have explained instead of arguing. With the first instant they stood unseen to each other in the crowding dark, relief flooded through him. "You see it now?" he urged them triumphantly. "You see it any more? Now let's have the lights back on," he said.

There it was again. The speck of light, but no longer so frightening.

Wertz swore. "A reflection! A damn reflection!"

McDonald said, "I don't mind saying it scared me stiff."

"What's doing the reflecting?" Wertz demanded. "You got any brilliant ideas on what's shiny enough around here to reflect light?"

"So we go see," Dane said. "We just walk up ahead and find out." A helmet. It had to be a helmet.

A few more steps and McDonald halted again. He pulled at his belt cloth and wiped the glassite of his vizor, playing his light on the dark shape of the thing ahead, now plainly roundish, with broad bulk near the ground. "It's not a man," he announced, moving on. "Whatever it is, it's not a man. Looks like a big pile of something or other."

They didn't have that much with them, Dane thought. Dr. Pembroke and his men couldn't have had enough with them to make any kind of a pile.

"Lichens!" McDonald burst out, not halting this time. He wiped his vizor. "Lichens. A big pile of lichens. Right in the middle of the ditch."

Dane kept his own light on the brightness that dulled as they approached. Something to the left of the pile. Whatever it was, it wasn't a helmet.

Twenty feet away he recognized it. "A specimen can! A plain ordinary everyday specimen can."

"It gave me a bang-out I'll remember for a while," McDonald said. "I really thought it was an eye or something watching us and shining up in our lights. You suppose they left it here on purpose?"

Wertz gestured at the waist-high mound of lichens. "Why cut all this stuff and pile it up here? If they intended to take a load of it back, why cut it here and not at the edge, closer to the spacecraft?"

"Yeh, how were they going to carry it out?" McDonald seconded him.

Dane said, "It must be another marker of some kind." He kicked at the base of the pile. All at once he was digging at the mass, scattering the plants right and left. "There's something buried under it!"

It was Beemis and Jackson. They lay on their backs, side by side in the dust.

"Dead?" Wertz threw his light around them, passing it hurriedly over the rows of lichens that rimmed them in above.

Dane went gingerly over Jackson's suit. It was intact. Apparently it was still functioning. Certainly there was none of the corroding moss effect visible that had eaten away the suit of Lieutenant Houck.

He brought his light full upon the face behind the vizor. He took his belt cloth and rubbed the glassite as clean as he could polish it. The eyes were open. Staring. If the man was alive, he thought the light would maybe contract the pupils.

Suddenly he saw it. "He's alive! This one's alive!" he exulted.

McDonald crawled over from the other body.

"Look at the nostrils!" Dane urged him. "You have to look close, but they're moving. He's breathing slow and hard."

They bent closer to Beemis, hoping to detect the tiny movement that meant life. The wide eyes stared up as though reproaching them for disturbing his rest.

"Yeh!" McDonald exclaimed. "Did you catch it? He's breathing too."

It came again beneath the bluish vizor, and again, the nearly imperceptible narrowing of the nostrils that had marked the widely spaced inhalations.

McDonald said, "What I'd like to know, was Dr. Pembroke hiding them or did he think he was burying them?"

Dane stood up, away from the quick thin face of Beemis. Rigidly unconscious behind the glassite shield, it retained the cold, contemptuous flair of the man. Dane felt a brief embarrassment at seeing him helpless in the dust, as if he had inadvertently interrupted him in the toilet. Even in his death mask the man would impart his own peculiar essence, as hard bright as the minerals of his profession. The philologist Jackson had collapsed to the average of the clay in which he was modeled. A lump with no other distinction than the commonest features of man. All his person had fled with the fatuous pulpit humor from below the eyes that never laughed at all. Brothers of the red dust of Mars, Dane thought, but no twins. Hell, it was daylight. In a few minutes it would be bright light.

Wertz said, "If he thought he was hiding them, this is about as good a way as in a young widow's bed. A pile of cut lichens in the wide open, in a place where there isn't any such thing as piles of cut lichens—"

"He probably did it so he could find them again," Dane said. "Maybe he was thinking the dust might drift over them." They were wasting time. "Let's get going. We've still got to find Dr. Pembroke."

From McDonald's stance Dane knew that he was talking with the spacecraft on the liaison frequency. He felt for his own selector switch. No, he didn't want to say anything. He knew why they couldn't seem to get moving. They didn't want to admit that they didn't know which way to go. After the certainty of a place they had to reach and to return from, there was now a vast uncertainty of where to look and how far to look. How *long?* He thought angrily. That's what you mean. How long can we look? How much time remains for looking? "None," he said.

"What?" Wertz demanded.

Dane said, "Nothing." He began to climb out of the gully.

Wertz said, "We've got to start back right away. We don't have time for any more looking. We've barely got time enough to get these two back."

Dane kept on climbing. Wertz talked too much. Dammit, the man ought to learn to keep his mouth shut.

McDonald cut in on intercom. "Major Noel says to take a quick look around and then start back. If Dr. Pembroke went any distance at all, he's hopelessly lost. We wouldn't have a chance in a million of stumbling onto him."

Damn Major Noel. Damn him, too.

"Even if he started back for help, he didn't make it. Once he's off his feet, there's a lot of square miles of lichens between here and the spacecraft to hide him."

Dane decided to begin with an arc of two hundred yards on the west side of the gully. Might as well begin on the side nearest the spacecraft. Thirty or forty-five minutes there. A like time on the other side of the gully. If the focal point of the spark fires had guided them to Beemis and Jackson, maybe there would have been another focus in the area, if Dr. Pembroke had gone very far.

He said, "You and Wertz start back with them. I'm going to hunt at least another hour. I can catch up with you before you get back."

"Not if you find him and have to carry him, you can't," McDonald said. "And if you don't find him, what's the use of it?"

"I stay and look thirty more minutes," Wertz surprised him. "Then I start back. Not one minute more. We've got to get out of these lichens. Anyway, it doesn't make sense to risk five men for the problematical chance of finding one who's likely enough dead already."

McDonald said, "I'm afraid he's right. We've got a duty to Beemis and Jackson. We know they're alive. We've got to give them their chance."

Daylight was brightening fast. As if it were being turned on weird stage scenery through a giant rheostat. It was an ugly, comfortless light, sketching in horizonless stretches of vegetation with broad, characterless strokes. Dane stared at the tangled masses of spike-like plants that crowded him in, up to his waist. The full hopelessness of it was as plain as the dirty green of their pigmentation. Dr. Pembroke could lie within twenty feet of him and be unseen.

It seemed like a yesterday of six months ago. Dr. Pembroke lolling on the cushions of the little cabin cruiser, pulling at a big glass of foaming beer and talking humorous argument with Old Grandfather Dane about everything the two restless minds chanced upon, while the boy fished for the lake perch and the boat swung lazily at anchor under the summer sun. And other long afternoons the boy and the man in the piney woods behind Old Grandfather's summer place, Dr. Pembroke vigorous in khaki trousers and sneakers, explaining Pleurococcus on the bark like a story of a hidden world, naming the polished pebbles showing treasure color in the creek gravel. And the day Old Grandfather died, Dr. Pembroke coming from Europe to put his hand on the young man's shoulder and look one more time upon the face of his old friend. "He was always living one more bright day. He didn't count any of them. He died young at ninety-four." Dane remembered as if it were a yesterday of six months ago how he had patted him gently on the shoulder and said, "Youth is the search. Time has nothing to do with it." Then he had turned away and walked out of the house.

These were the things that strangers could measure and put a value upon. A half-hour.

He fought out against the rubbery barrier, lifting his knees against it like a man wading into deeper water. When the half-hour had gone, he would stay. Not thinking too hard against the futility of it, he thought he would stay another hour…yes, not before then would he leave off and go back, ending the search…thinking it was a hell of a gift to the yesterday. If you didn't think about it as only an hour more than the half-hour that strangers gave, if you thought about it as very close to life itself, maybe it was enough. I'm tired drunk, he decided. Daylight coming is a little dying all in itself.

The light was flooding all around now, so soon, with the odd brightness, as if a storm came with it, that they knew as the Mars full dawn of day. He turned to look for the Earth helmets, far apart and questing through the improbable brush like treasure divers out of their element. A little luck would do it. A little luck, he thought, just as he angled off and came upon the tiny clearing of cut and strewn lichens with the helmeted figure sitting in the middle.

He went deliberately up and peered in at the white-mustached, Irish-pink face before he said, "Dr. Pembroke! Here he is. Over here. Here he is. We've found him."

He exulted over the same flutter of deep inhalation beneath the wide-eyed stare.

CHAPTER SIX

Major Noel switched off the command speaker. That did it. They were going to make it. McDonald would bring them in.

Colonel Cragg wasn't going to look too good on this one. Not the way the newspaper guy would write it up, he wouldn't. All Dane had to do was stick to the facts. Not that he could be expected to miss playing up his own part. If he didn't do it, Amalgamated Press would do it for him. They would want to make a hero out of their own guy.

The colonel had been wrong to let him go out at all, even if the guy practically forced it on him by his newspaper connections. It was a mistake to let any civilians go at all. The business of the sortie was search and rescue, not any last-minute observation or specimen gathering. For that matter Major Noel had a pretty fair scientific reputation himself, and who had a better right to lead the sortie? But he "couldn't be spared."

It was a cinch. Exactly where the guy Dane had said they'd be. A guy named Noel would have found them, with or without Dane, given the co-ordinates, but it sure looked like he wouldn't get much out of the trip except his name on the crew list.

He explored the back of his scalp, pressing gingerly at the area of the old wound. The ache was worse, pulsing dully every few seconds. Maybe the low gravity pull had something to do with it. It had started up right after they had been on Mars a little while. It had certainly been aching the second night. He remembered it hurting that night, all night. Hell, that was only night before last. Monday night and this was Wednesday morning. It seemed plenty longer than that. Still it couldn't be anything serious. They had told him he oughtn't to have any trouble, and he hadn't in all the three years. No aches or pains, except from the sight of a hospital. No more of that ever. That was wish number one. When you thought about that and all the things that could happen to a guy and every day you see the guys all around you that have already had it that made you hate the sight of a hospital.

It was uncomfortable and unnatural enough to have to live in a ward with five other men for three months. Without being sick and weak while you were doing it. A man who was well and in good health was deemed to require the space and privacy of his own three rooms to sustain him for effective duty. What formless asininity of military medicine decreed that it was good for him to share his bedroom and latrine with five strangers when he was sick and flat on his back on his bed the whole long day and longer night—that even the docs themselves didn't pretend to know. Except that it wasn't good for patients to be too much alone. When else does a man want to be more free than ever from the slashed, the smashed, and the diseased! And their stupid, interminable yammering. You shut it out with a book, but still it flows on, around and over you until the indignity of your public exposure, even to their visitors, combines with the unnecessary wakings in the mornings and the enforced early dousing of the lights so the five fools could sleep until no wonder a guy even hates to go near a hospital for his annual physical. Seeing the captain with his eyes smashed out fumble with three-weeks-blind fingers at Braille solitaire cards or grope for the latrine door and to know he didn't have the guts and imagination to destroy himself wasn't as bad as listening to the colonel with the mysterious sore back bray about his communications difficulties in Africa, interspersed with the careful detail of his daily treatments.

Father had been shocked by what he considered the trappings of poverty when he had torn himself away from Westchester and his broker's desk in the Street and found his son deep in the outlands of Georgia in bed in a room with five men and an unclosed archway yawning at the public hall. He had been too dispirited to explain to him that the normal and easy paternalism of the Air Force and the somewhat shabby beneficence of its Air Medical Corps did not proceed from exactly compatible points of view. You were either a man or a patient. One apparently couldn't be both, except for purpose of assignment to wards. He knew the Old Man was thinking of the nine years of Stanford technical education, as far across the country as you could get from Westchester, and the nine more years in the Air Force, not undistinguished years and characterized by rapid promotion, then to be treated for an honorable wound in the style of a charity patient. That was one thing he and Father had found to agree upon. It was a species of indecency.

And even that agreement had led inevitably to the old thing, and the Old Man had left angry again, angry as he could be under the circumstances, over a son demonstrably bright enough by his own record to realize the stupidity of wasting his life in uniform, as he had from the very beginning of the idea plainly told him he would be doing nine years before, when the choice was made in a quick afternoon of a California June. "Free life, hell," he snorted, snatching his hat up off the floor. "You're just playing a silly and dangerous child's game, and in costume at that. You see what it's got you, don't you? Even a fool can see that," he shouted for the edification of the blind captain and the communications colonel and the three empty beds whose tenants were obediently sunning themselves on the terrace. He turned his red-flushed, white-haired face away and stomped his still-squared six feet out of the presence of his dark, twisted-featured changeling.

Most of all there was the uniform. You knew the first time you put it on that you were made for it and for a pride in wearing it. It would be unthinkable to think of a time when you wouldn't wear it. How do you wear a hat after you've worn a cap? You going to settle down in a place like Westchester with a neighborhood of super-salesmen, and super bank clerks, and junior executives, and half-assed word and figure merchants and entertain their hungry wives at their parties and contribute to the Episcopalian Church? After Paris one day and Buenos Aires the next? You'd rather ride up the left bank of the Hudson every night right on schedule or drop in at the officers' mess bar after duty and lose yourself in the never-ending goings and comings of a thousand friends? The good old game of look-who-came-in-on-us-today-I-guess-they-must-not-have-any-guards-on-the-gate-today. You want to leave spit-and-polish cleanliness and military orderliness for paper-littered civilian streets and soiled, unsanitary civilian buildings, and ill-groomed, half-washed civilian mobs? There were lots worse things than being a perpetual executive officer or navigation officer or some other kind of an officer and somebody else always getting the command jobs. Back to research and development, Noel. That's your dish. You can't be spared. Not enough men with your background in uniform. Maybe not, except when they were handing out the promotions. There were always a lot of qualified ones then. With some kind of qualifications. At least they got the promotions.

The clock said twenty more minutes. Then he could get some sleep. A good nap and maybe he would feel a lot better.

At straight up 0700 Colonel Cragg stepped smartly into the command post. He sped the customary glance over the long workbench before he checked the instrumentation banked above it. The frown, Noel supposed—hell, he knew—was for the chart spread untidily askew before the commander's chair. Noel got up and laid it out smoothly on the chart desk, answering the good morning and watching the colonel pick up the log sheet.

The guy wouldn't ask what had happened. Not him. He would get the officially recorded information first. Through channels, even with the two of them in the room together.

"Very good," Cragg barked. "McDonald has found them. I won't say I'm not surprised. It looked pretty hopeless. Their being alive, I mean. Fill me in," he added. "If they don't talk or move, what makes them think they're alive? They can't get inside the suits to check."

Noel told him about the breathing. "McDonald said they found Dr. Pembroke sitting up like a Buddha all by himself out in the weeds. They couldn't rouse any of them at all. Dane thinks they're in a state of shock."

"Captain King had better watch out for that man. Next thing he'll be in the flight surgeon business." Cragg sprawled down in his chair and put his feet up on the workbench. "Sounds like an overdose of that static electricity to me. They've been in the middle of the spark fire for two days."

There was one for you. Even if the guy didn't have any scientific training.

Cragg shook his head and scowled at the log sheet. "This estimated time of arrival you've got here of 1230 hours. They've got to carry three men."

"They think they'll make it. McDonald thinks so." He told him about the carrying sling made out of specimen bags. "They've got a pretty fair chance of making it."

Cragg got up and went to the chart desk to make his own measurement, "Carrying sixty to seventy pounds of man a piece, they'll really have to crowd it."

"They can haul them in their specimen cart when they get out of the lichens." Anyway, you could damn well bet that the colonel would never take off with them in sight, coming in over the red plain. And they would be in sight in the glass as soon as they left the lichen beds. No matter what time it was, he'd never take off with them alive and kicking and right under his nose. No commander could do that.

Cragg found his easy chair again. "Stand by for 1300 take-off as planned. If they're late, we've got to give them a break, but I want to be ready to go the minute they're inside. Unless the penetrations build up. If it does, then they've had it anyway. Now you'd better get a little sleep," he added, the finality of his tone choking off Noel's remark about the lack of data on the lethality of the radiation. "You're going to have a busy afternoon." He began the business of lighting one of his cigars.

Noel opened the door of the radio room to tell the watch to call him at 1000. He went back to the chart table and picked up his pencils. At the exit he stopped.

"Well?"

Noel hesitated. The colonel was obviously disinclined to talk any more. "There was one other thing."

Cragg waited him out.

"On the report McDonald made just before you came in—some of the things they said didn't make sense, or I didn't understand them. But when I queried them, they only laughed."

Cragg spit out a puff of smoke. "Major, please come to the point!"

Noel said, "It was just that it was peculiar—under the circumstances."

"You losing sleep to talk nonsense?"

Noel regretted that he had introduced the thing. Now there was no help for it. "McDonald reported that they were making good time, considering the difficulty of wading through the lichens. Then Dane cut in and said, 'Once I was very happy. There was soft black soil at the edge of the orchard and we made a garden.' That's all he said. I couldn't get another word from him."

Cragg snorted. "That settles it. The radiation is getting them too. He's jetting off wing. Not that he had far to turn."

Noel thought a moment. "I'm sure I remember it exactly word for word. Then McDonald laughed and signed out." He hesitated a second. "Maybe we ought to mount a party to go meet them."

The colonel poked the cigar at him. "Not another man leaves this spacecraft. Not one man. Not even to go outside for one minute. We've very likely lost seven men already." He puffed rapidly at his restored smoke. "Put an operator on them. I want to know as soon as he can contact them. I want to talk to McDonald myself. I want to give him a good laugh."

Noel went back into the radio room and gave the order to the watch. Then he went to his bunk. In two minutes he was asleep.

In no better than two more minutes he was fighting the buzz of the intercom. It was already 1000. He fumbled for the right key and called

Captain Spear at the command post. "What's the news from the McDonald party?"

Spear came on. "None, sir. We've been unable to contact them since your last contact at 0654."

Noel calculated rapidly. They should have reached the edge of the lichen beds by now. Or be very near to it.

He pulled on his heavy boots and climbed the ladders to the sunlit lookout chamber in the peak of the spacecraft. He stood for a moment, ringed with glassite ports and 110 feet aboveground, and looked out at the red emptiness before he waved the observer aside. He swung the three-inch refractor at the near horizon of the lichen forest and put his face against the eyepiece. He followed the low line of the vegetation slowly to far left and then to far right. Then he began to scour the reel plain in front of it. The dust flat was as bare as the perimeter of the lichen land had been uninterrupted by alien form or movement.

It was not good. He kept at the search until the hands of his watch crawled around to 1020 hours. Finally he relinquished the telescope to the observer. He had the six decks below to inspect before take-off time. He had to go over the entire 80-foot sphere perched 24 feet high on its truncated drive cone. Opening on the circular corridors of the five decks above the drive deck were nearly two hundred rooms and quarters. Not all, fortunately, housed equipment essential to the maneuvering of the spacecraft, but all merited at least a professional glance.

He climbed down through the hatch to 3-high deck immediately below. Its storerooms and compartments delayed him only a few minutes. All but two displayed either their initial seals or those affixed in last night's inspection.

Two-high deck bore laboratories equipped for the scientists and the hospital. Not much to be held in readiness here either, although he did want to stop in the radiation laboratory to get a reading from the cloud-chamber monitor.

A round little thick-lipped man by the name of Spivak handed him the graphs. Noel let out a low whistle.

Spivak nodded. "One-point-three above yesterday this time." He seemed cheerful about it. He fished out a pencil and pointed at the red line that rose at a steep angle over yesterday's blue line. "They're diverging sharply."

Noel handed him back the clipboard. "Calculate the rate of divergence based on the last hour and give me predictions for 1200, 1300, and 1400 hours. I want it right away."

Spivak picked up a greenish pad. "I've already got it. Rate of divergence, point-one-four-five. That's from 0900 to 1015, but from 1000 to 1015 she went up to point-one-five-eight. Take the last rate off, and here's your curve."

Noel didn't like the way the man said it. He snatched the graph pad from him and scanned it hurriedly. Fear confirmed, he examined it more carefully. Twelve o'clock: 11.2 percent intensity; penetrations .0083 per second. Thirteen hundred hours: 13-7 percent intensity; penetrations .0136. Fourteen hundred hours: 16.6 and .0291. He looked up at Spivak. "What do you think?"

The man shrugged. "You really want to know what I think? I think we'd better get the hell off this Godforsaken ball of nothing fast. We can't take it. She'll pour through our insulation like a sieve."

Noel thought of Dane and young McDonald. Wertz with his heavy humorless stories. Not a chance. Not even the diamond-hard timageel that sheathed the spacecraft and the magnetic zoning could arrest the invisible bombardment.

"I'll tell Colonel Cragg. There's no word from McDonald since 0700. He'll more than likely move up the take-off."

Spivak said, "I know. He just left. He's checking your take-off settings right now."

"You know a hell of a lot," Noel snapped. "Why didn't you tell me?"

"Did you ask me?" The man grinned. "Look"—his face darkened savagely—"I want to go. We all want to go. We've made the trip and proved it, and this stuff is hot. The hull won't turn it. We got no time for lifesaving. Except our own, and damn little for that. The colonel's got good sense."

Noel strode to the call box and flipped the all-stations key. "Noel to Colonel Cragg."

"Noel." The reply was crisp-toned and meaningful. "I was about to call you. The big computer is out. Edwards can't get it to function, but I want an immediate take-off. I assume you're ready. We'll have to use the settings for 1300. Man all stations and charge the drive."

"They're not good for two hours yet!" Noel remonstrated. "The settings are computed to a tolerance of no more than 120 seconds."

The speaker blasted. "I am well acquainted with take-off settings. They'll have to do. We're going off in less than thirty minutes. That is, if this spacecraft is ready, as ordered. It is, isn't it?"

"It is," Noel answered grimly.

"Then we use the 1300 settings and correct when we can after take-off. It would take the rest of the day to work out new settings by hand with a slide rule. Do you read me?"

Noel looked at Spivak's broad civilian grin. "Yes, sir."

"It's 1043. We go off at 1100. I'll stand by for your clear. Take over."

CHAPTER SEVEN

Dane waded through the lichens. During the first few minutes of it, he had thought that it was going to wear them down quickly. The weight itself wasn't too bad. The inert forms of Dr. Pembroke, Jackson, and Beemis swung in the triangular hammock devised from specimen bags joined together and suspended from ropes knotted in baldric fashion around the waists and shoulders of the three bearers. By leaning outward against the weight of the three points of the triangle they could support the hammock off the ground fairly easily.

But the going had been awkward, until they caught the cadence of it. The sling fought its suspension among them, sagging and bumping the ground with every unevening of the pace. After a time they mastered the technique of keeping the suspending cords taut by an approximation of military step and with response to any slackening of one of the cords by leaning harder against the other two. The lichens now slid smoothly underneath, and even with frequent pauses they were making almost as good speed under the thin daylight, coming out burdened, as they had made on the way in under darkness.

Dane noticed that his thermometer had already climbed to -15° Centigrade for the ambient atmosphere. The pressure-suit air conditioner would soon be loading to hold down his body heat. He sniffed for the faintly chemical odor it imparted to his air when the temperature began to climb. His mouth was unusually dry, it occurred to him. He thought briefly of a malfunction. But his inside temperature was normal, so the thing had to be all right, even if he couldn't smell it.

Sniffing like that reminded him of spring air and the fresh scent of newly turned earth. He was glad it was time to rest again and let the tiresome thing slip to the ground. He was thirsty. Mars and spring gardening. You think of funny things sometimes.

Now they were marching again. He must have been thinking of something when they had started. No one had said anything for a long time, so that the starts and stops and the marching were all about the same, except for the work of the carrying. It was a lot like wading in waist-deep water. The lichens offered a retarding inertia, rather than a clinging obstacle that had to be pushed forcibly aside. The sparsely entangled meshes of the rubbery plants parted for their advance with small resistance, bearing a shapeless shadow of the strangers effortlessly ahead of them and closing as effortlessly behind them into renewed entangled meshes. It was simply the matter of taking steps, one and then another and another. Uncomfortable and tiring but certainly possible. After a while he noticed that his mouth was open again and turned his head to the water tube.

But now it was something that Jane said about the sailboat. He couldn't remember. He was surprised at his watch. How did it get to almost nine o'clock? If McDonald and Wertz would stop talking, he would be able to remember what Jane had said.

Ahead over the green stuff he saw one of the bare places. They could rest there awhile, and he would remember about the sailboat and tell them about it. The smallish sun was up pretty high in a blue-white sky. Hazy. Looked like snow. But they certainly had time to talk awhile before they went in to lunch.

"Take a break," he muttered, coming out of the weeds into the open red dirt. He let his burden sag to the ground and sat down, deciding that Washington was a poor place for a man to live when he could be on the mesas and plains of Texas. Fatigue rolled over him. It was good to rest. Why had he thought about Jane Slocum? He hadn't seen her for seven years. Since the weekend of the prom and he had gone back to Texas. It could be very dark in Texas, camping in the big deer lots. In the loneliness of late night it was dark in the camp, where the thick brush shut off the stars. It was dark, but the sleeping bag was snug-warm and the air was clean and easy to breathe.

Dane sat up, realizing at once where he was. It was midnight dark. With a quick pang he stabbed his light around, spotting the recumbent forms of Wertz and Lieutenant McDonald and the ones in the carrying sling. According to his watch, the hour was 2041. Maturing despair knotted around his bowels and jerked him wide awake with a clear realism. The spacecraft had been gone eight hours! He looked up for Earth, but the high haze was thick and the heavens were blindly unrelieved.

He threw on his radio and called. Over and over again until he had to admit the certainty. There was no answer. There could be no answer. The Far Venture was long beyond the range of their feeble radio packs. They were alone. Unthinkably abandoned. Never to see Earth again.

With three days' oxygen, he thought bitterly, they would not become old inhabitants of their alien world.

"This is it for John Dane!" he said unbelievingly. Unfortunately you don't just go conveniently mad and rail at fate, as in an ancient tragedy. With a flash of relief he thought that the ultimate action always awaits. It is always at hand—just ahead of the intolerable. He thought about the old Roman Stoic, with his room too full of smoke for ease. One can always leave the room.

It was a short comfort. How could it happen to John Dane? He bent his light over the lieutenant. The eyes were shut, the features composed and natural behind the visor of the helmet. Looking close, he saw the systole and diastole of the lips expressing a normal breathing. He shined the light on Wertz. They were both asleep. Nothing but asleep.

Well, he had his pistol. It would be kind to put them permanently to sleep. He fought the numbing impulse to review the delight of being snug aboard the onrushing spacecraft—amid the familiar confinement—already thousands of miles along course. The challenge of the endless emptiness to be traversed would be welcome; the nagging thought that the perfect flight of the spacecraft might be imperfect, a minor trouble.

It was panic thinking—make-believe—absurd. They were here. On Mars. Colonel Cragg was human. Like all men, he was human. If he had to choose between saving himself and his crew and waiting out three overdue wanderers in a forbidding mystery, he would make only one choice.

Yet you have to do something. At least you have to know for sure. You have to confirm the fearful certainty. As a man who suspects himself in a fatal disease compels himself to seek the certainty of the doctor's verdict, dreading to go only a little less than dreading to stay away and risk the loss of a possible cure.

He saw McDonald stir. Then Wertz. Then he realized that he was shouting into his microphone for them to wake up.

"My God!" he heard Wertz's voice rumble. "It's night!" The man got stiffly to his feet, an ungainly mechanical figure in the beam of light.

McDonald was already calling to spacecraft.

"It's no use," Dane told him. "I tried it. Either Colonel Cragg has taken off and left us, or maybe they're not listening in for us."

They knew that was unlikely. They did not like to say impossible. The operator might be snoozing at his post. But not on Colonel Cragg's crew. Maybe something might have gone wrong with the equipment. Radio long range had been out with Earth ever since they had come close to the planet. Maybe there had been some kind of a blankout on the liaison wavelength.

Dane said, "I'm not going to believe he left us until I see it for myself. We'll go see if they've gone."

Wertz said, "We were fools to come out here. He warned us."

"No," Dane said harshly. "Somebody had to come." Lieutenant McDonald said, "I guess we lost the toss. But it's a hard way to get it."

Dane picked up his rope's end and put it over his shoulder. "I say let's go see. We'll call every ten minutes. It doesn't matter much about the power now."

The others bent slowly to take up the load. Wertz said, "I don't think it was natural sleep. I had some awfully silly ideas running around in my head while we were walking. You want to know what I think, this radiation effect is working on us. Before long we're out like them." He jerked an armored hand at the three unconscious men.

"We're going to get out of these lichens," Dane told him. "By a straight line. As fast as we can go."

"I remember I thought I was going down the beach at Clearwater, Florida," McDonald said. "I was looking for a place there called the Seahorse Tavern. You men were off your orders too. How do we know what direction we've been going?"

"All we have to do," Dane told him, "is go straight west. That will bring us out on the dust. By then we'll see the beacon light. Maybe before. If it's still there, we'll see it."

"We ought to see it now," Wertz objected. "Unless we've been backtracking."

"There's a lot of dust haze, maybe." Dane threw his light ahead. "The lights don't penetrate very far."

The others tried it, shining their lights in sweeping arcs.

"Maybe you're right," McDonald said. "At least it's a hope."

They made one more call. Then they started into the west, the only direction that could be conceived as friendly. The loaded sling swung clumsy and slow against their urgency. Talk was over. They needed their breath. There was nothing to say except the things that a man has to keep within himself.

After an hour the lights were thrusting ahead against a thicker dusty ground haze, quelling at least the fear that because they could not yet see the beacon light, there was none to see.

At 0057 they came out of the lichens and stood all at once with unreasonable surprise on the broad dust plain, flat before them, denuded and barren as the bed of an old salt sea.

"Which way now?" Wertz wanted to know.

Dane had been thinking about that for an hour. "Unless we're hopelessly off, we should be northeast of the landing place. If we follow the edge to the south, we ought to find our specimen cart. Then we'll know our course exactly."

They went south for a half mile, then another half mile, and then at least another. The straight edge of the plant land still ran empty before them as far as the lights would shine. Rest stops were coming closer together. As the distance fell behind, nobody said anything about how far they had come into the south.

At 0245 Lieutenant McDonald finally called a halt. "I hate to think it, but we must have turned the wrong way. We've come more than two miles. If we'd been walking in the right direction, we'd have come to the cart by now."

They eased the sling to the ground.

Dane said, "I don't think so. I mean I don't think we had any reason to turn north. Unless we walked a long way straight south this morning, we've got to be right. If we were wandering around off bearing, we could just as likely have gone northerly."

"Look," Wertz said, "we know the spacecraft is gone, but even if it isn't, it's five miles out from the lichens. It's five miles out there in the dust someplace. North or south from here, we don't know which. I say we strike straight out. After we get out in the dust about five miles, we wait for daylight. We couldn't be too far off. We'll see it all right, if they waited for us. What's more important, maybe they can see us. This way we can walk ourselves completely out of their sight. Even if the dust settles."

It wasn't a bad idea. Except for the cart. The cart would relieve them of their load and double their speed. "Maybe it's only another hundred yards in front of us," Dane told them. "If we turn out now, we know for certain we've got to carry this sling all night."

"Maybe I ought to scout ahead," McDonald said. "I can go twice as fast if I don't have to lug anything. You two wait here and I'll come back with the cart if I can find it in the next mile."

"No!" Dane said sharply. "We stick together. You saw what happened to Houck."

"What are you trying to do?" Wertz exploded. "You starting that up again!"

"I don't know what I think. Except that it's obvious Houck was coming back for help. Maybe he was even coming to warn the rest of us. Something happened to him. Or maybe again, something got him."

McDonald whistled. "Jesus! You mean maybe something didn't want him to get back to the spacecraft?"

"He's nuts!" Wertz growled. "Nothing living could exist here. Except the damned lichens."

"I hope you're right," Dane said. "I hope to hell you're right. But what you really mean is that something like us couldn't exist here. Something that our experience can describe. That's all you can mean. It's extremely probable that a lot of things exist in the universe that our experience is too limited to describe. Why not here?"

"Nuts again," Wertz said.

"Just the same," Dane persisted, "there's a kind of pattern to the things that have been happening here on Mars. Maybe it's a conscious pattern trying to impose itself upon us. Maybe we were deliberately kept from returning. Maybe Dr. Pembroke and the others were kept from getting back to the spacecraft."

"But why?" McDonald demanded.

Dane picked up his rope. "Who knows? Maybe if some kind of conscious beings do exist here, they're curious. Curiosity is the mark of consciousness. That's why we came to Mars ourselves, isn't it? Curiosity."

"Curiosity killed a cat," Wertz said grimly.

It's an obsession, Dane told himself. It's a kind of pathetic fallacy. I'm forcing my own thoughtways upon events to make them conform to my own experience. But he could not help finishing out his idea. "If there is curiosity here, it could be observing us. Like specimens, so to speak. That's what we would do in its place."

"Cut it out," Wertz snapped. "You'll have me believing you. Not that it matters a hell of a lot. Cragg is long gone."

"We don't say that until we know it for sure," Dane said. "Let's go."

They took up the three-part load of the sling and resumed their grind along the edge of the lichen beds. At 0305 hours they rested for five minutes. At 0310 they headed again into the south, with McDonald on point at the apex of their little triangle.

At 0319 McDonald checked abruptly, hand upraised in the signal to halt. "What's that up ahead?"

CHAPTER EIGHT

Dane strained to see. There was nothing for him but the vague curtain of the dust haze. Nor for Wertz, behind his thick-lensed spectacles.

"It's a fence, looks like!" McDonald exclaimed. "Right out there. Straight ahead. Can't you see it!"

A hand came out of nowhere and gripped. Dane strove to speak. He heard himself say in a tight voice, "Let's get a little closer."

They freed themselves from the weight of the sling and huddled.

"We ought to spread out a little," Dane told them, "and move up on it slow. Keep one light steady ahead. McDonald's. He's got the best eyesight. Wertz and I'll cover us around the sides and behind."

He snapped his own light on and began to play it to the right and right rear.

"Wait a minute," he added. "Remember our basic briefings. If there is something alive and conscious out there, don't fire at it until it is definitely hostile and dangerous."

"Jesus God!" Wertz rasped.

"We don't know." Dane forced himself to speak calmly. "They could be friendly. Wouldn't we try to be friendly on Earth, until the unbelievable monsters from another world attacked us? We've got to remember that if the things are monsters to us, our appearance is for that very same reason monstrous to them."

"I don't want to take any more of this," McDonald spoke out. "Let's go on ahead and get it over with."

They inched forward, deeper into the fantasy. McDonald's beam gouged the dust that sifted through the night until it was diffused, dissipated, and throttled at the limit of vision. Playing his own light steadily to the side and rear, Dane wrestled with desire to face into the fearful front, if only for the briefest assurance.

It was unbearably long. Then Dane saw it himself. A long low barrier hugged the ground athwart their path.

Suddenly McDonald broke ahead, striding swiftly at the thing.

"Lieutenant!" Dane yelled at him, forgetting the helmet and the microphone.

A raucous reply burst in his ears. "Here's your fence!" McDonald sounded as if he were choking on the words. "Completely without monsters. It's only some more damned lichens."

They went up, clammy with the draining suspense. Blocking further advance to the south, a long line of lichens stretched out as far to the right as they could see.

Wertz played his light about. "Looks like we're in the pocket of a bay. They must have been falling back gradually to the left."

Dane checked his compass quickly. "What do you get, McDonald?"

"What do you mean, what do I get?"

"Your compass. What direction does the edge of this bed run?"

McDonald raised his wrist to look. He shook the instrument and looked again. "East and west, according to this."

"Mine reads the same. How about yours, Wertz?"

"East and west," Wertz answered. "I don't get it. The lichen beds run almost due north and south for forty or fifty miles. Something must be wrong with the compasses."

They checked the instruments against each other. If they were in error, they were no more than a degree apart on the error.

Wertz said, "It's probably a small promontory we overlooked."

"Then we're long miles away from the landing place," McDonald said. "From the observation deck you can see the edge of the lichen forest runs north and south from horizon to horizon."

"A small promontory could fool you from a distance," Wertz argued. "It probably only runs out a hundred yards or so and then bends back to the south."

Dane detected the taint in his voice. "You thinking what I'm thinking, Wertz?" he went on. "About the carts?"

"Where else could they be?" Wertz burst out angrily. "First we can't find Dr. Pembroke's cart. Then we can't find ours. Now we find lichens where lichens are not supposed to be. Only they couldn't grow that fast."

Dane said, "What do we really know about them? Remember how fast the green areas on Mars have been observed to expand in the spring? Only an extremely intense metabolism in the plants could explain it. Maybe to cope with their environment they have a metabolism comparable to our rate of living raised several powers."

"You saying they grew out around the carts?" McDonald asked.

"I can't think anything else," Dane said. "We should have thought of it sooner. There wasn't any place for Dr. Pembroke's cart to be except in the lichens, and he wouldn't have dragged it into them. That goes for ours too."

McDonald pointed at the plants in front of them. "In there someplace?"

Dane hesitated. Then he made up his mind. "No. Not in there. Somewhere behind us. I think we must have passed the place a long way back. I think these lichens grew out today for another reason. I think we're directly opposite the landing place at its closest point to the lichens. I think this stuff is growing out towards the spacecraft."

"The metal?" Wertz fumbled with the idea. "The metal, maybe? Attracted by it, maybe?"

Dane knew he was thinking about Houck's pressure suit. He was thinking about that corroded, crumbling metal himself. "Or maybe by the power emanations of the spacecraft's equipment," he said. "Last night there was a significant spark-fire pattern pointing directly at the spacecraft. If we follow this line on out, I'll bet it will point directly at the landing place."

Wertz said, "So what?"

A little more and Wertz would give up. "We don't know that," Dane told him sharply. "Until we do, we've got to keep trying. Maybe Colonel Cragg set a new time to wait us out. It could be daylight. We've got to hurry until we know he's gone for sure."

They retraced their steps to their burden and angled out to follow the lichens.

After a while Lieutenant McDonald said, "This is no promontory we overlooked. Not this big a one."

The lichens ran on west for a quarter of a mile before they cut off and bent sharply back in the direction of the main beds. At the apex the peninsula was narrow. Fingerlike.

They slogged on. Out into the open dust plain, glad to leave the cursed lichens behind. Even if only a vast emptiness of rolling sand dust lay before them. It was, Dane noted, 0355.

Apathetically he listened to McDonald make the 0400 call and waited without hope for an answer. Dog-tired, he thought.

They now rested every ten minutes. Still the pace dragged. The load they bore was not backbreaking, but it had clung to them for so long that it was like the old man of the sea—unrelenting—endlessly swinging among them and trying to draw them down into the dust. At best they were making scarcely a mile for every hour of fighting to stay on their feet.

It was 0500. If his hunch about the lichen peninsula was correct, Dane thought, they could not be more than three miles from the landing place. No faintest imagining of beacon light had they seen. Perversely the dust settled more thickly over their own probing light rays.

"We couldn't see the top light if we were within a thousand feet of it," the lieutenant essayed. The note of hope was faint.

They rested and went on again. There was no end, Dane thought. They were marching in a non-time. The minutes and hours they measured on watches made no sense. Purpose was reduced to putting a foot forward, then the other, then the first, then the second. Except for the blessed stops.

At 0630 daylight was palpably in the air, but they still lived in the ocher folds of the dust storm. "Just let it stop," McDonald swore. "Just let the damned wind stop blowing and we could see something."

They could feel no wind, no familiar movement of air, but it was there, three or four miles an hour of it, stirring the feathery dust into vague billows. Like tired smoke. If it would stop, the dust would settle fast in the thin air.

At 0900 they stood together in the haze and agreed that they had come at least five miles. They ought to circle and search. Maybe they had already passed the place. Even if they had been coming out along the right line.

"What's the use?" Wertz objected. "If the spacecraft is still here, we could be close enough to spit on it and not see it."

"It's getting lighter." Dane tried to sound cheerful. "Maybe it's settling out."

"It's just the sun climbing," Wertz came back. He pointed up at a brighter spot in the eastern sky.

"We might as well rest awhile and see," Dane decided. "There's no use wandering around in it. We can't go much longer anyway."

With added gentleness they lowered their burden into the dust. Probably for the last time, Dane thought, not caring much about the fatigue. This is it, he decided. He sat down first and then stretched out full length on the red-dirtying soil, which had long since coated them with its own-claiming color. Waves of relief laved his numb muscles.

CHAPTER NINE

He was bouncing around in a boat. Fishing? Somebody was shaking him.

He looked up into broad daylight. At a pressure-helmeted head bending over him. Memory flooded back. The dust had settled!

Then he saw! Behind the transparent visor was the face of Major Noel! He croaked at his microphone.

"Take it easy," he heard.

Dane sat up. He saw the massive happy shape of the spacecraft, geometrical on the red plain. Not a half mile away. He pointed. "Brother, am I glad to see that! We thought for sure that Cragg had left us."

"He couldn't," Major Noel said.

Dane got stiffly to his feet. "Maybe he's human after all." He saw that Wertz and Lieutenant McDonald were sitting up, their visors wiped clean of red dust. There were three men with Noel and two carts.

"Couldn't you hear us calling you?" he blurted. He was appalled now at the fright. Radio blankout, and a man left past hope. Anyway, he was happy. He was happy as all hell, with a great, lightheaded bubbling of spirits. He was thirsty. He was starving. He was everything that was being alive. He decided against the relief tube. In a few minutes they would be rid of the suits. And never again!

Dane, old boy, you made it, he exulted privately. You made it!

Noel said, "I may as well tell you now. The colonel didn't wait for you. We couldn't raise you, but the colonel was going anyhow. We couldn't take off. She wouldn't fire up. The activators are dead as a last year's pullet." He went over to the carts to look at Dr. Pembroke and the others.

It was the way the little major had said it. Dane had no intimate knowledge of the intricate organs of the great spacecraft, no familiar kinship with the immense tubular rocket engines or the squat nuclear activators that topped them. Knowing their names and even with some precision the manner of their workings and the long history of ordered thought precedent to their devising was not ample to imagining the detail of the diagnosis and cure of their ills with wrench and customed know-how. Yet a machine was something a mechanic could fix. With time and effort perhaps but, by virtue of his calling, surely. For certainly a machine stood beyond the realm of organic decay or disease or accidental death. Wear and fracture and stoppage were all susceptible to the specifics of new parts or cleaning or adjustment.

It was the way Noel had said it. The specifics had been applied and applied again and had failed. There had been finality and violence to the utterance that bespoke the man too disciplined to rail at the inevitable but too sensitively vigorous to accept it. Again he thought, like one who hears from his physician the inevitable, impossible sentence passed on his own selfness.

"What's the matter with them?" he asked.

Noel started the procession off towards the spacecraft. "We don't know," he said shortly. "We can't find anything wrong with them. Except that they won't react for more than ten to twenty percent power."

He cut the explanation off as definitely as the slamming of a door and went back to questioning McDonald. Dane decided that only military conversation was desired. He didn't want to talk anyway. He just wanted to get in the Far Venture and out of the suit as soon as he could. Before he starved to death. No ration pellets this close to the mess room. His watering mouth conjured with the taste image of a thick Air Force steak. With fried potatoes. With pan gravy made from the steak drippings. With ice-cold milk. With homemade bread and yellow butter. Maybe some of the mess cook's specialty, the baked beans in tomato sauce he always had ready for snacks. It was the best thing about the whole oversized junket, eating in an Air Force mess again, day after day. If he didn't quit letting his appetite run away, it would be more than a few pounds he had to lose.

Then the airlock was closing and there was the struggle to get out of the suits. Why all the quiet? He saw one or two of the rescuers glance at him and look away without smiling while they jostled out of the stiff suits and passed them up through the manhole for storage, mounting the ladders one by one, manhandling the inert bodies.

"You all quit talking?" he demanded.

Noel nodded at the last two crewmembers. He waited until they had stowed their gear and started up the ladders. He kept on waiting, his swarthy squeezed-up face contemplating the manual acts of bringing his cigarette to his lips and taking it away again to emit short exhalations of smoke. "To hell with it!" he grunted.

He swung on Dane. "This is it. The top rocket man on board this can is a Pembroke man. Like you. And a civilian. Like you. Now that you're back on board, do we go?"

Silence swelled thick between them. The little major's eye did not waver.

"Colonel Cragg?" Dane demanded.

"There are 125 men on this spacecraft," Noel snapped. "Officers, crew, and scientific personnel. Six were out on the sands. That leaves 119. Besides your friend Vining, that leaves 117 or 118 who think you and Vining messed up the engines."

"After Colonel Cragg suggested it, I suppose."

"Suggest hell! He put Vining under arrest."

Dane stared at him. "How stupid can you fellows get? How could Vining put the engines out? You've got rocket engineers on your crew. What's the matter with them? Wouldn't they know?"

"That's just it. They can't find anything the matter. They're tearing them all the way down now."

"Migod!" Dane exclaimed. "What I know about mechanics is how to open a can of sardines, but I do know a man couldn't do something in a few minutes to those engines that couldn't be found and fixed in a hurry. He wouldn't be able to make any noise. He couldn't use any heavy tools."

"That's not what the engineers say. If he is the top rocket man in the United States."

Dane snorted. "It doesn't make sense. I want to see this guy Cragg. Now!" Burning up, he reached for the ladder.

Noel said, "Maybe you'd better wait a minute. He's looking for you, too. He'll wait. But here's something you want to think about before you shoot off your mouth. As soon as we spotted you out on the plain this afternoon, the colonel released Vining and put him to work on the engines. That puts your Mr. Vining on somewhat of a spot. You right along with him. If he gets them working, the colonel will probably prosecute the two of you for sabotage or willfully risking the spacecraft. If we get back to Earth, it's a trial and maybe prison. Of course if Vining can't start them, it doesn't matter much one way or the other."

His foot on the first rung, Dane turned half around. "What about you? What do you think?"

Noel laughed without mirth. "I know what I want to think. I hope to hell the colonel is right. I want to leave here. And quick. But I'm scared. I don't figure you're smart enough for it. I don't mean you're dumb. I mean just not sharp smart. I don't think you're hard enough to think of giving yourself or Pembroke an ace in the hole with those engines until you could get back here. Vining maybe. But I don't figure you for it."

"Thanks for not too much."

Dane went on up the ladder. Was it possible? Vining was a square-shaped man whose frame must have been bulge-muscled in his younger days. His hands were spatulate and heavily calloused, but on top his bulky body was the curiously delicate face of a cloistered scholar, suggesting even in its habitual repose a latent frenzy. The man's lifelong passion was nuclear rocket engines, but in an older century he could have been a learned monk, dashing his fine-drawn intelligence against an intricate scholasticism instead of the calculus of thrust and fissionable fuels and the heat-resistant qualities of recondite alloys. To judge him, one would have to weigh the sacred idea of the tremendous motive power, to the design of which he had contributed so signally, weigh it against his love for his old friend Pembroke of an earlier generation of space enthusiasts. When Dane thought of the withdrawn, hazel-gray eyes, seemingly remote from the close at hand, as if the man continually forced an abstruse mathematical-chemical-physical conjunction into focus, he said to himself, No. Vining would never chance it. Not with the penetration rays mounting, perhaps to kill them all before his engines could prove themselves by the great fact of the successful voyage from Earth into the far unknown and return. For no personal glory but for the triumph of the idea he served, he would permit nothing to endanger the voyage.

Dane was very much afraid that Colonel Cragg was wrong about Vining. And if he was wrong, why couldn't the engineers start the engines? Some internal breakdown of the complex nuclear parts, where enormous reactive forces were confined to a balance as delicate as that of a chronometer? Requiring complete disassembly to discover and correct? But why? There had been no malfunction in the drive since its system-testing phase. Not one in flight tests. No sign of maladjustment in the outflight or the perfect landing operation. He mounted rapidly to Colonel Cragg's quarters.

Lieutenant McDonald and Wertz were already in the little chamber.

Cragg's lips thinned. His face, rough and stubborn as fired stone, twitched at the long scar that ran across his cheekbone to the tip of his ear. When he was angered, officially or privately, as he frequently was, the scar flared red. At the sight of Dane it began to burn. He threw down his pencil. "That's all, gentlemen, I want to speak to Dr. Dane." Dourly he watched them get out.

"Dane," he lanced out, "I've got only one thing to say to you. I intend to prosecute you to the limit of the law for delaying the take-off and exposing this vehicle and its crew to grave danger in willful contradiction of the orders of its commander."

"Possibly I ought to remind you," Dane restrained himself, "that I am not in the military service. I may be technically under your command for the duration of this voyage, but at its end I shall be as free to sue you as you are to charge me. If I were you, I wouldn't make any wild charges I couldn't prove."

"Through no fault of yours," Cragg ignored him, "we are all still healthy. Yesterday the penetrations came within point five of critical. For some reason, or good luck, they leveled off just in time. Today they are a little lower. Now that you and the precious Pembroke are safe inside, I suppose Vining will be able to repair the drive."

Dane decided to try to be reasonable. "Colonel, have you given any thought to the possibility of intelligence on this planet? Hostile intelligence? Spark fires concentrating around our personnel. Men mysteriously unconscious. Radios mysteriously dead when you need them most. Lieutenant Houck mysteriously dead. Fire patterns pointed at the spacecraft. Engines mysteriously inoperative. It just might add up to God knows what."

Cragg surveyed him coldly. "This conference is over."

Dane said, "That's okay with me. Our plain ordinary physical troubles are bad enough for me. Now maybe even the lichen vegetation is reacting to us. If the lichens really are attracted by the spacecraft metal, you had better give a lot of thought to stopping them before they get in contact with us."

Cragg spoke contemptuously in four letters.

CHAPTER TEN

From the ports of the high observation deck Dane watched the Martian night unroll itself from the east, as visible as a blue-black storm moving in wide brush strokes to paint over the sunset. Occasionally a metallic clamor intruded, but otherwise the spacecraft, huge and solid, seemed to doze, unfolding its people for sleep and untroubled security. The hour of evening slowed, nodded—deceived. Dane knew that in a dozen tactic positions men were alert.

Not only the engineers pursued their mystery. An officer stood watch at the command post, very probably Colonel Cragg himself. Power spun out of the dynamos for the lights and the living equipment, the radar that probed their environment, and the diverse complexes in the laboratories that stood by to record and interpret it.

Not only the crew and its officers, but physicists, biologists, chemists, astronomers, botanists, zoologists, mathematicians and statisticians, mineralogists strove in their tiny workshops with their instruments and their learning to bend a new world to the discipline of ordered inquiry. Doubtlessly the medic still lingered at his task of restoring Dr. Pembroke, Beemis, and Jackson. The cook and his helper must be busy with the evening rations.

And even as Dane contemplated the quiet and his aloneness, Airman First Class Humphries climbed into the chamber and busied himself with the searchlight, bringing on the piercing white beam and making trial sweeps over the near terrain. Afterward he switched it on automatic, so that the bright light ground tirelessly through 360 degrees of the darkness that shut them in.

The kitten-friendly Humphries was himself unusually reticent. In fact he had not spoken a word, greeting or otherwise. "You mad about something?" Dane asked him.

With patent care Humphries continued to monitor the sweep of the light. "I'm on duty," he muttered.

"That mean you can't even say hello? You've been on duty up here before and spoken your piece."

"Colonel Cragg ordered a special watch."

"What does he think is out there to watch against?" Dane tried.

"He didn't say." The remark was rudely short.

"Look, fellow," Dane spoke out sharply, "I may as well begin with you. There seems to be an idea running around that somebody fouled up the engines. If that's what you're sore about. Just for the record, I didn't. And I'm convinced that Mr. Vining didn't either."

The man stopped his fiddling. "Then why wouldn't they run?" he said. Surly disbelief canceled the question.

Dane decided that he might as well get to work. He toggled the power switches of the radar photo plane table. "I don't know. We can only hope they find the trouble soon."

"The grease is we'll take off in the morning. Now that you got back with Dr. Pembroke."

"I don't seem to have many choices," Dane observed. "If Vining and the engineers can fix the engines, he and I are guilty of sabotage. If they don't, we rot here." He worked the keys that inflated the balloon and released the antenna reel. In the attenuated atmosphere, even with the peanut scanner and the tiny photo-electric pickup button, the balloon could carry the finest and lightest of lead wires scarcely a thousand feet aloft.

Through the ports he had seen visually that the spark fires were exceptionally profuse, but when he tuned the plane table and threw both the radar and the photoelectric pickups on it, he let out a low whistle. Masses of the spark nets glowed twice as bright as he had yet observed them, and the great overriding bolts flung themselves from the nets to the horizon line every few seconds. Without any plotting Dane perceived the insistent and superior intensity of a pattern that converged toward the spacecraft. When he measured the peninsula of lichens that had thrust out into the plain, it was over two thousand yards long. In one day it had grown two thousand yards!

While he watched, an odd blip of light formed at the tip of the peninsula's image on the glass. To his amazement he saw it wink once, then twice, then three times, then repeat the cycle. After a pause the light winked again. Steadily the phenomenon repeated itself.

Why had Colonel Cragg sent a party out after dark to explore the lichen peninsula and why were they signaling with lights? He didn't recognize the signal. One dot, two dots, three dots spelled out *E-R-S* in radio code. It meant nothing to him.

Then he noticed that the phenomenon could not be a light signal. It was not being picked up by the photoelectric scanner. It was being picked up by the radar antenna. It had to be a radar signal, and the impulse that bore it was not originating with the spacecraft!

He fumbled at the keys of the intercom and called the command post. "Captain Spear?" he called, recognizing the answering voice. "Dane. Has Colonel Cragg got a patrol out? Near the lichen beds?"

"No." The reply was coldly official.

"Could any of the scientists have gone out?"

"That would really take the colonel off! Didn't you get a copy of the order he passed out?"

"Get this!" Dane said. "This is important. Check everybody and see if anyone is missing. It's possible someone might have slipped out without your knowing it."

"Jesus," Spear exclaimed. "If they did, the Old Man will fry them when they get back. Your little trip was enough for him." His voice changed. "Say, your crowd up to something 'scientific' again?"

"Check, will you?" Dane insisted. "I'm picking up a signal from about three miles out. On the radar frequency."

Spear swore again. "Will the Old Man ever fry 'em! I'll run down who it is."

"And let me know, will you?"

"Okay, okay." Spear signed off.

Immediately he broke in again. "Dane? Spear to Dane. Say," he said, "what kind of a signal did you say?"

Dane repeated. "A signal on the radar. A blip. A blip winking on and off like code."

"That's what I thought you said. Radar. You're seeing things. We don't have any communications equipment that would make a signal like that."

"That I know. At least I was pretty sure of it," Dane told him, his excitement mounting, "but I'm not mistaken about the signal. I'm looking at it right now. It might be interference from some piece of equipment someone has taken out there and is operating. Check, man," he shouted at the intercom. "We've got to know! Airman Humphries is here with me," he added, somewhat out of sequence.

Dane was appalled at his neglect of witnesses and the record. "Humphries, come here," he called. "Look at this." Quickly he brought the movie camera to bear on the luminosity of the plane table and started its motor.

He needn't have worried. The phenomenon persisted steadily, as unvarying as if it emanated from a timing device.

"What have you got?" the airman asked him.

Dane had to talk to someone. "It could be a query. One, two, three. One, two, three. The simplest form of a statement and a query. One, two, three. Over and over again. Something out there could be counting up to three for us. For us to notice that it is counting. For us to recognize that if it can count, therefore it exists. It's not saying one, two, three. It's saying, 'I am! I am! Do you recognize me?'"

Humphries looked startled. "There ain't nobody out there. You heard what the captain just said. You feel all right?"

Dane thought for a minute. "I don't know how I feel."

The intercom rasped. "All present and accounted for," Captain Spear sang out, like a group commander at retreat. "Nobody outside. You'd better get your equipment checked."

It was a letdown. He hadn't thought of a malfunction in his own device. He pushed the camera out of the way and studied the winking point. He decided to call the radio engineer.

Lieutenant Yudin had fat, moist-looking hands and a pallid round face that he appointed for an air of effectiveness with a small dark mustache and glasses in circular frames of black plastic. He liked to talk brusquely and firmly. "Must be in the antenna," he pronounced, like a suburban medic rounding out a diagnosis for the solider commuters. "Better reel it in. Couldn't be outside interference. Nothing out there to cause it." He began to manipulate switches.

"Hold it," Dane ordered. "I want to try something first. Can you rig up a make-and-break switch so we can interrupt our transmitter beam and send out some signals on it? Like dots and dashes?"

Yudin's smallish eyebrows went up. "What for?"

"I want to try something," Dane repeated. "Can you do it?"

Yudin looked as if he had just remembered what he had been told by his wife not to forget. "Sure I can, but what are you up to now? Some of your friends out there again?" He peered out a port at the flashing horizon.

"No, but it looks as if we're getting a signal." Dane pointed at the scope.

"What do you mean, 'No, but it looks like we're getting a signal'? If nobody's out there, how could we?"

"That blip." Dane pointed again. "One, two, three. One, two, three. It's too regular for a malfunction. It's exactly the way an ordered, reflective intelligence might approach a supposedly intelligent intruder. It could be a way of saying, 'I'm here. Do you recognize me?'"

Yudin's jaw slacked. Then he laughed raucously. "I'd better call the colonel and tell him you've really gone off your nut."

"Okay. Okay," Dane checked him. "First hook up the switch. Then do your calling. There's a chance something might be out there we didn't bring with us. Someone, if you want to call it that. I've got an idea."

"Migod, he really means it!" Doubt slanted toward bewilderment. "You really mean it?"

"The switch!" Dane insisted.

Yudin pointed at the control panel. "You can use the main power switch. It won't burn up on you. There's not enough juice."

Dane tried it. It was awkward, but he could do it. If he went at it slowly.

He waited until the mysterious blip showed and then interrupted itself. Trying to work the switch in the same cadence, if not at the same speed, he sent out answering pulses. One, two, three. One, two, three. Then he stopped.

The blip came on again. One, two, three. The same as before.

"Next will be our Brooklyn hour. After a few dozen scenes with our sponsor." But Yudin was caught up in the experiment, staring nearsightedly at the table scope.

Again Dane repeated the signal, striving to mock its tempo. A thought occurred to him. "I'll reverse it." He sent, three, two, one. Three, two, one.

They waited a minute. Another long minute. "Look's like you signed him off," Yudin said, relief in his voice. "Fooling around with that switch probably upset some impedance in the antenna circuit that was causing it."

Dane felt the knot of tension loosen. "Maybe you're right." Was he disappointed?

Yudin picked up his tool kit. "You didn't really think there might be something out there watching us, did you?"

"Look!" Dane shouted. The blip was on again. Winking furiously. Then, while he stood stiffly, arm half raised to point, it settled into the signal. One, two, three. One, two, three.

"I'd better pull that antenna in," Yudin said. Suddenly he whispered, "Migod!" He stared at the scope.

The thing was winking the reverse signal. Three, two, one. Three, two, one!

Dane leaped for the switch. Four, two, three, one, he signaled. Four, two, three, one.

Immediately the answer came. Four, two, three, one. Even the slower tempo of Dane's sending was imitated!

"I'll try a word on it!" Dane seized the switch handle and spelled out *c-a-t* in code.

Back came the answer. Dash-dot-dash-dot, dot-dash, dash. *C-a-t!* Then the identification signal was repeated. One, two, three.

Beginning to perspire, Dane sent the word that associated itself. Back came the answer. Dash-dot-dot, dash-dash-dash, dash-dash-dot. *D-o-g!*

Yudin stepped away from the radar table. He swore softly and looked at Dane, not framing the question in his eyes.

Dane felt a weird stroking against the nerves in his back. "There's something out there," he said hoarsely. "Something out there is aware of us."

Yudin took off his glasses and examined their cleanliness. "What do you think it is?"

"I'm going to ask it," Dane told him. He called Airman Humphries from his task with the searchlight. "I'm going to transmit the question 'Who are you?' Watch the radar carefully and remember what you see." He went back to the switch. "You read code, don't you?"

Humphries looked at Yudin.

The lieutenant nodded.

Humphries said, "Some."

"Watch it closely, then," Dane said. He took hold of the switch. "We ought to make a record of this." He indicated the charting table. "Both of you take pencil and paper and write down exactly what I send and what comes back."

He waited until they had picked up the writing materials, watching them with vivid attention as they selected pencils and handled the scratch pads. Then he began to send, *W-h-o a-r-e y-o-u?* He repeated, *W-h-o a-r-e y-o-u?*

He saw Yudin's face and Humphries' distorted by the effort of concentration. Then he was no longer aware of anything around him but the opaque glass mask of the plane table, veined with the fitful pattern of the spark fires over the map pickup.

At last the signal began to wink. Dane followed it breathlessly, feeling his lips spell out the letters like a child in school. *W-h-o a-r-e y-o-u? W-h-o a-r-e y-o-u?* His own signal had merely been repeated.

"He wants to know who we are," Humphries said uncertainly.

"Tell them," Yudin said.

Dane shook his head. "It couldn't know English. It's only repeating our signal."

"Maybe it's an echo," Humphries suggested.

"Not from this planet," Yudin said. "Not with radar waves traveling 186,000 miles a second. Too slow. It couldn't be an echo. Impossible. Look," he added soberly, "I don't like this. Supposing there really is some kind of Martian. Underground cities and that stuff they used to write stories about. What are they going to think about us? What do they do next? Maybe they're getting ready to come after us!"

Humphries said, "Jesus!"

"That's a point I tried to make with Colonel Cragg," Dane said. "But if they're really intelligent, they're curious. They will want to find out about us. Study us. Like we came to study things here. If they're intelligent enough to try to communicate with us, very likely they wouldn't want to destroy us. At least at first. It would be half-intelligent things, like primitive tribes on Earth, that would be dangerous."

"What do you mean, 'at first'?" Yudin demanded.

"They might decide we are dangerous to them." When he had said it, the little room contracted to a point of conspicuous light in the black darkness that peered into the ports. The expanse of red dust and drab green lichens was no longer the monotonous scenery of a barren, dead landscape but alive with watchful eyes. A place to be gone from.

Dane pushed the thought away. "There is one language that's universal. We'll try them in mathematics. Let's see if they can add."

He began to send again. He sent one dot, then another dot, and after a pause two dots. He followed with two dots, then two dots, then after a pause, four dots. Finally he sent four dots, four dots, then after the pause eight dots.

An answer came back at once, an exact repetition of the dots and pauses.

"E-E I. I-I H. H-H. And a string of dots. That doesn't make sense," Yudin complained.

"I wasn't sending code. Something Martian wouldn't know code numerals. I'm using one dot for the number one. Not for E. Two dots is for the number two. Four dots is the number four. I sent three equations. *One plus one equals two. Two plus two equals four. Four plus four equals eight.*" He rested his hand on the switch. "Now we'll see if they get the idea. Their first signals showed us they could count. Now we'll see if they can add."

He sent, *One, one…two. Two, two…four.* He waited a few seconds and sent, *Three, three…*then stopped. "Let's see if they get the idea and add three and three."

"I wish you wouldn't stand there and talk like a professor lecturing," Yudin broke out. "You've got me believing this thing! Not that it's possible."

"I'm surprised at myself," Dane told him. "Considering what we have discovered, I don't see how I can stand still at all. Wait!" he exclaimed suddenly. "We forgot all about it!"

Yudin jumped. "What!"

"The camera. We should have been recording— There it goes!"

"One, one...two," they counted. *"Two, two...four. Three, three...six."*

"Six!" Humphries shouted. "They added it!"

He knew then. "They're there!" he exclaimed. "Whatever they are, they're there. There's something alive and intelligent on this planet, and they're trying to communicate with us."

Full realization stabbed him with wild pride of accomplishment. He had done it! For the first time in the history of mankind, a man had established a mental union with a being from another world and had exchanged intelligible information. He had been that man!

Yudin clutched at his sleeve. "They're still sending!"

"Four, one...three," they counted. *"Four, two...two. Four, three"*

"They're subtracting!" Dane exulted. "They left the last equation incomplete. Now they're testing us!" Quickly he sent back the answer, *Four, three...one,* and got confirmation in reply, *Four, three...one.*

"One more test," Dane told them, "then we send for Colonel Cragg."

Yudin was reminded of his duty. "I'll have to tell him now. He'd better know right away."

"Better not use the intercom," Dane advised. "With the engines dead it might be smart to keep this quiet."

Yudin decided to polish his glasses once again. "I had forgotten about the drive. This thing drove it out of my mind. If we're really getting signals from the Martians, we could be in a helluva fix. We could if they take a notion to be mean."

"You thinking 'be mean' like Earth people?" Dane was surprised at how he resented the man's remark. After Yudin left, he called again across the tenuous bond of the radar waves. He tested the unknown signaler in multiplication and division and was exuberant when it sent him like problems in return. Then the winking responses became uncertain. They flashed on a time or two again but made no sense, then ceased.

Dane sat on the observer's stool and spun out his dream. His friend, his mind friend, had got the confirmation it wanted. The strange visitors from space were intellectual and rational. They seemed to be friendly. At least they had tried to exchange identification. Perhaps when this good news was digested, the unseen would show themselves. What the morrow might not reveal! Maybe yet tonight. It was unfortunate that the expert in the patterns of languages was lying unconscious in the hospital.

The rasp of heavy boots on the ladder broke his reverie. He thought of the difficulty of explaining all this to Colonel Cragg. If Dane knew his man, Cragg would call for battle stations.

When the hinged cover of the manhole pushed up, it was followed by the curly blond head and athletic shoulders of Captain Spear.

Half emerged, Spear held the cover back and ran his eyes once around the observation deck. "Dane," he said abruptly, "follow me. You're wanted."

Some more of Cragg's officiousness. Nobody, particularly the scientists, was going to forget who was boss. Well, it wasn't Spear's fault. Dane put his foot on the ladder and swung through the deck, wondering a little at Cragg's sending an officer as messenger. "Yudin tell you anything more?" he called down to Spear treading just below him. He rather liked the guy, for all his everlasting physical exercises. The American girl's dream, he thought. And in an Air Force uniform too. That took away the extra ten years, even for the junior misses.

Spear didn't say anything, running on down the rungs with the familiarity of an acrobat, or if he did, it wasn't audible over the noise of his boots. When Dane set foot on main deck and turned around, Major Noel stepped stock in front of him. Behind him on the open deck with Captain Spear, Dane saw Lieutenant Yudin and behind him an airman named Jerves.

They're jittery, Dane thought. They know. Yudin must have told them.

Noel's arm shot up. Dane felt the hard slash of the palm edge at his neck. Lights showered. Something hard drove into him. Then he realized that he was sitting on the metal deck and that Jerves was holding his arms. He felt a little sick from the neuralgia that streaked down his shoulder. When he cleared a little more, he found that chain-linked steel cuffs bound his wrists.

"Lock him up," Major Noel ordered. "And strip him clean of any metal he's got on him."

Dane stared up at him. "What the hell goes on with you!" He tried to make sense out of things, wondering at the hard plates he sat upon.

When he remembered the blow, he got up on his feet and surged at Noel, fighting against the weight of the two heavy men hanging onto him.

"I don't like a damn murderer," Noel snarled. "Especially when he tries to murder my own commander."

Through his hurting temper to beat the man down, Dane saw him dimly. "Colonel Cragg?" he heard himself say thickly. "You mean Colonel Cragg? He dead?" he added ungrammatically.

"You ought to know, damn you!" Noel shouted. He shoved at Dane's shoulder. "Get the hell to your bunk. I want to see you tied down and out from underfoot."

Dane conquered the urge to strike at him with the chain they had strung between his wrists. "How did I do all this?" he demanded. "Who made you the judge and jury?"

Noel turned on his heel and began to mount the ladder. Captain Spear and Jerves shoved at Dane, pushing him along the narrow corridor to his bedroom, thrusting him against his bunk while Jerves pulled the gravity boot off his right foot and snapped a leg shackle around the ankle and then around the rod that anchored one corner of the bunk to the deck. Then they took off the wrist irons and locked him behind his own door, doubly bound within the four-foot radius of his chains.

His weariness was sudden and refused to cope with it, riding even over the indignity of the restraint. He was leg-weary, arm-weary, back-weary, and mind-weary. The hours since he had lain on the bunk stretched behind him into far memory. He counted them vaguely while he got out of his clothes, momentarily wondering what they had expected to find on his person. Since 0600 Wednesday to 1930 Friday. Not counting the long sleep in the lichens and the shorter one on the red sands, it was nearly seventy-two hours. Six dozen hours. He grimaced. Sounded like a crate of eggs. A lot of eggs.

He put it off, all of it, until tomorrow. Except maybe the signals. In two minutes he was asleep.

CHAPTER ELEVEN

Lieutenant Yudin didn't like to mull over his experience on the observation deck, but he couldn't dismiss it. Even if he had been tricked.

It was 2100 hours. Throughout the Far Venture the Air Force crew stood their posts sharply, but under the ordered discipline, Lieutenant Yudin knew, things were in an uproar. The civilians, he observed with a faint distaste, knotted in gossiping all-civilian huddles with even more than their usual gregariousness. Still he would have joined one of their groups that flowed together, then dispersed in favor of a new combination, if it were fitting for him to discuss the casualty, his commander, with them. Though he scarcely knew any of the men, he would not really mind a word or two about the colonel, if he might in turn talk about Dane and find out what they really thought of him and his signals. The civilians were important in their fields, most of them, and he would like to tell them about the phony signals and get their reactions. They were an aloof and casual bunch, though, not concise and mannerly like the military. He felt that they looked upon the crew with supercilious and secret amusement. Civil but always smiling about it.

After a while he packed his small hand tools with neat order and took them out of his little workroom. He climbed with some difficulty up the ladders to the observation deck. There he stood for a long time, looking at the photo plane table and trying to make up his mind. Finally he laid out his tools and began laboriously to disassemble the apparatus. For an hour he took down tubes, condensers, transistors, and impedances. He traced wiring and hunted for inductive taps. He searched the cabinet, the stand, the surrounding deck, the backboard. He went below to the next deck and painstakingly examined every inch of the ceiling. He found nothing. But somewhere was the source of the interference. It had to be somewhere, but on his own he couldn't go over the entire spacecraft, crammed with apparatus and each instrument zealously watched by some one or other of the specialists.

It was a foggy mess. One way or the other he had a duty. If Dane had gulled him, he had done it for a reason. If he could figure it out, it would all tie in with the stalled drive and the attempt to kill Colonel Cragg. If they really were Martian signals, that was a hell of a big thing, too, requiring the full and careful attention of the commander and his staff. He grimaced at the thought of even going to Major Noel with an unsupported story of signals from an uninhabited planet. But it was plain that he had a duty and a responsibility that now ran far beyond his assignment as electronics engineer of the Far Venture.

He thought of getting them to let him in on Dane for a little quizzing, but then he was unable to think of anything he might get out of him if he did. He went down to the main deck to his own bunk and lay across it, dozing a little, not thinking things out as he had intended to do, until he was brought wide awake by the three long buzzes and the three short of officers call on the intercom speaker. It was immediate assembly.

He hurried around the circular main deck and climbed up to 1-high deck and the command post. Captain Spear and Major Isbell, the astronavigator, were ahead of him.

Major Noel looked at him coldly. "Where's your sidearm, Lieutenant?"

Yudin was not quick enough to prevent his hand from straying ineptly toward where his shoulder holster should have hung.

"You are aware that officers and crew are to wear sidearms at all times while the spacecraft is at rest on this planet, aren't you?" Noel prodded.

"Yes, sir," he mumbled, realizing that he had not answered smartly. "I was asleep." He should not have added the excuse; he knew that too, as soon as he had uttered it.

Noel turned from him contemptuously.

Major Beloit, the engineering officer, came up the ladders with his assistant, Captain Schofield, followed by Lieutenant McDonald and Captain Finerty, the supply officer.

When the officers had assembled, Noel led off. "Finerty, what did you find?"

"One's gone, sir."

Noel pursed his lips, nodding as if the reply were laden with profound wisdom. The conceited ass is play-acting, Yudin told himself. Now the airmen get blamed for it again. Why doesn't he accuse the civilians? They can get at the stores as well as the crew.

"Pembroke has disappeared from the medical room," Noel said deliberately, dwelling on each word and waiting for his effect. "Captain Spear and Major Isbell have made a preliminary search of the ship without success. Captain Finerty now reports that a pressure suit is missing. It looks as if Pembroke has slipped outside. On the other hand, maybe he removed the suit and hid it to fool us." His look sharpened. "I want a thorough search of this entire ship. I want every locker and storage space looked into and all stores and equipment searched through. In other words, if he is aboard, find him. Watch yourselves and caution the crew. He may be dangerous."

They all waited to see if he had anything to add. He's got them, Yudin thought. He not only assumed command as senior officer, he really is the commander.

Major Beloit spoke up. "He must be off his beam. How about the others?"

"Still unconscious," Noel said. "Still in the hospital."

"You think maybe…?"

"I don't know," Noel interrupted him. "It's possible. We don't know for sure how long he's been gone. Captain King checked on his condition at 1600. He was there then. Still out, according to King."

Yudin looked at the flight surgeon. King was the assertive sort he had no confidence in. Pembroke could easily have fooled him. Chances are he looked in, felt his pulse, and went back to a drink and a nap. Trust a medic to provide for himself.

"He's undoubtedly a suspect," Noel went on. "We don't know the exact time the attack on Colonel Cragg took place, except that it had to be after 1800. Captain Spear relieved him at the command post at 1800."

"He couldn't get more than a few yards away from the spacecraft without the beacon and the lookout picking him up," Lieutenant McDonald objected. "He must be hiding on board. It's as light as day when that thing sweeps over you."

Yudin thought how Dane had made a point of distracting the airman from the searchlight to witness the signals. The time could have been prearranged and Pembroke could have made it away then. Something was very definitely peculiar about those signals. Maybe a plot to take over the Far Venture. Dane and Pembroke and the civilians. Why? What could they get out of it? Unless they had found something out on the face of the planet. Precious metal? Gold? Diamonds? That could explain why they wanted to delay the return. While they found some more and brought them inside without anybody knowing it. When Colonel Cragg refused to stay, they tried to kill him. Maybe he found out how they had jammed the drive. And why. Yet they couldn't really want to take over the ship. They had to have the crew to get them back to Earth. They could only have wanted to delay the return. Noel was a fool. An officious little fool. He'd better be careful or he'd have a knife sticking in his own back.

"Let's find him first and talk about it later. Alert all crew on the search," Major Noel ordered. "Let's go. I want Pembroke in fifteen minutes, or I want to know he's outside."

Yudin hesitated after the others had gone. Major Noel had pulled out the swinging stool and sat at the bank of command instruments, drumming his fingers against the writing desk. He was given to quick, bitter sarcasm, as Yudin well knew. Still, later would be too late. He had better tell him now.

"Sir, I have a report to make," he essayed. He told about the signals. He decided he had better work in some detail about his own thorough check for hocus-pocus with the equipment.

Noel heard him without interruption, waiting perceptibly after he had finished. Then he looked at him as if he were something crawling into sight. "Thanks for the information." He stressed the last word unpleasantly. "Captain Spear reported Dane's actions to me the minute he learned about them." He pointed at the watch on his wrist. "That was shortly after 1830. It is now almost 2300. Promptness is one of the elementary military virtues. How do you think I happened to find

Colonel Cragg unconscious? I went to report to him that Dane was active again. Now go on about your duties."

The dogmatic fool! Yudin went up the ladders to the observation deck. He ran over his sure knowledge of every item of communications equipment in the whole damned Air Force. Ten years a first lieutenant, yet whom did they tap when they wanted a real specialist for a tough assignment? Like this Mars flight. Men like Noel could bluster commands over an intercom. They got all the promotions, the few there were after Congress slashed the appropriations, but the specialists did the work. Not that Noel wasn't a technical man himself, but he had convinced the powers that he was also the command type. So he played soldier worse than an Air Academy colonel.

Dr. Pembroke wasn't hiding on the observation deck. Who would expect him to be? Where? Under the radar stool? He went down to 3-high deck and peeked into his own parts lockers. Three-high deck in the collision area near the top of the big sphere was principally a ring of food storage bins. Under the secondary meteor shield the bins were individually sealed off by airtight doors for tertiary protection. He plodded methodically out and back the five passages radiating from the central core that held the ladder wells. Most of the lockers were packed tight, a solid mass of cartons flush against the bin doors. Just as certainly Dr. Pembroke was not in any of the others. Yudin called Major Noel and gave his negative report, learning that he was to stand by for the 2400 watch, which would be doubled. Noel wasn't taking any chances.

Less than an hour left before his duty. He decided to go down and see how the engineers were making out. The drive would not start tonight. You could bet on that. Nor any time until Vining was ready for it to start. Vining and Dane and Pembroke. They were in it together.

He tried to piece together a theory of Dane's movements after he had come in from outside. He could not have brought in anything of any size without its being observed. So Pembroke had found something, and Dane had got in on it someway. But why want to kill Colonel Cragg? He couldn't take the spacecraft off until Vining decided to fix the drive. Unless they had let the colonel in on their find and he had refused to do whatever it was they wanted him to do. It had to be something big. That was one thing for sure. It had to be something big. And dead men tell no tales. But maybe Cragg wouldn't die after all.

He went down through the high decks, past the main deck to 2-low deck, where the great truncated sphere of the spacecraft's body sat on the squat truncated cone of its base. Most of the 2200-odd feet of 2-low deck was occupied by the square bulk of the nuclear drive that rose from the base deck below and thrust all up against the floor of 1-low deck. Nesting over the 41 take-off blast tubes that thrust down in the base cone like a bundle of giant dynamite sticks, the monster battery of generators was more like a windowless blockhouse than the live thing in a moving vehicle. For all its unfunctional design and the knowledge that it was dead, Yudin shuddered when he stepped into its opened passages and sought out its internal chambers.

It was something of a bank vault and something of a rectangular labyrinth. Narrow passages branched off at right angles. Lighted here and there, they plunged darkly into nonhuman bylands. Open manholes went down into pitch black, and ladders climbed into obscured recesses overhead.

The central chamber was deserted. Yudin strained quietly to hear. If anyone was working, it was a cerebral labor. His watch's ticking made him think of a Geiger counter. He turned around and hastened out of the thing.

Vining was just coming up from the tube deck. He glanced curiously at Yudin. "They have down here already searched."

Yudin nodded at the big generator housing. "Gives me the creeps. You making any headway with it?"

Vining swept his hand torch at the blind, black wall. "Here is nothing wrong, but the power. The power is weak. The power will to the take-off ratio not develop."

"That's what Major Beloit said yesterday," Yudin told him.

"It is also the truth tonight." Vining thrust up closer. "You think I do this?" he shouted.

Yudin saw the fatigue lines and the bloodshot eyes. "Take it easy. Your job is to tend to this baby. You built it. Why can't you fix it?"

Vining grabbed the lapel of his uniform and shook him.

"Take it easy, I said." He pushed away the man's hand. "I just asked you what's the matter you can't fix it."

"*Ja, Ja.* So you do." Vining kicked a bench around and sat down heavily. "All you want is me the drive to fix. So I build it. So I know to fix it. Here are all the parts. Here are all the quantities and correct. But here is not the power. Here is fission. Ten percent critical we get. Sometimes twenty per cent. That is all. Here is no take-off power."

"But why?"

"Why! You ask me why! Why grows all at once the healthy body cancer? My drive has cancer. But to cut the cancer away, the surgeon must first find the cancer."

He got up. "Now I sleep. Tomorrow I recalculate the quantities, but it is no good. You want to know what I think?" The words came hoarsely, like a loud rough whisper. "I tell your colonel, but he swears and orders me to get the power. He orders me to fix my drive that he says I have destroyed. Then I work more hours and I tell him again. We are in some force field caught. An unknown force field. It has to be. A force field that destroys the balance of the drive!" He was shouting again now. "A force field, I tell you. It has to be. So he laughs at me and says, 'Who is the fool, you think?'"

Yudin said, "He's just about dead now, you know."

"*Ja,* I know. A force field. Does Major Noel believe? *Nein!* Major Beloit? *Nein! Ich? Ja!* I must believe it. Here we die. On Mars we die. I must have years to solve new quantities for the unknown force. Else it gives one big explosion. Today I come maybe many times close to one big end for us all. Who knows it, the unknown force?"

Yudin had not heard Vining spill out so many words during the entire flight to Mars. Everybody on the spacecraft would end up crazy. No, that wasn't what he was thinking. He was getting afraid. These high-powered civilians were getting on his nerves. Was it really possible the planet might exert a field that would merge with forces aborning in the generators and cumulate with them to bring about freak mutations? God, they were sitting on a huge bomb! It could let go, like this crazy Dutchman said in his crazy accent, any time he altered the firing piles.

He gave Vining a short good night.

"Life? What is a life?" Vining detained him. "Life can go. There is to a life no urgency. That you live, it is not urgent. It is death that is urgent. Who says 'no' to death? You have urgent business for living? Who says 'yes'? More lives are coming. What is strange about your going? You do not like that thought, Herr Lieutenant? You come to me about the drive to see? No, Herr Lieutenant, you come about life. And I tell you I have not life for you. So you think I am crazy, when I am only sleepy."

CHAPTER TWELVE

At 2400 Captain Spear went to the command post to take over from Major Noel. He began the watch with a check of all guard and alert positions. As he bent his lean body to the ladders, he felt an alert kinesthetic pleasure in the movements, tingeing it consciously with regret that he had now aged to thirty-four years. Not much longer would his muscles take on a fine tone, in spite of exercise. Likely enough, some decline had already set in, hidden from him now but next year or a year or two later to emerge in sagging abdominal bands and slacking stamina in thighs and calves. He rapped on his hard gut, dismissing his rapidly retracting hairline. As long as the old body was in condition, a man looked young and felt young.

He went over the log with the major and got the "good nights" said without more than the usual catalog of admonition the guy always dished out—just like they both didn't know it all by heart. Noel gone, he ran through the intercom positions and settled down to wait for 0600 hours. Once or twice he thought about home, wondering idly what Alice was doing. What time was it on Earth? In the time zone of the apartment, that is, he corrected himself. Brother, would she be having a running duck if she knew they were stalled on Mars, even if there wasn't any danger of not getting the thing fixed. Radiation permitting.

Anyway, the thing was reliable. It had had hundreds of tests, and there were enough engineers and rocket boys along to build another one out of the bins full of parts and such junk if they had to. So it took time to find the trouble. Eventually it would be found. The Far Venture was provisioned for at least six months' good eating. Any major sabotage would have been spotted right away. Like Beloit said, something was out of adjustment and it wasn't always easy to find. Let him worry about it. That's what he got paid for. Hell, if they had to take the thing down to bare wire and metal or anything else it had been put together from, they could do it. Still Beloit and his boys had better get their damn drive to frying while the radiation was behaving itself.

He took out his wallet and looked for a moment at Alice's blond, wide-eyed smile. She was a good-looking kid, all right enough. She had come out of that movie theater in Albuquerque, practically bumping into him. For a minute she looked straight into his eyes, shocking him with her appeal for him. He could almost see the late afternoon sun on the flower pattern of her summery dress when she switched around him and hurried away, down the wide main drag, her corn-silk hair lifting off her shoulders in rhythm with her walking. Without any other thought he followed the blond head weaving through the crowd. They got married three weeks later, in the base chapel, at noon, and drove away to Mexico City for two weeks. He had been a little startled by her eagerness, but it was good. He smiled. Good girls had to sit on it too long. No wonder they couldn't get enough of it at first. Alice was a good kid, no doubt about it. No fuss about the temporary duty and the long trips away from home. After ten years in bachelor officers quarters, married life tied a man down a lot. A guy missed having plenty of money in his pocket and all the time in the world when he wanted it. If he was going to have a wife, though, he was glad it was Alice he had.

At 0200 Major Beloit came up from below for some chow. Spear put an airman at the command-post intercom and went along with him. Beloit sat for a long time on the bench, sipping at his mug of coffee. He looked plain tired. After he had eaten the two sandwiches he had fixed, he stretched out his legs and sighed. "That hit the spot."

"You getting anywhere yet?" Spear asked him.

Beloit was willing to talk now. "We're still getting less than twenty percent power. That means that fission is way down from what it ought to be. We're checking the generators now, one by one, but we haven't found anything yet."

Spear wanted to ask him about Vining, but he didn't think that it would be a proper question. Colonel Cragg had shown his own suspicions all right, but Beloit was peculiar. Like most of the technicians. Besides, he was outside the command channel. Maybe he hadn't been briefed on Vining. You couldn't deny, though, that he gave you a feeling of confidence in him. You didn't have much doubt that he would eventually find the trouble and repair it. In a way it was a shame that a guy like Beloit, with everything he knew about his specialty and all his experience, couldn't expect very rapid advancement. He was buried in his rocket drives. Outside the command line. Forty-five at least and over fifteen years' service, well known in the Air Force, and only a major. Best he could ever hope for was colonel. Probably he would retire as lieutenant colonel.

"About all I know about a rocket drive is that it works," Spear said.

"It isn't very complicated," Beloit protested amiably. "Maybe the underlying concepts are a little difficult, unless you're up on atomic theory, but the main idea is pretty simple. It's a nuclear-fission drive, and in a way it's like the old internal combustion engine, except that the nuclear explosions exert their energy directly in a battery of rocket exhaust tubes instead of driving pistons down and turning a crankshaft. Fundamentally the drive works from an extremely rapid series of small explosive fissions in each of the forty-one rocket tubes, one at a time and in practically instantaneous rotation. We control the thrust by directing a precise quantum of atoms of one of the radioactive isotopes of iodine into each of the rocket chambers for each explosion. These fission quanta are like the charge of powder in a cartridge, regulated for what the tube can tolerate."

Spear grinned at him. "You've got me a practically full charge already. Or should I say, 'Whatinhell did you say?'"

"The idea is simple enough. It's the engineering that really took the doing. For example, the fission explosion is not a critical-mass-type chain reaction but the fission of each nucleus, or practically every nucleus in the quantum, caused by the impact of neutrons in an extremely large and dense beam, which we pass into each explosion chamber simultaneously with the quantum of nuclei it envelops. It's like turning a fire hose on a teaspoonful of sugar. The neutrons also bear a negative rider charge. The neutron beam is so large and so dense with slow neutrons that a very high percentage of the nuclei, which bear a positive rider, are struck and split. We develop immense thrust in each rocket tube in rapid succession. More important, we control it exactly."

"It's as clear as the mud the hop frog jumped into," Spear told him. "So why don't you fix whatever needs fixing?" He wished the guy would just say in so many words that everything was okay. Still it was encouraging that he was so cheerful. If he were worried, it would probably show up plain enough.

"That's what we're going to do." Beloit smiled. "But not until we find it. There are hundreds of transistors and relays in the feed devices. Really several complex and synchronized electronic calculators. There's the extremely critical device for diverting the nuclei and the neutron beams into the successive firing chambers. There are the enervators and the energizers and the accelerators that create the two meson fields. There are the moderators that slow down the neutrons. There are the tubes and the fields that strip the nuclei from the radioactive isotope. And last but not least, there are the 943 neutron generators, each one of which is as delicately balanced a little gadget as you would want to tear into. It takes 943 of them to make a dense beam of neutrons for the fission chambers. We might be looking for a week yet. Maybe it's even a combination of things and won't show up right away in any particular one of the components."

"Okay," Spear said, "you go to it. You trying to give me a headache?"

Beloit laughed. "Oh, it's not that bad. What man can build, man can take apart and put back together again."

"Yeah?" Spear said. "You ever try that on one of your alibis to your wife?"

"Not married," Beloit answered shortly. "Women and engines don't mix. Both of them want all your time."

Spear laughed comfortably, thinking that Alice was really a good old girl, about the Air Force and everything.

They talked on for a while until the phone rang. Spear said, "It's probably mine." He went over and lifted the instrument.

Spear identified himself.

"There's something moving out on the dust!" The words tumbled out of the receiver.

Spear tingled with a quick clarity, the diverse complexity of the spacecraft and its defenses falling into precise order for him, ready for his commands. "Range? Bearing? Character?" he snapped. If it were Pembroke, even Yudin would have told him so at once.

Yudin gulped audibly for breath. "About three miles. Radar bearing, 47 degrees. On surface. Range 4950 yards."

"What is its character?" Spear demanded. "Come on. Give!"

"Yes, sir," Yudin said with better control of his breathing. "Small object. We have both the search beam and the telescope on its location, but we can't make it out. On radar it shows slow approach toward the spacecraft."

"It's likely Pembroke," Spear decided. "He's been back out to the lichens. Stand by. I'm coming up." He switched to the command post. "Sergeant Purley," he ordered, "sound off battle stations." He switched to Major Noel's quarters. "Sir, Yudin has blipped an unidentified small object approaching on the surface at 4950 yards, coming in slow. It's possibly Pembroke. They've got it in the light and the telescope on it, but they can't resolve it."

"Stay at the command post," Noel ordered. "I'm going up there."

Spear swore against the strident buzzers sounding battle stations all over the Far Venture. He would! He tossed a word of explanation at Major Beloit and pulled himself up the ladder to the command post. He pushed Purley out of the way with a friendly elbow and sat down on the stool before the control banks. He listened to the familiar chatter of the turret guns clearing and took on the rush of "ready" reports. The Far Venture was adequately armed to take on one small blip, whatever it was. Settling back easily, he noticed Purley's tense face. "Take it easy, man," he advised. "It's probably only Dr. Pembroke trying to get back to us."

Purley said, "Yes, sir." Hesitantly he added, "Captain?"

Malassignment to put him on this crew, Spear decided. "What is it?"

"About those signals Dr. Dane picked up. Do you think there's something else out there? I mean besides Dr. Pembroke?"

"Where'd you get that?" Humphries, of course. "Never mind," Spear added, not unkindly. "It was likely only a malfunction of the equipment."

"They say he got a message that made sense," Purley objected.

"Dr. Dane is also now in confinement. Maybe he just pretended to get a message." He saw that the man was not satisfied. "Whatever might be out there, we've got the fire power to take care of it. We ought to have. We mount six machine-gun turrets, four recoilless 140's, a couple of dozen missile tubes, a ring of flame nozzles, and four bins of guided thermal and nuclear missiles. We can wipe out that blip in a couple of seconds any time we want to. Anything living we can kill. They couldn't get near us."

"Excuse me, sir, but that's the point," Purley said. "Supposing it wasn't something alive?"

Now there was one for you. An Air Force sergeant who believed in spirits. "Come off that," Spear told him firmly. "If there's anything on this planet that wants to send messages, it's nothing that can't be blown up or burned up, not to speak of a dose of fission bomb."

"Yes, sir," Purley said.

The blip came in slowly. At 0245 it was 3700 yards out, still on 47 degrees. It was making about two miles an hour straight for the Far Venture.

At 0253 Major Noel called. "It looks like it's Dr. Pembroke. At least we can make out the pressure suit plainly now. I'm not taking any chances. I want that thing covered with all arms you can bring to bear until we identify Dr. Pembroke and get him inside."

"Wonder why he won't answer?" Spear asked.

"No calls answered. Maybe his radio's bad again, but radar is very clear. I want Major Beloit to cover the entry lock with automatic weapons and fire grenades. Get him in and don't take any chances. Get him out of that suit and have him brought up to your post."

Spear acknowledged the order. "Supposing he doesn't make it all the way. I mean not answering and all of that. I suppose he's off his mind again."

"That's his bad luck," Noel said. "We're not risking anybody outside. Spear," he added, "this may sound silly, but we've got to remember where we are and all we don't know about this place. I want you to pass this on to Major Beloit too. Confidentially. Tell him to be careful. We don't know for sure what's in that suit. Maybe it's Pembroke and maybe it's something else."

"Migod, you don't think that!" Spear couldn't believe he was hearing it. Not Major Noel!

"I'm not taking any chances," Noel repeated emphatically. "I don't want you to take any, or especially Major Beloit to take any. Impress on him that he's to find out what's in that suit before he lets it through the lock. He's not to risk anything himself. Not with the drive out. Tell him to get a look inside that helmet before he opens the lock. Get me?"

"I get you," Spear said. "Christ!"

CHAPTER THIRTEEN

Vining had come down to his post at the main reactor control heavy with interrupted sleep. Major Beloit watched him narrowly now that the grotesque pressure suit trudged very near, trailing a cloud of dust from its awkward steps back to the edge of the spotlight cast upon it. Earlier they had taken down the big panel of controls, for the third time in fact, seeking some disorder in its dense vinery of tubes and wires, and there was little point in Vining watching his post at the dismantled mess. Except that the emergency standing operating procedure stipulated his being there.

The first time Beloit had taken it down he would have bet his reputation, such as he had, that nothing was wrong in that panel. Or in the auxiliaries. It had to be in the neutron generators themselves, as Vining, the old fox, well knew. He would really bet a reputation on that. At first he had thought Vining might have altered the input of atom quanta. Not anything so easily detected as altering the mass of the quanta themselves, which were subject to constant and exact measurement, but conceivably he could have lessened or in some way neutralized the rider charge on the nuclei of the target atoms. Input of normal nuclei would reduce the hits from a theoretical one hundred percent to less than ten per cent, and correspondingly reduce the simple fission. Nothing approaching take-off power would be released.

He ran the nuclear equations mentally. Twenty percent fission before reaction leveled off. Not enough for take-off but enough to indicate a fairly sizable positive rider on the nuclei. Of course Vining might have partially dispersed and weakened the positive meson field that attached the rider charges, but he would have had to alter the big tubes or their input, and that could be detected. You couldn't miss anything that easy to see.

It had to be in the neutron generators. Certainly the neutrons had to be slowed down and given their negative rider, but again, the moderators could scarcely be tampered with, and any substantial reduction of the negative meson field would also demand physical alteration of its generative tubes or their input. He could not have missed that. But the 943 neutron generators themselves were infinitesimally critical reactors in their own right, tiny as baseballs and delicately commingling unstable masses to fine proportion. Disturb or adulterate those critical balances and the fat stream of neutrons that poured into the explosion chambers to bombard the nuclei could be attenuated.

They had already completed checking more than a third of the generators with no success, but Vining was one of the pioneers of thimble fission. He might be a hard man to thwart if he put his mind to disrupting the neutron generation. Actually they had no way to check the massivity of the neutron beam except by its effect on fission. The massivity could be substantially less, and the only evidence would be a decline in the fission, which was exactly their trouble.

The telephone gong jangled sharply.

It was Major Noel. "Beloit, under no circumstances are you to come personally close to Pembroke. You are to stay out of the entry lock. Pembroke is to be brought up to the command post on the hoist, and you are to stay out of that too. I don't intend to risk my chief engineer. That's all."

Beloit acknowledged and stood back to the port. The suit was at a hundred yards, walking very slowly. His mind flashed back to Earth and thirty years ago. It was New Year's Day, 1991. He stood on a fishing pier on Dauphin Island and watched the tide roll out of Mobile Bay into the Gulf. There was a blond girl with a long surf rod, casting her line gracefully and far out into the water. A year or two older than he was, he guessed, nineteen or twenty maybe, and her figure was full and good against a yellow sweater. He wanted her pretty bad, but she had only looked at him once, quickly unseeing after perception of his squat, stocky figure and coarse face. Acutely aware, he reeled in his line and went back to the cottage, where he was master of a slide rule and the sophomore engineering problems in his texts. She would be fat and fifty now, wherever she was, smug over a couple of grown offspring. He himself had no particular trouble in getting plenty of girls younger than her own children. Funny if he had run on to a daughter of hers sometime around Mobile and never known it. Not any odder than standing in a spacecraft on the planet Mars and looking out on the sight of a grotesque, humanish object come up over a bizarre red plain to the mouths of their guns.

The intercom rasped. "Suit at fifty yards. Open entry," Noel ordered.

Beloit went down to the observation port that looked into the entry lock. The outside hatch hung open and the ladder was out. Automatic weapons in hand, two pressure-suited guards stood over the opening, motionless.

The seconds ticked off, until there was a shifting of posture by both guards. Beloit knew that the suit was below. They could see it. He wouldn't want to be Pembroke, stepping into sight under that entry. A jumpy finger on the trigger and the shock of seeing the thing all of a sudden, and reflexes might go off, in spite of disciplined control.

They were backing away from the open hatch. Slowly a monstrous head rose above the opening in the curving side. An extraordinary hand reached through and grasped the highest rung. Then the suit was inside and the hatch was closing.

Beloit blinked, straining to see through the hazy transparency of the small port. He took out his handkerchief and wiped at the dust that covered the pane. The suit was turning ponderously from one guard to the other. Finally it raised its corrugated arms and worked at its helmet, passing misshapen paws ineffectually at the collar wing nuts.

It ought to take off the gauntlets, Beloit thought. If it was one of us, it would twist the lock joint of its gauntlets. Pembroke would know to take off the gauntlets first.

Beloit snatched at his microphone. "Can't you make him out?" he demanded. "Who is it?"

"It's Dr. Pembroke, sir," the answer came. The man sounded surprised.

Beloit wondered about it before he recalled that the men would have no reason to expect anything else. They had been told only to be careful. He was now surprised at his own suspense. What else could have been in the suit except Pembroke?

It took a little time, but the suit finally managed to get its neck locks loosened. When it lifted off the heavy helmet, the massed white hair of Dr. Pembroke and the wizened face, small for the large head and hair shock, were plainly revealed. Beloit phoned Noel. As far as he could judge, Pembroke's actions were normal. Perhaps he had forgotten about the gauntlets until he had managed to get his helmet off and the guards had told him. He pulled off the rest of the suit briskly enough, leaving it in a heap on the floor. One of the guards had his helmet visor open and was motioning to Pembroke to get into the lift. As soon as the panel slid shut on him, Beloit heard the faint grind of the mechanism. The lift was ascending.

That was that. Beloit felt the fatigue hit him and thought of his bunk. Damn, it was a quarter to five. He needed more than the couple of hours' sleep he was going to get. Maybe Noel would hurry it up with the all-clear so he could go to bed. Officious little squirt—really. But a competent technician. Still not the man for commander. When the phone rang, he picked it up quickly, blowing his breath out against his thrust-up lower lip.

It was Noel all right, but now he wanted Beloit to come up to the command post. Bed? What did Noel care about Beloit's rest?

Beloit picked a path through the litter of the control panel. It was going to be a helluva job to put all the stuff together again and check it, not to speak of tracing through the remainder of the generators. The better part of a week. Anyway you looked at it. Hell, he was just tired. Nothing could look good at five o'clock in the morning. After the whiskey faded out, the blonde's face looked dirty.

No use climbing ladders. He went over and punched at the call button of the lift. The indicator showed the car at 1-high, but no responsive whir came from the mechanism. Somebody had propped the car door open, a favored malpractice. Let the other fellow climb the ladders, I've got a can of beans to deliver. Half the crew under military discipline and the other half civilians. What else could you expect? One thing you could say for Colonel Cragg. He had been tough, but he handed it out to them all, and all alike. Military or civilian, he was in command. Whether they liked it or not, you had to have a strong commander on a junket like this. Noel would never cut it. Doctor this and doctor that would drop in their big words here and there until the poor bastard didn't know which way was which. Not that he would have picked John Dane for a murderer, but it just showed what could happen when things got out of hand in an emergency. Confinement neurosis, the psycho men called it. Everybody on edge and every man for himself or what he thought was the right thing to do.

When he climbed out on to 1-high deck, Noel was waiting for him.

"Come on," he ordered, "I want to show you something." He led off around the curving passageway.

Crumpled in the corner of the lift car was the body of Dr. Pembroke. Half the side of his head was blown away. A service pistol lay in the blood on the floor. Captain Spear was standing by.

"What I want to know," Noel demanded, "is why you would let this man who was obviously out of his mind retain possession of firearms?"

Beloit focused on the image of Pembroke entering the lift. The old man must have had it in his pocket. Maybe a shoulder holster under his garments. "Suicide?" he asked.

"Look to you like he was run over by a truck?" Noel snarled. "Why was he allowed to retain a weapon? Or didn't you think of it?"

"He didn't have any visible." Beloit said. "Your orders were not to come near him."

"I said *you* were not to go near him. I said no one was to touch that suit. You had men down there. You should have had them search him after he got out of the suit."

Beloit swore at himself. What was the use?

"I'll have to enter that in the record against you," Noel said with an air of dismissal.

These unpredictable things happened. When they happened, they happened swiftly and out of control of anything but good fortune. This one would dog him the rest of his career. Maybe not neglect of duty, exactly. Under the circumstances no board of officers would pin that on him, even if Noel chose to put a charge against him, but certainly an entry for ineffectiveness in a critical situation, and boom! There went the silver leaves he should have won out of this damned expedition.

"Not that you didn't make an understandable mistake, especially after the way you've been loaded with work," Noel echoed his thoughts, "but I don't expect a field-grade officer to make mistakes, particularly when it comes to security. I'm not going to prefer charges, but I am going to give you a reprimand. That's all," he added abruptly. "Spear, have the body removed and record what you found when you opened the lift."

Captain Spear said, "Major Noel, can I speak to you a minute?"

Beloit watched them draw away, excluding him from their official circle. His sour hatred flowed out toward them, like a mist that froze into a wall and left him standing alone and shut out. He didn't want to go to bed. He wanted to say something. But there was no one who could appreciate the vast knowing he had of intricate apparatus, tremendously essential apparatus, no one who could appreciate that fully and at the same time who also owned power to command things to be different.

CHAPTER FOURTEEN

Dr. Jose Ruiz Cruzate smacked the heel of his palm against his forehead. *"Non! C'est impossible!* It cannot be!" He snatched up a sprig of the lichen stuff and ran around his lab bench to thrust it under Wertz's nose. "It is living. Even now this piece, it has the life! Do not talk to me of your chemicals. With the life there are the ways of life. It is not required that we understand, for them to be."

Cruzate was a little squirrel of a man. Wertz was pleased with the pertinence of the metaphor. Cruzate had the bright darting eyes and the quick pose of a squirrel, as if he were ever ready to scurry out across the lawn for a nut and back up a tree into his hole. Except that a squirrel does not suggest the pedant, and a pedant Cruzate undoubtedly was. An excitable, Frenchified, poetizing pedant, but pedantic as the multiplication tables when it came to his beloved "subject" of botany, as he always referred to it. Not the "discipline" or the "science" of botany or simply "botany," but always the old-fashioned term, the "subject" of botany.

"The 'subject' of botany," Cruzate loved to say, pronouncing the word *sujet,* as in French, when he was excited, "the *sujet de* botany is like the drama of Racine. *La botanique* she is *classique*. She has the order. But also she has the poetry. What surprise! What variation of form and theme!"

What the guy really meant, Wertz supposed, was that plant life—it's a wonder he didn't call it the vegetable kingdom, or whatever the French for that would be—what he meant was that plant life is capable of reduction to reasonably systematic classification but displays a wide spectrum of deviation from the systematic norms. The man was provincial. Consider the carbon compounds and their isomers, endless, almost mathematically infinite in their number and their diversity of properties. Cruzate knew too much botany and not enough anything else. Even so, you couldn't help liking the little guy a lot.

"Why does a Spaniard like you talk French when you get mad?" he asked him.

"I have tell you, I have tell every man on this madman's venture I am so blindly vain to adopt, I have tell you all from the dawn to the dark, Spanish I am not. My name, it is Spanish. My father's father, he was Spanish, but my father and my mother and I, even one named Jose Ruiz Cruzate after my father's father, became born in the glorious city of Paris, where I am even now, if not for my insufferable pride in my poor attainments and the blandishments of you Americans. Paris! Not canned up like the herring in an impossible place with the fear of the machinery trouble and the listening to the talk of the nonsense. And why do I speak French? I know no Spanish for my native tongue. You Americans, perhaps with your atomic drives and your United States Air Force and your Expedition Mars you have better reason for a man to be speaking French than it is his own native tongue?"

"Okay, Ruiz," Wertz told him, "I only wanted to hear you explode. Now what don't you like about the idea, except that it's a chemical concept instead of biological?"

"Non!" Cruzate shouted. "It is you who do not understand. Not I. It is impossible. You do not comprehend either the lichen or the life."

"You want to tell me why they grow over more than a mile of bare dust in a day?"

Cruzate threw the lichen branch back on the bench. "You want to tell me why the spring corn breaks through the soil crust, to come out for the sun?" He shrugged dramatically. *"Non,* my friend, we see these things, we describe them, we give them the names, but let us not ask ourselves why they come to be. That is the way of things. Why does a man become old? Why does the stone fall? Perhaps it should likewise fly up? You find the answer in your test tubes? *Non.* You tell me only that the stone falls. You tell me only that it falls in such a way."

Wertz creaked the chair back. "You and I are going to have to have a talk about operational analysis one of these days. You're talking words. Your distinctions are verbal. The distinctions I would like to make are distinctions in the understanding of activity of one kind or another. Either we perceive and recognize things by our senses and attempt to understand them, or we make deliberate physical manipulations and try to understand them, or we make deliberate combinations of thoughts and attempt to arrive at greater understanding. The subject of our scientific analysis is what happens, and the object of our investigation is to discover activities we have not been aware of. In any situation upon which we direct our inquiry, a complete analysis of the activity involved would satisfy our inquiry. Maybe there are other things to analyze than activity, but they have not proved necessary for our purposes. Take the question of meanings. If I want to know the meaning of a term I wish to use, I think I must know the conditions under which I will use it. If I want to know the meaning of a term you use, I have to know the conditions that caused you to use it. So I say meanings are operational. They grow out of activities. Don't talk to me about 'life' as if it could exist isolated and pure, like a substance. Talk to me about the activities you want to associate and characterize by the term 'living,' which is therefore itself a term naming an activity."

Cruzate exploded a *bah!* "You give me the headache. You should be in the Sorbonne."

"Okay," Wertz said, "I'll split hairs with you. You tell me why you're so sure these things have Earth-like life; then I'll tell you *how* they act. Once we see what activity the term 'growth' describes here on Mars in the case of the Mars lichens, perhaps we can also discuss the terms 'living' and 'generation' more calmly."

Cruzate exclaimed, "So now we play the game! I tell you what you already know. I describe the lichen plant. Then you tell me I am wrong, because these lichens are different. That I already know." His voice was climbing toward the Frenchman's octave. "I know also they are of the lichen family. Any botanist recognize these thing at once as a variety of lichen. Ascomycetous fungus living symbiotically with protococcalous algae. Fruticose thallus body, erect and freely branching, like *Caledonia,* the reindeer moss, except very much more large and more coarse. A first-year student recognize it immediately. Thus are the principles of plant life exhibited here in another world, even as your elements and compounds are to be found the same."

"Except that there are countless millions of possible chemical compounds and combinations, few of which we know naturally on

Earth—or here. And don't forget your living things are merely expressions of these combinations, each with its peculiar arrangement of the elements of substance. We have every reason to expect life to be vastly different wherever it is found, with chance resemblances merely conditioned by similar environments. Sure, we've found a fungus-like body drawing its sustenance from the chemical soil in a lichen-like manner, breaking down the compound of the soil with lichen-like acids exuded through the mycelium-like sheath of the thallus, as you call it. Sure, there are chlorophyll-bearing, plant-like cells captive within the plant to supply the photosynthesis. The whole thing looks like a lichen. Superficially it acts like a lichen in many ways, but make no mistake, it's not what you call a lichen at all in its most significant activity. I mean its growth and reproduction. Or have you found the customary spores and sex organs?"

"It may be they are characteristic of another season. By analogy the plant should have them."

"Look, Ruiz, how many planets in the solar system? How do we know? We don't. We count those we observe. We don't establish an ideal number in our minds, like the ancients, and say there are five, or some other number that fits a harmony of the spheres. We count them. Likewise there are no sex organs or no spores until we observe them. You can't establish a phenomenon by analogy with a preconceived pattern. You have to establish it experimentally."

"It may be that you have established your explosive generation experimentally? Is it not more likely these plants have what we call the fast life and convert the soil food into the lichen cells with a great quickness? It is common to observe the mycelium of a fungus to grow across the entire field of the microscope while we watch it. In forty-eight hours a speck of fast-growing fungus can advance at a rate of $1/8000$ inch a minute, a rapidity incredible. Every advancing cell, it can put out a new side branch every thirty to forty minutes, and each branch, it can advance at the same rate and put out new branches. In twenty-four hours the fungus colony has produce one half mile of mycelium strands. In forty-eight hours it has produce the hundreds of miles of cells. By the analogy why can we not expect these big lichens to grow in large size, as the microscopic Earth fungi can grow in the miniature?"

Wertz said, "Look, Ruiz, just as I told you, you're talking in words. You can't predict events by analogy." He got up on his feet, the old soreness bearing out against the base of his spine. He was going to get a regular program of exercise going when he got back to Earth and put himself back in some semblance of shape. There was always the threat of diabetes to the thickset man who let himself get fat. Martha would have to quit making so many biscuits and good fried meat gravy. A man couldn't help stuffing. But a man ought to do something for himself besides live in a laboratory. Had been almost ten years since he had even so much as played a game of golf. "Ruiz," he said, "come down to my lab. I want to show you something."

Wertz noticed the disorder of his place after Cruzate's neat workroom. Both benches were cluttered, and most of the jars and impervious flasks on the self-stowing shelves would need careful attention before the take-off. Still, he had his luck. Without his old good luck he might have drudged along for weeks without turning up the Mars isomer. That's it. I'll call it the Mars Isomer, he decided. Get a supply of the lichen things back home in good condition and throw a new idea to the annual A.A.A.S. meeting for a change. Dr. Rudolf Wertz of the National Institute will now present a paper on "The Mars Isomer, a Chemical Life Principle."

He took up the test tube that held his centimeter or two of the isomer, the product of a truly original attack, if he did say so. "I isolated this stuff from the lichen tips. Now watch." He put a small pinch of a yellowish-brown powder on a filter paper. "Hydrous ferric oxide. I brought along a quantity in the natural earthy state on the possibility that the Vaucouleurian theory might be correct, that it is the constituent of the soil of Mars that gives the planet its red color. I wanted to compare the natural Earth substance with the Mars soil, but they don't quite match. The Mars mineral is more like the amorphous substances we call ferrite, metallic derivatives of the ferric hydroxide $Fe_2O_2 (OH)_2$. Now the lichen type of plant, as you have just said, consists of two dissimilar organisms, a fungus living married with several algae."

Cruzate said, "Symbiosis."

"You have the term," Wertz admitted. "Now, as I understand it, the fungus offers protection from the cold and provides inorganic substances by exuding acids that can decompose what the plant is growing on. The protoplasm of the algae cells at the growing tips manufactures enzymes and organic acids that diffuse through the cell wall into the host material. If the fungus is growing on wood, these digestive chemicals diffuse out into the wood host and break it down into simple sugars. These in turn diffuse into the fungus mycelium and are converted into more fungus. In the lichen the digestive acids, so to speak, can even break down rock as a host to secure what we might call their food. That is correct?"

"But certainly," Cruzate said. "You put it *exactement.*"

"Now on Mars these lichen plants grow in sand and dust. They break down the ferrites in the soil and absorb principally iron and silicates. The Earth-like algae bodies supply oxygen by photosynthesis. You have checked that?"

"Correct." Cruzate nodded. "And also build up the organic substances."

"Well, back to our problem. How to account for the extremely rapid growth. The speed at which the green areas expand in the spring has been a puzzle for generations. Now we ourselves have seen them shoot out toward the spacecraft and grow over a hundred yards of bare sand in an hour. Now look."

Wertz put a pinch of the ocher-colored powder under a large bell glass. "The ferric oxide will serve as a concentrated form of the iron food the Mars lichens find in the soil. I next dampen it with water bearing finely ground silicon dioxide, the pure form of silica. Water is an unknown elixir of life for our Mars lichens accustomed only to the meager H_2O they can draw from a trace of mist. At best a light dew is their only experience with water, and they are extremely hydroscopic. Next I replace the bell jar over my souped-up synthetic Mars soil. It has these inlets by which I can introduce an equally souped-up atmosphere."

He connected a tube running from a small metal gas cylinder. "The atmosphere in the spacecraft is regulated Earth atmosphere, rich in oxygen, such as the Mars lichens have never known. He turned the petcock at the end of the cylinder for an instant and then closed it again. "This introduces a little more carbon dioxide, about the same as its percentage in the atmosphere of Mars."

He took up the test tube. "Now, my botanist friend, for the climax of our little drama. I have provided a small bed of highly concentrated lichen fertilizer, so to speak, under an enriched atmosphere."

Cruzate shrugged. "You make the *beaucoup* talk. You belong, I say it again, in the Sorbonne lecture *salles*. This 'lichen fertilizer,' I do not comprehend."

Wertz laughed. "A figure of speech. The silica and the hydrous ferric oxide are very similar to the minerals the Mars lichens decompose in their native sand for their own growth. Only much concentrated. The water seems to work like a catalyst. Just watch."

He held up the test tube. "In this solution I have concentrated a substance that I've been able to extract from the Mars lichen plant. I haven't been able yet to formulate its exact structure, but it belongs among the carbon compounds and isomers. For the time being I just call it the growth element. As a matter of fact, in spite of the tremendous research in the organic compounds, their practically infinite possibilities have barely begun to be synthesized. All that we know about most of them is that they are theoretically possible."

Cruzate cleared his throat hesitantly. Wertz ignored him. The demonstration would settle his hash, but really one had to have a little of the background. To attain a reasonable understanding of experimental phenomena, one must be prepared to grapple with principles.

"Let me take one example," he went on. "The simplest group of carbon compounds is the paraffin hydrocarbons, composed of only carbon and hydrogen. The simplest compound in the series is CH_4, with one carbon atom and four hydrogen atoms. The next is C_2H_6, followed by C_3H_8, then C_4H_{10}, and so on. The thing to remember is that with the exception of the first three members of the series, the formula for each compound does not represent a single substance. There are five different substances represented by the formula C_6H_{14} and nine by C_7H_{16}. The simpler members of the series have familiar names, like butane for the fourth. But there are two butanes, normal butane and isobutane. They may have the same molecular formula, but they are very different in properties. Even though they are both gases under ordinary conditions, normal butane liquefies at about zero Centigrade, isobutane at about minus 17 degrees. And every chemical compound made with normal butane is different from the substance with the same molecular formula that is made from isobutane. Follow me?"

It didn't matter. Cruzate was smart enough to know that the other man knew his own field. Wertz went ahead with it, savoring the symmetry of his exposition, glad over the compactness of the explanation. When he really wanted to, he could explain the complex in terms easy enough for anybody. "Such varieties of a compound are called isomers," he went on, "and for the higher members of even the simple paraffin series chemists have not yet prepared all the possible isomers, each of which, remember, has its own properties, different in at least some fashion from all the other isomers and compounds in the entire range of organic chemistry. Chemists have calculated that there are over three hundred thousand isomers represented by the formula $C_{20}H_{42}$ and about seventy trillions of isomers—that's seventy million millions—represented by the formula $C_{40}H_{82}$. And that's in only one series of simple carbon compounds. They have not even calculated yet the number of possible carbon substances that result from the isomers of the many series of possible compounds, say with from one to forty carbon atoms and hydrogen and nitrogen and oxygen atoms in all possible combinations.

How do we pretend to know what can be? Who knows what mysteries may be among them?"

"It is enough!" Cruzate cried. "Desist. I whirl in the head!"

"Here you are then," Wertz said, "one more idea, then I will demonstrate what strange properties some of these infinite combinations may conceal. In the Mars lichen I have found an isomer of a carbon compound that has the same property for self-reproduction or self-copying that we find in the protein structure of the sexual genes of Earth life. Now I have established that this carbon-hydrogen-nitrogen-oxygen isomer is a profuse constituent of the body of the Mars lichen, and that it and two related isomers are capable of exploding into an immense multiplication of their own kinds, resulting in the formation of the over-all shape and substance of the complete lichen plant. Explosive generation, as I told you. And explosive generation you are about to see."

Wertz reached for a pipette and drew up a few minims of the straw-colored isomer from the test tube and introduced it into a glass tube that stemmed through the shell of the bell jar. The liquid ran slowly down until a drop formed on the inside end of the tube directly over his tiny pile of fertilizer dotting the filter paper.

While the little spheroid swelled heavy and pendant on its glass stem, Wertz watched Cruzate. He was characteristically intense. This he won't like, Wertz thought. It's going to upset his allegiance to a one-way passage between the living and the dead.

The surface tension of the drop could no longer sustain its weight. Grossly large by any standard imposed by Earth gravity, it drew down an obese, pyramidal umbilical stalk, ruptured it, and fell upon the waiting powder. Immediately, as if spark had fallen on gunpowder, the reaction exploded into a cluster of dwarf Mars lichens, a bush-like bunch as large as a grapefruit.

"Mon dieu!" Cruzate breathed. *"C'est incroyable!"*

Wertz said, "Maybe. But there it is. Explosive generation of the whole plant. Bypassing the entire process of cellular growth. You still think they are what you call normal plants or what you call living organisms producible only by parent living organisms?"

Cruzate lifted the bell jar and fingered the lichens. "I will examine this." He broke off a sprig, murmuring, "It is the perfect replica. I see lichen thallus. I feel it, but I must at once make microscopic sections. We shall see if it really lives. It cannot grow and reproduce its kind, unless somehow your liquid was alive. Maybe in it virus-like submicroscopic organisms."

Wertz said, "Don't try to go down that street. There was nothing under that bell jar but what you or anyone else would call purely nonvital substances. I obtained the lichen compound by crystallizing it out of an acid solution. It has been redissolved, boiled down, and recrystallized, over and over again, an even ten times. It tests to carbon, hydrogen, nitrogen, and oxygen and nothing else. Before that, it was extracted from the macerated plant by chemical reaction with dilute sulphuric acid and precipitated with caustic soda. In fact the entire procedure was practically identical with the textbook method of deriving quinine from the native bark. The crude extractive sulphates were dissolved in alcohol and deposited with sulphuric acid. They were repeatedly dissolved and recrystallized fractionally to separate them, and finally the pure isomer was precipitated by ammonium hydroxide. The explosive generation I stumbled on by trial and error, in trying to find out the function of the compound in the plant. No, I don't think there is a virus or anything that you mean by the term 'living' left in that solution. But if you don't think that plant you see is alive, look at this."

He thrust the tip of a spatula into the container of hydrous ferric oxide and lifted a small quantity into a test tube, then added a like amount of silica. He put a little water into the tube and shook up the mixture, thumb over the mouth of the tube. "Lichen fertilizer suspended in water," he said, displaying the murky liquid. "I'll pour a little of this around the plants, and I'll bet you say you can see them grow—rather see them expand by the instant addition of new branches and new stems."

He tilted the tube carefully and poured a few drops at the base of the miniature Mars lichens. The cluster of plants snapped to triple its size so quickly that it spilled the tube out of his fingertips. Instantly the things crackled into being all over the end of the bench. Now they were the size of the plants out on the Mars plains. Wertz jumped back. He swore mildly. "It got away from me, but it's damn convincing, isn't it?"

"It is unholy!" Cruzate exclaimed. "If it is true, it is not good. I would rather not believe it. I must test it for life. Now. With no more the delay!"

Wertz said, "Test away all you want. I have already made sections, naturally. But maybe you can see something I didn't. For anybody's money, that stuff's what you call alive, and get this, it's indisputable that it came from nonliving substances."

"Virus, subvirus, whatever it is, it had to be in the solution. There is no other explanation."

"By your theories, maybe. But a theory is only good as long as it reconciles the evidential data. Also, there is the matter of the principle of economy. Why assume a complex, unverifiable hypothesis, like the passing of what you call life through several chemical reactions and physical processes, when the much simpler and understandable answer stares you in the face? We have found a certain chemical substance that under certain conditions erects itself into shapes and substances in combination with other substances and then the result displays the activities we have always called living. Where was your mysterious life added, to these nonliving substances and nonliving preliminary activities of simple chemical and physical formulation?"

Cruzate said, "That I cannot tell you. I only know that it must have been there or it must have been added."

Wertz suppressed his exasperation. "Now you're merely expressing a faith. In a preconceived idea. It has to be there, you say. Nothing has to be anywhere, until we establish that it is there. 'Has to be' is optative and absolute. Frankly I have very little patience with optatives, and in the universe of physical events I have none. There they are intruders and the cause for most of our blunders."

"Maybe so," Cruzate muttered. "But you, do you not really say by these same words that I ought not to accept optatives? That itself is an optative!"

"Medieval. Any good apprentice logician would be able to demolish that. While you look through your microscope and do…"

Cruzate's eyes were bulging.

Wertz followed his outstretched arm and pointing finger.

The entire top of the bench was crowned by lichen plants. Instruments and glassware tumbled crazily among them. "It must be feeding on the silica in the glass!" he exclaimed.

A sharp cracking snapped like the ultra-rapid staccato of a dozen firecrackers. The embedded bell jar vanished in a swipe of transmuted color. Gray-green arms struck out at them.

And then Wertz was fighting. Shoulder-high, all over the laboratory, protruding from the benches and the shelves, from every point of security, the lichens had exploded into a jungle profusion. Except for the small air space in the geometric center of the room, they were drowning inside a great stinking puffball. Walls, floor, ceiling, all familiar shape of the room had gone.

"Cruzate!" Wertz shouted. "Watch out for the acids. The tips are loaded with it. Cover your face and eyes. We've got to get out of here."

It was thickly clinging. Yet it yielded, like a seaweedy maze. Wertz covered his face with one arm, and plunged at the door, like a fullback hitting the line.

"Come on, Cruzate!" He fumbled for the latch against the tingle of chemical activity on his bare face, at the same time noting methodically the mildness of the action and reflecting on the high selectivity of the plant's acids for the substances the organism had affinity for. Instantly dissolve glass but only gently irritate the epidermis.

He burst out, reached behind, and jerked Cruzate through with a heavy pull. "Christ!" He slammed the door behind them.

"Some of that stuff got out!" He pointed to the lichen bits and severed strands at the sill. "Look! We've got to get it. If it starts to spread out here, we're done for."

Cruzate stooped, grubbing for the particles. "In the next lab we burn it. Or the acid."

"No! Leave it there. We don't dare lose a crumb. It could explode all over the ship."

"It cannot eat of this metal," Cruzate protested. He stamped the timageel deck.

"We don't know what it can do. It ate into Houck's suit and killed him. Maybe timageel will resist the acids. Maybe it won't. Maybe the things might mutate under the conditions inside the spacecraft. You saw them hang on the walls and ceiling inside the lab. It had to find something it could corrode well enough to hold it. Probably the insulating panels. Maybe something else. We can't take a chance."

No, it wouldn't do. The stuff would stick to their clothes. Small pieces. Also, the plants he had created might differ in subtle ways from the outside, natural ones. He might really have induced a mutation himself; that is, more exactly, some alteration in the molecular structure of the growth compound. His synthetic plants might be themselves a kind of isomer plant to those outside. With altered properties. He couldn't take the chance.

He yelled for help, shoving words of explanation at the dancing Cruzate between shouts.

A much-surprised airman eventually showed and wanted to know what the noise was all about.

"A blowtorch," Wertz told him. In the geological lab next door was Dr. Judah's blowtorch. On the tool bench.

The man gave him a hard look.

"I can't move from here, dammit!" Wertz told him. "Neither can he. We've got lichen tips on us. Now get me that torch quick, and I'll explain it to you later all you want. We'll have to burn up our clothes too. Right here."

The stare turned blank.

"Move, man!" Wertz slashed at him. "Then we'll put on a good show for you."

The airman shook his head, but he did turn around and go into Judah's laboratory and he came back with the blowtorch. Wertz told him to set it on the floor and stay away from them.

"You got a match?" Wertz demanded. When the man had found a package in his pocket, he tried to remember how to light the torch.

The airman moved in. "Let me."

"Get the hell back away from this stuff," Wertz said. "You tell me. One step at a time."

Between them they got it lighted. Wertz picked it up and poured the blue flame over the lichen fragments, carbonizing them, all that he could find.

"Next we burn our clothes," he pronounced. "Then we take a bath and wash our hair in a good neutralizing base."

"It is frantic!" Cruzate sputtered. "These things here, that you have somehow made. They cannot grow. The green plants need the light of the sun to live and grow. Where is the sun in this metal monster that bring us here?"

"Maybe so. But we don't know."

Cruzate's face lightened. "The heat! That is it. The fungus, it cannot survive the heat. The cold, yes. Indefinitely. But the heat, *non!* One hundred fifty degrees they do the work. Then they are dead."

Wertz wondered if the little guy thought he would make himself ridiculous by taking off his clothes.

"Oui," Cruzate said firmly, "the heat. It is all is required. The 150 degrees. It is easy. Pouf—they are dead!"

Wertz thought a moment. "Is that established? The 150 degrees, I mean? Fahrenheit? Is that the theoretical limit for fungus plants?"

"On Earth, but certainly! Here many things are different." Cruzate waved a grand gesture of uncertainty. "Perhaps this also. But with the general temperatures lower than the Earth temperatures, so also would I expect to be lower the maximums for the living plants."

"Okay, okay." Wertz had the idea now. A few coils of heating element thrown into the close-sealed lab ought to do it. "Isn't your name Whipple?" he asked the gawking airman.

"Yeah."

"Okay, Whipple. I want you to do two more things for me. I don't want to leave this spot and maybe scatter some of the stuff around. Please call the flight surgeon and ask him to have a strong solution prepared of sodium carbonate. Two big buckets of it, and send them up to me. Tell him it's important and I'll explain later. Then call the commander and ask him to do me the favor of coming up here. Will you do that?"

After reflection Whipple allowed that he would.

"Okay. There's a phone in where you found the blowtorch. Ask them to hurry. Ask Captain King to send a couple of bath sponges too."

While they waited, Wertz got out of his clothes, feeling the amazing lightness no human could ever accustom himself to when he had shucked his heavy gravity belt and footgear. Finally he persuaded Cruzate to follow his example. "We'll throw all these clothes inside when we open the door to introduce the heating elements. We'll foul up the place if we try to burn them up with the torch. Then we soak ourselves good with sodium carbonate, and it neutralizes the acids in any fragments in our hair or sticking to our bodies. Then we swab down the floor with the same stuff, and I think everything will be sterile. The damned things can't grow any more without their acids, that's for sure."

Cruzate grunted his disgust. He moved delicately about with his weight off, as if he were afraid he would soar up and bump his head.

When the two buckets of solution and the sponges came up, they further amused Captain King's grinning medical orderly by bathing in the milky liquid, sloshing it freely over their bodies and squeezing it out of the sponges on each other's head. As soon as the orderly saw Major Noel come through the bulkhead, he departed abruptly.

"I guess all this has an explanation of some kind," Noel commented.

"We're not exactly playing games," Wertz told him. "We've got trouble enough for everybody."

"I hope it's not a brand-new one."

Noel sounded tired. Wertz felt a twinge of sympathy for the man. He had his load, all right enough. "It's about the lichens," he said. "We were experimenting with them and they literally blew up in our faces. I'm afraid now that they could be dangerous to the spacecraft if they grow up to it and get in contact with it." He began telling him what had happened.

Noel listened soberly.

With the reflective man's disturbance over directness, Wertz struggled against Noel's interrupting queries that chopped off his explanations. It would take only a few more minutes to report the incident adequately, with some indication of the historical and analytical detail of the experiment.

Noel wasn't having any. The basic facts were enough for him. Obviously he was getting excited under the official mask. In spite of his annoyance Wertz noticed with some admiration how his manner crispened. He also regarded his own inevitable prolixity with a certain additional annoyance.

"The lichen peninsula is only fifteen hundred yards away now," Noel said. "It's still growing straight toward us. Now we've had fair warning what the plants could do to the spacecraft's skin, if they really can chew up metal. And it looks like they can. That means we've got to play it safe and keep them away from any contact with the Far Venture."

He shook his head. "This is just among us. We could likely spend several more days here. With the lichens growing all the time. You men are the experts," he said abruptly. "I want results. I want to know how to stop those plants growing and kill them off if they turn out to be dangerous to us. My resources are at your disposal. You tell me before tomorrow morning how you recommend we do it."

Wertz threw his sponge into the bucket. "Just like that, you say!"

Noel looked at him without expression. He pushed out his lower lip. "You know everything now you'll know in the morning. Tonight you'd better think, because tomorrow you experiment. Outside, that is. I'd make it good if I were you."

Why the sudden antagonism? He acted as if something had suddenly made him sore about something. What came to the tip of his tongue, Wertz didn't know before he said it, but he said it. Maybe fending off his embarrassment, he thought. "John Dane tell you anything about thinking there could be intelligent beings here that don't want us to get away?" he had blurted out.

Noel said, "I'm far from convinced these so-called signal effects are emanating from any Martians. We've scouted the lichens where they're supposed to be coming from. If they're coming from there, they're coming out of some damned thin air. There's sure no transmitting equipment of any kind there." His face twisted still tighter. "Could be some bright genius boy among us has rigged up some fancy kind of inductive tap on our equipment to play games with us."

"Why?" Cruzate exclaimed. "But why?"

"Did you ever think it could be just a plain nut?" Noel said. "Nuts don't have to have reasons."

Wertz said, "Just supposing there really were Martians. Then supposing they are fertilizing a path for the lichens to grow in towards the Far Venture. I have just proved how they react to an enrichment of their environment."

Noel said, "They keep themselves pretty damn well hidden, for my money. If we've got Martians, then as long as they hide out as well as they've been doing, they'll play hell doing anything to us."

"I'd say just the opposite," Wertz said.

"Look," Noel said. "Speculate all you want to. I like to theorize myself when I've got plenty of time for it. Right now I've got plenty to think about without imagining up any Martians. Sure, we're trying to check the signals out. You've got to. But for my money we've got a nut. No offense meant to present company, but a scientific, very expert nut. If I can put two and two together, we've already had one nut, and a pretty close call for the colonel it was, too."

"I'm getting tired standing around here naked and half floating, like a goldfish," Wertz told him. "Especially if you're going to give me that routine about Dr. Pembroke being the one who stabbed Colonel Cragg."

"He's the best guess I can think of."

Wertz shrugged. "So you keep John Dane locked up."

"Precaution," Noel said. "Things have changed a lot since I had him confined. Then the finger was square on him. Then Pembroke pulls his act and all at once things are different. I'm still going to hold Dane in confinement until the colonel comes out of it. Then he can tell us himself what happened. Till then it's my personal opinion that it was Pembroke."

"It's not mine," Wertz said stoutly. "I'd rather think it was John Dane, and I damn sure don't think it was him."

"Your privilege," Noel said. "But somebody pushed that knife into the colonel, and Pembroke was floating around at the time. Undoubtedly mentally unbalanced."

"He's dead and buried now." Wertz thought of the metal box under the Martian sand and the burial party of pressure-suited gravediggers hiding something away in a secret place on an imaginary world. It was not impossible, he conceded, that the old man had broken down out there in the lichens before they found him and brought him back. Radiation madness, like they said. Or something like that.

"He was a great man," Cruzate pronounced. "If he did wrong, he did not know what he was doing."

"I'll let it rest there," Noel said, not unkindly. "We've got a lot of more immediate troubles. We can go before a court and give testimony and hunt out the guilty after we get back home. Right now our problem is to get back home." He turned on his heel. "While you're getting dressed, I'll arrange to heat up your lab and get rid of your lichens for you."

CHAPTER FIFTEEN

Wertz eased his light body to his bunkroom and got into a fresh suit of coveralls. He snapped on a weight belt and pulled on gravity boots, and he felt normal again. At least the normal he had become used to, of dragging heavy feet. The ideal outfit would have shoulder weights, he decided, molded plates of lead, like epaulettes or football shoulder pads. Too much of the weight in this harness was low on the body for a feeling of freedom.

Noel was already back at the lab door. He had a coil of heavy cable, one end snaking away toward a heavy-duty outlet in the next lab. Four small coils of heating element were fashioned and waiting. Two men stood by.

"We can't just leave the door open a crack for the cable to pass in," Noel told him. "According to what you've said, I want this room sealed off. Can a man get in there and plug in these heaters inside your lab?"

Wertz thought about the acid tips. They hadn't injured him or Cruzate, but it would be taking a chance. There ought to be a safer way. "We could drill a hole in the door for the cable. After it was passed through we could seal the hole up around it."

"We'll still have to open the door to get the heaters inside. How about that?"

"Get one of your small flame throwers up here," Wertz told him. "First we drill a hole in the door and pass the electric cable through it. Then we open the door and spray the inside of it with flame and also all the plants close around the door. Then we attach the heaters to the cable and throw them into the middle of the room. We shut the door and seal up all the cracks. With fire shooting in the door while it's open, the plants can't come out."

"It could work," Noel admitted. "But why not just burn out the whole room?"

"The fire will kill them," Cruzate put in, "but so will the heat, and you do not destroy the laboratory."

"To hell with the laboratory," Noel said. "We wouldn't take a chance on unsealing it anyway. Whipple" —he dismissed them—"bring up an M-6 flame thrower. We'll burn the place out," he decided. "It's simple and it's sure. If heat would work, fire ought to work better."

The notebooks. The samples! Wertz thought. "You can't do it that way. You'll burn up everything I've done on Mars. My notebooks are in there. The records of all my analyses."

"You'll have to do it over. What you can't remember. You can remember most of it, can't you?"

Wertz felt the yes-sir compelling tone. "You know better than that," he said sharply. He thought of the painstaking, intricate analytical operations on the planet's atmosphere. "If we should escape tomorrow or next day, I'd never have a chance to repeat the work. You want us to go back without even determining the—"

"I want us to go back," Noel snapped. "That has priority over everything else. This ship's got to return."

"Okay! Okay! I'll open the damned door and go in after my stuff! Then burn all you want to!"

"Let us try the heat for a few days," Cruzate intervened. "I can assure you that these things are the lichen-type plants. They do not survive the temperature 150 degrees. Then the work of Wertz, it is not lost. I think even after a few hours it is quite safe to go in. They are of my profession, these lichens, you know," he added gently.

Noel turned to his airman. "Bring me an electric drill. I want a one-inch hole through that door. Okay," he added to Cruzate, "we'll proceed on your advice."

Wertz wondered why he had made such a point about it. Who could know what Pandora's box of tricks he had unlocked? Cruzate lived in another time. A much older time of the twentieth century. He was almost early twentieth century. Systematic. Categorical. Everything subject to classification. Definable classes, admitting no penumbra. A fairish jolt of his mental kaleidoscope and it wouldn't surprise him if Cruzate began to find teleological patterns in his ordered arrays.

Wertz was disturbed when a mind like Cruzate's agreed with him. For any reason. Not that one couldn't proceed from faulty principles to right spot judgments. It was just that it was accidental. Noel had the right kind of mind. He cut right to the core of the question. The primary object was to return to Earth. Without return nothing else mattered at all. Investigations, learnings, notes, all were written in the red sand dust. Left there like the body of Dr. Pembroke. Whom they could all very likely join. Without benefit of burial.

The airman was a long time coming back. Apparently one-inch drills were not found in every tool chest. After he had rigged it up, Noel directed him to pierce the door panel.

The man flexed broad shoulder muscles. His husky forearms and hands fondled the heavy tool gracefully, with an odd suggestion of its buoyancy. He tried the security of the chuck before he pressed the trigger switch. Then he addressed the casehardened point to the timageel surface of the door. The whirring deepened as the tool took hold and he put some weight behind it.

Suddenly he bent forward. Wertz thought the drill had won through, even as he saw a large area of the solid door crumple into pieces, like breaking a pane of painted glass. The airman lurched into the green rose that blossomed full-blown through the hole. He cried out hoarsely and staggered back, rubbing at his face.

Wertz shouted, "Lie down!" He grabbed his belt and pulled back and down. "Get down on the floor!" He snatched up a bucket of the sodium carbonate. "Cover your eyes!" he yelled at the cursing, rolling figure.

He poured the bucketful over the head and hands. Then he took up the soaking sponge out of the other bucket and swabbed at eyes, ears, and neck, laving the livid acid marks. The man was severely burned. The acid tips had turned viciously caustic since he and Cruzate had plunged out through them.

He heard Major Noel snap out an order for flamethrowers. When he looked up, the evil rose had doubled. It grew visibly before his eyes, expanding its circumference and thrusting forward its protrusion, its surface shaking and stirring chaotically in a slow, Brownian dance. He grabbed the blowtorch, which mercifully still stood on the floor nearby, and fumbled with its pump. Any second the things might explode throughout the whole corridor.

"Let me have that!" Major Noel demanded. In the same breath he ordered Cruzate to get away from the danger. "We can't risk you two. Get going!"

"The hell with you, sir!" Wertz shot back. "Commanders are not expendable either. Besides, this is my baby!"

At last the torch roared. Its nozzle hissed out a blue-white dagger.

Noel said, "Whipple, take this man. I want that torch."

Before he could get out of his crouch, Wertz felt a choking arm shock around his neck, and a weight from behind dragged him irresistibly back, sprawling and locked in some kind of judo hold.

He saw Noel take up the torch and thrust it at the lichens. "Cover your eyes! Your eyes!" he gasped against the choking arm.

Under the moving blast of the torch the lichens blackened. A stultifying smoke arose, gray, heavy, and stinking with chemical vapors. Wertz thought of the possibility of cyanogen compounds. Hydrogen cyanide...formed when carbon is strongly heated in temperatures of the order of 2000 degrees in a mixture of hydrogen and nitrogen. There had been no opportunity for exhaustive study of the complex organic acids in the tips. The charred stems were certainly carbon...but the open flame…that was combustion. Anyway, one whiff of cyanide and they would all have been dead by now.

Noel went all around the circumference. Then he passed the flame over the center in slow, smooth brush strokes. Wertz decided that he was holding his own. And the sinister trembling of the plants was no longer visible. "Okay, fellow, you've done your job," he said. "You can let me up now." The smoke was getting chokingly thick. "Better layoff that, Major. You've breathed enough of this stuff. You'd better get some masks before you burn out the laboratory."

"I have attended to that," Noel said.

Neither of them wanted to say much about the condition of the walls and surfaces inside. The door was of thinner metal than the decks and even the bulkheads, but then, maybe the acids were concentrated against other areas inside. Even now lichens could be erupting. The entire laboratory could be a sieve, leaking acid lichens into all the adjoining rooms and spaces.

The corridor filled rapidly with crewmen and equipment. Captain Spear came up. "This has got to be fast," Noel told him. "I want two men in asbestos suits and one for myself. You will take the rest of the men out, including these civilians, and seal off the corridor. First I want all the doors opening on this corridor sealed. This is going to make a big chemical stink. Then we're going to pour Wertz's laboratory full of fire. That will be all for the lichens."

Captain Spear said, "I'll take the M-6 in."

"Don't waste time, Captain," Noel answered levelly. "You can instruct me in my duties some other time. Carry out your orders and clear out of here. On the double! I imagine that, armed with a flame thrower that can burn out a pillbox, I am the match for a small roomful of plants."

Spear smiled wryly and began barking his orders.

Wertz grudgingly gave the devil his due. He didn't like the guy, but Noel had the stuff in him. Wertz realized that all the others, officers and crewmen alike, had known without a word being spoken who was going in with the flamethrower. The guy was not only their commander, but he was a leader to be followed. Somehow he did look different from the others now. Just a guy, dead pan, pulling on asbestos overalls, but he emanated an easy confidence and a competence that gave the operation the assured outcome of a planned drill.

There was something about the professional military it took a long time to become aware of. They cherished their little dignities and made ostensible show of their obligations, but when the issue confronted them, they drew up together in a tight-knit band for the attack, all the way through from buck airmen to commander, relying on their commingled merits. There was a clue to it in the way Noel had ordered the "civilians" out. It was not just solicitude for the well-being of civilians; it was that civilians didn't belong where the military stood in danger. A kind of unworthiness to meet the foe. Wertz felt a touch of disgrace.

A phone jangled sharply at the end of the corridor. One of the men ran to it. "It's for you," he reported to Major Noel. Wertz noted that he came back properly close before he spoke. "Emergency from the command post."

Noel shook off the man who was adjusting the flame-thrower harness to his shoulders. "I'll take it," he directed Captain Spear. "Check these men in their suits. I'm about ready to go in."

CHAPTER SIXTEEN

Lieutenant Yudin hitched up a leg over a knee. "I shouldn't say it, I guess, but I don't think Major Noel ought to keep you chained up like this." He looked quickly down and away from the links around Dane's ankle. "It's already been three days. Most everybody thinks Dr. Pembroke did it anyway."

Dane lay back easily on his bunk. "You get used to it. Especially when nobody's going anyplace anyhow. Thanks to you, I've had plenty to keep me busy."

Yudin twitched his black-rimmed glasses at the sheaf of notes and the stacks of photographic prints that cluttered the pipe-legged bunk. "I tried again today to get him to release you and put you in charge of the deciphering operation, but it's no go. He says no go until he hears what Colonel Cragg has to say."

Dane wanted to be left alone with the new prints. "How's he doing today?" he asked, knowing the fellow wanted to talk. He did owe him Noel's permission to have access to the materials.

"Captain King won't say anything. Except that he's doing as well as could be expected and he has a chance. You never get anything out of a medic. Not them. They never give themselves a chance to be wrong. A couple of hundred years ago they stalled you with an 'in-God's-hands' and alibied with an 'it-was-God's-will.' The modern ones just keep their mouth shut and pretend it's all too complicated for the ignorant layman to understand. If the patient dies, they expected it all along, and there was nothing that could have been done to save him. If he lives, they cured him. It's a good racket. They can't lose."

Yudin got out his big curved pipe and began to stuff it, settling down for a chat. "I don't like this whole thing. Not one bit do I like it. Item one, not enough power to get off the ground, and they're no closer to finding out what's the matter. Item two, those lichens growing so fast you can see them. You actually can see the things grow. Right across the open sand. Straight for this big can we're sitting in. Why? Item three, these signals. Are they phony or not? If they're not, where the devil are they coming from? They've got to be straight-line transmissions. Like any radar beam. They're coming straight from the direction of those lichens that are growing out toward us, but there's no antenna tower that we've been able to spot or anything else. Noel's had two scouting parties out. One party went fifteen miles into the lichens, and damn the risk, and never spotted a sign of anything but lichens. So maybe it's not line-of-sight beaming after all. Maybe they're just plain phony. Like Major Noel says, maybe we've got a screwball. Huh-uh. Not for me. I don't think so. What kind of a tap they going to put on my equipment and me not find it? But then what I say is, if there are Martians here, why don't they show themselves?"

"Maybe they're afraid of us," Dane said. "Maybe they're observing us by some method we haven't any idea about at all. Maybe they're some small insect life hiding in the lichens like small villages in a big forest. Maybe anything. How can we tell?"

Yudin laughed a little. "You got ideas, man. But even if they could be that little, they'd have to have equipment. To send the messages."

"There again, how do we know what they have to have? It doesn't take a bigger particle of matter than an atom to emit energy. Supposing their entire transmitter was the size of a pinhead. You think a scouting party would find it?"

Yudin shook his head tolerantly. "The power would burn it up."

"What kind of power? Electrical power as we know it? Or maybe power as they know it? What about a microscopic civilization using subatomic power? If it takes 200 million hydrogen atoms lined up in a row to measure one inch and then a hundred thousand electrons side by side to reach across the diameter of one hydrogen atom, it isn't too hard for me to conceive of an intelligent being so small that we would have to have a lens to see it and yet with a brain as complex as ours."

Yudin sprang up from his stool. "I've got to report this to Major Noel. They might be invisible and all over the spacecraft! We'd be at their mercy!"

He was an odd duck. Somehow his parts didn't just quite jell. A tangential type, rather than direct and purposefully controlled. No wonder he hadn't impressed the military.

"It's just a speculation," Dane assured him. "I suppose we could think up a dozen more, all with some plausibility."

"I've got to report it to him anyway. The commander has to be informed about all possibilities." Yudin fell back on his starched sententiousness.

"Just one second more. While you're telling him about possibilities, you might try to get across another item to add to the three you're worrying about. That's this. I know I didn't knife Colonel Cragg. I know that for sure. I am also as sure as a man can be about another man that Dr. Pembroke didn't do it. Under any circumstances. That adds up to an item for us all to worry about. There's a murderer loose on this craft, and he's no Martian either. Somebody on the Far Venture is a murderer, and my guess is he'll try again. For my money I'd want a guard over Colonel Cragg all the time."

The absurd mustache danced above Yudin's pursed lips. "All right," he said. "I'll tell him that too." He locked the door carefully behind him.

The little devil! Bringing duplicate prints of the signals received, getting friendly in his clumsy way, so maybe he might learn something. Had Noel really given Yudin an important role in the attempt to decipher the signals? It had struck Dane as an inept appointment from the first. Even though, technically, communications was Yudin's responsibility. The likelihood was that Noel had marshaled the intellectual resources of the entire party on the problem. Even Dane's, although unwittingly and through the left hand. But Yudin was only sweating to do extra duty as a detective. No wonder he hadn't been excited by Dane's progress to date. The simpler things Dane had told him could easily have been inferred by any intelligent mind. Very likely the answers he had instructed Yudin to send were duplicates of those already sent by order of Noel's team.

Dane was anxious to exchange his full findings with the other investigators. Maybe his conviction of a Martian source for the signals was in fact the product of too much unrelieved introspection. Both evidence and hypothesis fare better when exposed to the objections and cross-examinations and countercheckings of other minds. The signals seemed to him to have an evident unhuman flavor. Another mind slanting into the examination of them from another angle might possibly have made a good case for human faking of the unhuman. It was damn well time to be loose from this damn bunk, he began to fume, and out

98

from behind a locked door to get at the thing completely and totally with all available information and assistance.

He rattled the shiny light chain attached to his leg and grinned wryly. "Not going anyplace at the moment, Dane," he murmured.

He picked up the morning's take in the box of prints Yudin had brought him. This batch was obviously different. There were 174 four-by-five photographic prints cropped and enlarged from each frame taken by the 35-millimeter recording camera over the radar photo plane table. As usual, each had been dated and numbered serially by the darkroom man in the order of exposure. All were filed neatly and in consecutive order in stand-up fashion in a light carton. What struck Dane immediately on his first riffle was that most of the prints in the batch bore what resembled a word in which the former single symbols stood for letters. After the first few prints the single symbols were paired in various combinations. At the end of the two-symbol sequence he came upon a sequence with three symbols to each exposure and finally one of longer combinations with as many as six, eight, and nine symbols. Also, for the first time no new symbols had appeared.

He began sorting the 174 prints into "alphabetical" stacks in which the same symbol appeared either singly or as the first of a pair or group. This gave him eighteen stacks. Most of the prints were in the seven stacks for the seven symbols he had previously decided were numerals. All the singles and pairs were made up of these: the small circle he took for the numeral 1; the two points of light connected vertically by a bar, like a dumbbell balanced on end, apparently the numeral 2; the tiny triangle of three light points and connecting lines that must stand for 3; the square, pentagon, and hexagon for 4, 5, and 6; and a tracing of a little seven-branched tree-like object, probably a seven-tipped lichen plant but almost certainly the numeral 7.

Most of the other symbols had been identified, if some only tentatively. All were made by the threadlike line that connected the dots of light in the manner that constellations are often depicted. A "fishhook," in which the line proceeded from one point of light and curved back toward its origin to meet another light point, had always appeared standing on its shank between two numerals. Dane assumed it meant "equals." Two bars joining ends at right angle he called "does not equal." The fishhook with a bar dropped from its point to the middle of its shank fitted in as "equals what?" The dumbbell laid horizontally was "plus," and shorn of its right-hand point of light it became "minus." A circle cut through its area with an irregular curve but with two plain polar arcs could be "Mars" or "Martians." A circle perched upon a truncated cone was obviously the spacecraft. There was a little stick figure, either "man" or "you." For three symbols he had no meanings: two dots of light placed vertically and joined by a zigzag line; a small logarithmic spiral unwinding from a central dot to a terminal one; a rimless wheel of spokes, each tipped with a point of light.

So far the "messages" Dane had been able to exchange had been mathematical, the simple equations of addition and subtraction. Again most of the new signals appeared to have numerical value. Several of the word-like groups, such as 2 plus 3 equals 5, were obviously the same simple equations now sent simultaneously as one signal to replace the halting succession of single-symbol transmission.

In certain of the equations now before him the number symbols paired like Earth numerals to make higher numbers. For example, "23 plus 32 equals 55" figured out. Other groups, seemingly the same, made no number sense at all. If they were equations, they did not solve by simple addition or subtraction. Certainly "22 plus 36" did not "equal 61." Or if "22" was read as 4 and "36" as 9, the answer was certainly not 7, as "61" would then consistently have to be read. To complicate it further, many of the equations were interspersed by the nonmathematical symbols.

For the first time the messages were not transparently meaningful. After an hour he gave up on both the individual signals and his sorted stacks. If there was a clue, he could not discover it in the familiar comparative process of cryptanalysis. He decided to put the signals back into the order of their reception and copy them off as a continuous message, treating each photo print and its group of symbols as if it were a word. Maybe there was a pattern extending beyond the individual signals.

As he went along, he inserted vertical pencil strokes to separate the individual signals, like bars in a staff of music. When he had copied the entire set of signals, he borrowed another black chamber technique, going through his copy and setting down his tentative decipherings under the corresponding symbols wherever they appeared. He had written in only less than half when he caught the evidence of a pattern. Triumphantly he filled in the remainder, supplying question marks beneath the unknown symbols. At the head of his sheet of paper he wrote, "Message of 27 July."

Before the longer groups began, there were 77 prints, starting with those bearing only one symbol and including those bearing two and three symbols. The pattern of these 77 signals was plain.

The Martians had taught him their numbering system. No wonder the equations had not solved. Sheepishly he admitted the unlikelihood of the

Martians using Earth's decimal system of counting. The Martians counted by sevens. Not a decimal system. A septuple system. Look at their seventh numeral. Like a seven-tipped lichen plant.

It fitted! It fitted beautifully! He had to be right about the source of the signals. A hoaxing tap of the equipment, for whatever reason, departed the plausible for fantasy. The simple staring-in-the-face fact was that something was trying to communicate with the spacecraft. Not trying to, actually doing it! How the symbols could be transmitted as complex units so that they could be received on a radar oscilloscope was another matter. Sufficient that they had been transmitted.

He began to devise a table of the 77 simple signals, writing under each symbol its value in a septuple counting system. After a few boggles, including a bout with the symbol he called the "zigzag dumbbell," which he tumbled to as "zero," he had it. Laid out in rows of seven, the 77 number signals themselves revealed the system. The Martian symbols for 1, 2, 3, 4, 5, 6, and 7 corresponded with the Arabic numerals, but Martian symbol 11 was Arabic 8 and 12 was 9, 13 was 10, and 17 was 14. A peculiarity of the Martian system was that it did not use the null or zero sign in numbers under three digits, nor use the seven sign except in the unit position. Then Martian symbol 21 translated to Arabic 15 and 27 to 21; 31 to 22 and 37 to 28. The Martian triad-symbol 101 gave Arabic 50, and 107 gave 56. The four-symbol 1001 gave 344 and 1007 gave 350. The easily filled-in gaps in the transmitted sequence were themselves evidence of economy of thought. The Martians were good instructors!

At the head of the table he had laid out, Dane printed, "The Martian Table." He was now ready for the puzzling equations that began with the seventy-eighth signal. From his number table he easily read "22 plus 36 equals 61" as 16 plus 27 equals 43. Other recalcitrants, like "33 minus 22 equals 11," correctly yielded 24 minus 16 equals 8.

The Martian Table also permitted him to derive the formula for computing the higher Martian numbers. If in the decimal system "2343" equals

$$2 (10^3) + (10^2) + 4 (10) + 3$$

then the Martian number "2343" equals

$$2 (7^3) + 3 (7^2) + 4 (7) + 3 = 864.$$

Bafflers like "33062 plus 15311 equals 5143" were now revealed by a quick computation in powers of 7 as 8276 plus 4271 equals 12,547.

The fiftieth signal after the Martian Table was a triad: the equal sign twice, followed by the 1. Looking ahead for a new pattern, Dane found that the next 22 prints all bore the equal sign as the second symbol, following an initial nonnumber symbol. He isolated another clue when he observed that only number symbols followed the equal sign on all, and that on consecutive prints the indicated numbers ran from 1 to 11 and then repeated the sequence. When he arranged the 22 prints in two columns of eleven, he saw that he had two identical sequences of nonnumerical "equations."

He copied one of the columns on a sheet of paper and down its side filled in the translation of the symbols, except for two remaining unknowns. At the head of the column he wrote for a title, "The Eleven Table." The eleven equations, or rather statements, were obviously the rudiments of a number code. The symbol for "does not equal" was to be signified by "2" and the plus sign by "4." The pictogram for Mars was asserted to "equal" the number "7." "Spacecraft" was "8." "Man," or "you," was "9."

The next four prints now became statement of the code, if the equal sign could be accepted as a copula to assert identity: *Symbol Mars equals Mars (or "Martians"?) Symbol Mars equals symbol 7. Seven stands for Mars.* The fourth again suggested the use of the number 1 for the equal sign or copula.

The Martians had begun to teach a number code that would permit reply to their pictograms and ideograms. With the "alphabet" of one to seven radar pulses, "men" could encode the symbols the Martians had power to transmit graphically. The numbers "9-3-7 sent as "7,2-3-7" would say *Men are not Martians* in a nonmathematical context. The lesson in code was concluded by the next print, which bore symbols that read *8-2-7 stands for spacecraft is not Mars.*

Eleven signals now remained, each of which Dane took to be a sentence. Most contained yet unidentified symbols, and the others were obscure, unless possibly one made up of the symbols for "man" and "equals what." This one he rendered as *What is man?*

He shuffled the remaining prints, scrutinizing them one by one, and hoped for inspiration. He dealt them out in solitaire rows and picked them up and dealt them again. Suddenly he stopped all movement. He was not alone in his locked cell.

It was like autumn-crisp leaves in a dry woods, a faint, persistent rustling of sere vegetation, a snake crawling over dried leaves on a gully floor. His eyes were drawn up, to whatever was above his head. Instead of the buff metal of the ceiling, a dark mass hung over him.

Dane stared at the trembling, vegetative look of it with amazement.

Lichens on the ceiling? Inside the spacecraft? He thought of the lichen peninsula. Was it corroding the hull? He jumped up to reach at the quivering bush.

Even before his hand flamed, he felt urgent alarm. This thing was deadly. Like sight of the coiled snake, it shocked him into reflex recoil.

He had barely brushed the stuff, but his hand was fire-burned. He shouted loud alarm. While he sniffed at the stinging odor, a slow liquid drop slipped to the floor. The friendly, familiar compartment was all at once invaded by death.

He snatched the blanket from the bunk and piled it over his head and shoulders, like a poncho without a head hole. With the same movement he grabbed at the metal stool and flailed the door.

The acid smell was strong. It dug into his nostrils until he had to stop to sneeze. Any minute the searing stuff would eat through the blanket fabric and attack his bare head. Maybe his heavy pounding was shaking acid out of the plants. Quick! he thought.

When interminably later his door opened outward, his wild effort struck a last blow against air. The stool's weight jerked him ahead sharply against his ankle chain—tripped him flat, face against the hard deck.

"Whatthehell's the matter with you, chum?" a rough voice lashed at him.

It was First Sergeant Peeney. "It drips acid. Get me out!"

The sergeant gave a startled look at the ceiling. "Jesus!" he said. The departure of his habitual methodism jarred the ascent to the final syllable.

With head and shoulders outside across the threshold Dane could afford to look too. The lichens had grown down halfway to the floor along the far wall. He had been lucky in their choice of a wall. Any of the others and they would have been on him where he had stood swinging the stool.

The sergeant wasted no more time. He charged down the passage with as close to a run as he could urge his square—shouldered bulk in gravity boots. "Gotta get the key to the irons," he trailed behind him.

This big man was quick and effective. He was back at once. Without fuss he got the right key in the lock on the first try, and Dane rolled the rest of the way out on the riveted deck of the corridor.

Major Noel came up on the double, two airmen hurrying behind. He was rigged in bulky asbestos coveralls, a flame-thrower tank strapped on his back.

"Whatinhell happened?" Dane demanded.

Noel took a quick look inside Dane's room. "Sergeant," he barked, "have this man strip and throw his clothes in there." He fiddled with the nozzle of the flame gun. "Then get back through the bulkhead. All of you."

"How about you or somebody telling me whatinhell's going on!"

"Hurry it up. It's bad."

Like telling a child to wipe his nose. He tore at the offending coveralls.

Noel pulled the hood over his face. The nozzle spurted fire. He hosed the scaring stream rapidly around the walls and floor of Dane's room, then poured it full into the main lichen mass overhead. A dense white smoke came backing out into the corridor.

"Socks and shorts too," Peeney rumbled. "You heard the major. Let's get out of here."

Bootless, Dane edged along the passage, skating each foot ahead in turn, trying to hurry and keep sliding contact with the deck. They retreated past the first meteor-tight division and dogged its door shut behind them.

"What about Noel? He breathes too."

"He's got a respirator in his hood," Peeney said.

"I've got to get some boots and some fatigues," Dane told him. "I feel goofy enough in this strip-tease costume, let alone feeling as if I'm going to beat my brains out against the roof every step."

A clap of steely thunder slapped them. The deck quivered.

Peeney looked at Dane with wide eyes. "That was a jolt. That did us some damage." He grabbed the bulkhead phone and punched the command-post button.

Yes. It sounded as if it blew half the side out. It was a damnable time to be naked and bootless—muscles unfettered.

Peeney stood listening. Finally he said, "Right," into the mouthpiece and hung up. "There's been a helluvan explosion on 2-high deck. Dr. Wertz's lab went up."

"What's the bad news?" Dane tried to swallow the dryness.

"I gotta tell the major."

"Tell him! You think he didn't hear that bang?"

"He's needed, and he ain't here, is he? I gotta report to give him. And he ain't going to like it."

"What's the damage?" Dane insisted.

"We issue a report when the commander says so." Peeney started lifting the door latches.

"Hey! You can't go in there," Dane yelled at him. "Not without a respirator. It's full of smoke by now. Maybe gas."

Peeney turned and looked at him. "Now where am I going to get a respirator? You got one in your pocket?"

"All the same, you'd better get one. Or wait till he comes out. It's too risky without one."

"Deck below," Peeney said. "We stand here jawing, we could have one up here." He looked at one of the airmen. "No. I'll go. I can put my hands right on it. You two get back up to 2-high. Make yourselves useful."

Dane started to prowl the adjacent quarters. Old Man Judah's. Maybe he had an extra pair of boots in his locker. Coveralls, anyway. He wondered why a man felt vulnerable to injury without the negligible protection of a flimsy thickness of cloth.

Boots? No boots, but two or three sets of coveralls. Geologists work in the dirt, he thought. Maybe better luck on the boots next door. Suddenly he caught up short, thinking out the floor plan. Wertz's lab? It would be right above his own quarters. The explosion had been right over Noel's head. Right on top of an overhead deck already eaten out with lichen acids.

That did it. Noel was finished. He would have come out in a hurry if he had been able. Dane skated out into the passage and wrenched at the bulkhead latches. When he cracked the door, wisps of white smoke seeped in around the edge. Ahead the corridor was blind with fog.

The door swung open hard, catching him sharply on the forehead. A fire-suited figure stepped over the coaming and closed the opening quickly behind him.

Noel pulled off his hood. "Where's Peeney? Where's Beloit? How come you're always underfoot?"

An airman hurried up the passage. He looked blankly at Noel.

Noel nodded at Dane. "He let me through right after I called you."

Beloit arrived. Then Wertz carrying what looked like a bucket of milk. "You okay, sir?"

"I was outside," Noel told him. "It knocked me down, and I got up. What's the damage, Major?" he demanded.

"The hull is intact, sir."

"Anybody hurt?"

"Yessir. Captain Spear is dead. Sergeant Gonzales is dead. Fritts and Lee got hurt. Not much."

Noel shucked his gloves. One at a time he carefully handed them to the airman. Abruptly he exploded, "Spear and Gonzales! Goddamnitohell! Pretty expensive experiment," he snapped at Wertz.

Wertz bristled. "I'm sorry about Spear and Gonzales. But the experiment was necessary. That's why we came here, to find out about things. You and I both."

Noel wheeled away. "Bring Dane along," he said. "I want to talk to him after I come back down."

CHAPTER SEVENTEEN

Dane waited at the command post. He was still in custody. That had been made clear by Sergeant Peeney, assisted by Airman First Class Merrick.

Both men ignored him. He was physically present and accounted for, and that, it was made obvious, was the extent of their concern. A flow of orders and requirements from the scene of the explosion on 2-high deck had to be entered in the action log. Dane sat back out of their way and listened to Noel come over the monitor speaker. Report and reply, decision and order, step by step he drove up the tempo of operations. Even over the wires he permeated the spacecraft with a definite presence, attending precisely to detail. It was a capable performance, Dane acknowledged.

Peeney and Merrick were steadily engaged by their duties, he also admitted, but not so much engaged that they couldn't have included him in their by-play of remarks upon what was going on. From their manner it was not hard to imagine a heightening of the corps feeling among the crew. It wouldn't be difficult at all to imagine their traditional, half-contemptuous, half-proud appraisal: "They make the trouble, and we have to settle it. We pick up the pieces."

He thought of the blond Mrs. Spear that Captain Spear had found in Albuquerque. The way Spear had talked about her, she was refreshing in an unprofessional-wife's way. Not a bright-chatter-with-the-colonel sort of woman with taut tendons in the back of her hands and hollow-ground smile. She would be the kind to take it quickly and deeply—maybe even permanently. If there was such a thing as permanency in human relations. Even so, better to be a live widow than a dead husband.

Gonzales had no wife, but he had sung the poetic border music in a clear plaintive tenor above the softly chiming chords of his guitar, surely a pattern of activity as alien in the vastness of the galaxies as this world upon which he had met oblivion and the end of all music had been to Gonzales, himself far adrift from the Rio Grande home in a universe where Rio Grande life was elsewhere impossibly ununderstandable. Whatever his manner of living, man had to return into the earth from which he had been born. It was some sort of saying, but said in all truth. Man is Earth, nor could there be anything else for him. Not even the old idea of heaven, unless it too was an image of Earth—the ancient Mother Earth.

Perhaps the far ventures of the dawning age of space travel would in actuality be discoveries of Earth itself and all the rich wonders it lavishes on man. Venturesome Columbuses bringing back the news, not of New Worlds, but of the rediscovered world they had left, with its familiar hills and homely plains, the still forests and the bright beaches opening on the fabled wine-dark seas, the man-refreshing seasons, and the good-seeming shine of sun and moon, and everywhere home, the home to which man was so bred that he too is an inseparable part of Earth. The beauty stored up in the ancient clichés, Dane thought, all around man, all over Earth, from his birth through his life. Like the soft chords of a well-played guitar under the Rio Grande moon, heard briefly and then the quiet.

Noel appeared at the thick door of the command post, his dark, squeezed features at last showing the strain of red eyes and slackened mouth. He nodded at Dane. "I want to talk to you."

Dane followed him around the passage to the commander's quarters. "How is the colonel today?" he asked, feeling himself an intruder among Cragg's vacated gadgets.

Noel pointed at a chair. "I'll get to that later." He sat his small body neatly down at the desk. "I want a complete briefing from you on this idea you have about a microscopic civilization here." There was a tint of contempt to his directness.

"Lieutenant Yudin must have made his report," Dane commented.

Noel picked up Cragg's straightedge and waved it Cragg-like. "I expect prompt reports from my officers and men. Also from the civilians on board concerning anything related to our mission. I know you know that our biologist hasn't found any microscopic organisms on this planet, not a single kind, except those we brought along ourselves aboard the spacecraft."

Noel's familiar face was suddenly strange. Dane paused, sensing a taut remoteness about the man that struck him all at once with the born authoritarian, the dedicated man. As a commander Colonel Cragg had been tough and hard; this man would be rigid. Undeviating from whatever line he might draw. With full command on his shoulders this was not the same man.

"I am. I am well aware of it," he said finally.

"So you think the biologist is wrong."

"I don't know. I do know there are keenly intelligent beings here. So far they have remained invisible to us. Either by design, or because they are remote, or because our eyesight doesn't pick them up. I was just speculating about microscopic beings. This is a large planet. We have explored only a tiny part of it firsthand. Forms of life are confined to certain zones on Earth, why not here? I also have other speculations. You must have some yourself. Have you considered the possibility of intelligent forces? Charges and potentials similar to electrical activations, for example? What about the spark fires? They could be something more than static discharges. Maybe in some way we haven't imagined they are what we call alive."

Noel's eyes slid into his and locked. "An hour ago I was told you had a record for imagination, but don't try to make a fool out of me with a bunch of wild ideas. I want to know two things. First, what you really know, if anything. Second, why have you been feeding Lieutenant Yudin a lot of stuff and nonsense?"

"What's the matter, Major? Your nerves acting up?" Dane said bluntly.

Noel laid down the straightedge carefully, feeling for the desktop, his hard eyes unswerving, staring at him as if a steel circle held the two of them immovably together.

Then a change, almost of friendliness, came over him. The official mask relaxed. "Maybe," he said. "I don't want to be peremptory with you, Dr. Dane. And I don't expect any man to take it lying down if I am. I lost two men this afternoon and two friends. I can't forget that I am at least temporarily responsible for an important mission of the United States Air Force that includes the safe return of this spacecraft and all aboard. Both that mission and our return are mysteriously endangered. I've got to know anything you might have learned or what you might really suspect about these messages we have been receiving. First of all, I've got to know why you're so sure they aren't just faked someway."

Dane thought a minute. "Well, in the first place, we would have to assume somebody aboard has capabilities we don't know about ourselves. Before they could fake the pictogram symbols, for example, and tap them to a radar screen. That's a pretty big assumption right there. And all because somebody's crazy? That's not enough for me either. Why go to all that assumption, just because it's hard to believe there are intelligent Martians on what we call a desert planet?"

Noel listened without interruption, with the skill of a man accustomed to detailed, factual briefings. Dane began at the beginning. He sketched in the background of the number table he had put together and explained the means it gave for reply to the Martians. He wrote down the symbols for the sentences he had solved, ending with the one that queried, "What are men?"

"With your permission," he went on, "I want to state again that I have had nothing to do either with the stoppage of the drive or with the attack on Colonel Cragg. I want my release from arrest. I want to answer these signals, and I want unrestricted opportunity to build up a vocabulary of symbols for the possibility of detailed communication. We are on the verge of one of the great events of human history. We have made first contact with minds from another world. The significance of that contact dwarfs everything else connected with this voyage. And everything else in our century. Even the fact of this interplanetary flight itself."

Noel said, "If you are right, there are two things that we've got to do—not just one. If there really are Martians, we've got to find out who and what they are. We've got to find out how advanced a civilization they have, and especially if they are any threat to Earth on future flights here. But second, and this is the one that counts, we've got to get the information back to Earth. To do that, we've got to get off this planet."

He smiled frostily. "I'm going to release you from arrest. You will give your full attention to developing friendly communication with the Martians, if any. I won't say I'm ready to agree with you that there are. But I'm going to follow through with you. For a working assumption, at least. I've got to. You will exercise your activity through Lieutenant Yudin. He'll be instructed to give you all the help we can."

Dane stood up, exultant despite a thought about how imprisonment scars a man's independence. Suddenly angry with his joy, he had to say it. "Am I to take it you've decided I'm clear? Or is it just that you need my help?"

"It looks like you're doing better with the messages than the rest of the staff. But there's one thing you can take for sure," Noel snapped. "You're not my candidate for the man who stuck that knife in the colonel. If you were, you'd rot before I'd turn you loose."

The lips tightened again. The mask was back. "One thing more I want you to understand. You civilians are on board as technical experts and advisers. You are not to interfere in any way with the operation of this spacecraft or the duties of its crew."

Dane said, "Have it anyway you like. I'm not looking for a medal."

"Good."

"Since you've been so thoughtful as to clear me of suspicion of attempted murder, you have somebody else in mind?"

"I didn't say you were clear of suspicion. I said I didn't think you did it. You ought to know who I've got in mind. I understand you've already put in your yell about it."

Dane grunted his disgust. "You'd better wash your face on that one. It's really out on a limb! Dr. Pembroke couldn't do such a thing, no matter what condition he was in. Mentally or otherwise." He struggled to hold his voice level. "I'll tell you what I told your stooge Yudin. There's a murderer on this ship. And if he tried for Colonel Cragg once, he'll probably try again."

"You ought to be glad I take Pembroke for my man. However"—Noel shrugged—"Colonel Cragg is not so sure about Pembroke."

"Cragg!" Dane exclaimed. "I thought he was still out."

Noel shook his head. "Negative. He revived enough to say a few words last night and he's better this morning."

"Well," Dane shot at him impatiently, "that ought to settle it. Who did *he* say it was?"

Noel shrugged. "It was dark in the passage and the knifeman got him from behind."

"You mean he doesn't know who stabbed him?"

"No, he's not certain. He's not sure at all. But he doesn't much think it was Pembroke. He seems to remember a last-minute impression that it was a big man. Too big for Pembroke. Say more your size."

"Wait a minute," Dane demanded. "What are you trying to say?"

Noel shrugged again. "I'm not trying to say anything. Except that the colonel doesn't really know who did knife him. But he does think it could have been you."

"Me!" Dane shouted. "That's impossible. He couldn't see anything that didn't happen!"

"That," Noel added, "is only his suspicion. Not a certain fact."

"Thanks!" Dane told him.

CHAPTER EIGHTEEN

Why did anyone on the Far Venture want to kill Colonel Cragg? Dr. Pembroke, because he was crazed by radiation? That one couldn't be entertained for a minute. But then who? And why? What was the motive? What was the gain?

There had to be a reason. A pretty strong reason. Therefore it was likely that the same reason yet existed. Somebody was going to be heard from again. Next time maybe he wouldn't be so lucky as to leave no more clues than a standard belt knife. A hundred extras over the Far Venture for a hundred reasons. Then again maybe he will be luckier. Cragg dead this time. By still undiscovered hand, with all his suspicions and maybe charges in the official record. That would be fine for John Dane. Just wonderful.

He couldn't take comfort in the support of Amalgamated Press.

Ames would fight official charges tooth and toenail for him if he thought the news value favored Amalgamated. Otherwise a trusted employee named Dane would meet the fate of the political appointee in high places who has, innocently or not, embarrassed his administration in front of the voters. The great managing editor would publicly beat his breast and righteously join the hounds in full cry after the hare who had betrayed the sacred honor of journalism. He could hear Ames saying it to his confidential staff. "Gentlemen, it's news with a capital N. The moral conscience of Amalgamated has always crusaded for the right, in public places high and low. We are also just as scrupulously intolerant of even the suspicion of wrongdoing by any person who represents, no matter how insignificantly, our own proud name. Now get to it and give it to me hot."

They had made him fairly snug in an emptied supply room on 3-high deck. A standard service cot had been bolted to the floor and made up with fresh white linens. Two blue Air Force blankets were tautly tucked in and turned down. A clothes closet with shelves and hooks and a wide shelf to serve him for a table had been contrived out of packing-case plywood and angle irons. He even had an extra stool for company and a folding canvas chair for reading.

A clothes closet was not much good without clothes, he decided. He went to the quartermaster's office and signed a chit for Air Force shirts, pants, socks, boots, underwear, sweaters, a kind of work jacket he liked, fatigue coveralls, toilet articles, a billed work cap, writing materials, and a stack of towels.

While he shoved the stuff into a duffel bag, he saw that he had omitted to ask for shoes. Once the spacecraft was underway and the thrust was converting inertia into the effect of gravity, crew and passengers would dispense with the weighted boots and return to conventional footgear. Maybe he had subconsciously lost all confidence. If they couldn't take off, he would certainly not be wearing ordinary shoes again.

Later he went up the ladders to the observation deck. It was already dark outside, but the eastern front flamed with the spark fires. The display was the most intense yet. The snapping long bolts leaped almost steadily from the ground in flashing arcs over the horizon.

He glanced at Airman First Class Humphries, stolidly on guard with the revolving beam of the sweeplight. He knew that the man was covertly inspecting him as much as the periodically illumined environs of the spacecraft.

There was a page in Old Grandfather's journal, written a full fifty years after the event of standing as a boy of seven in the graveyard of the old Indiana village home. It was Decoration Day and already the flowers were on the graves of everybody's folks and the small stiff-clothed American flags had been thrust into the grassy mounds over the Union soldiers. Then somebody said, "They're coming!" The boy heard the far beat of the drum, and as they came nearer, marching out from town, the fife vaunted once again the notes he later knew as "The Girl I Left Behind Me." He shouted, "The Old Soldiers are coming," was admonished to be quiet and restrained only by a flick of his own grandfather's hand from running through the long grass down to the gate and out into the dusty road to see them come. Then they did come. The Grand Army of the Republic. He guessed the score or so of blue-coated, kepi-topped men as more than a hundred, wishing he were marching at their head with the sword. They did come, in double file behind the flag and the color guard and the fife and the drum, past the long row of horses and carriages tied outside the graveyard, through the gate and up to halt and form ranks at the flagpole. While all the folks stood respectfully back, the drum crashed into the long roll and the flag ran up in the hot sun to the top of the pole, then sank, as the drum cut with one sharp beat and it was so quiet you could hear the pulley squeak, the flag slowly floating down to half-mast. Then again the long roll of the drum, and quick commands and three cracking rifle volleys fired slanting up into the air. And no one moved or said anything while they wheeled and marched away, out the gate and down the dusty road, vanishing around the curve, and the marching music going away with them until it was gone and Decoration Day, 1912, was over. Old Grandfather Kenneth set down fifty years later that for him the highest, most poignant poetry of his life was the fife notes of "The Girl I Left Behind Me," half heard in the old-time sunshiny noon above the far meter of a drum.

"Write yourself a book like this, boy," he said when he gave him the journal. "Put down yourself and what made you your own self. Then you can hold it in your hands and read it over again. It's right to keep alive what you really belong to. The world keeps changing fast, and you won't change fast enough to keep up with it. Before you know it, you're a stranger in the world and you think everything is worse than it used to be. And you're right. It is worse. For you. Because a lot of you doesn't have any meaning except among the things you remember. Like sunlight in the city, shut out by the walls instead of spread over open fields and beating down on red clover and making shade under the trees. Sunshine doesn't make much sense in the city."

Dane thought that was a funny thing to say, but he took the book carefully because he loved the tall old man with his funny-looking short white hair. Nobody could read out loud like Old Grandfather or knew all the things he knew. "Just you ask my Old Grandfather, if you don't believe it," he would say.

"That boy will worry you to death, Sir," Father said almost every day. "He's keeping you from your rest."

Old Grandfather roared with good humor. "Grandson," he would shout, "don't try to tell your grandfather when to take a nap."

One day—it was spring vacation in his third year at the university—he took down one of the three fat ledger volumes of his great grandfather's journal, for the first time. He read until far into the night. The old-fashioned handwriting unnoted while the familiar voice lived again, choosing its rounded phrases. Old Grandfather and his world well loved!

"We are a vast and beguiled field of folk who are graduated from simplified learning into common understanding. But among us also stand the trueborn who cleared the wilds, always ready to cut at the new wilderness and show us again as we may be. In all of us—so much alike and yet so much different that every man, and nay to the poet, is indeed an island standing alone in strange waters—in each of us is our own strength and beauty. For not wealth nor power is the danger of nations but denial of the nature of man."

One of his professors, the man of learning, had said, "That's early twentieth-century romantic liberalism. You can trace it back to the great Romantic period in literary history. Last half of the eighteenth century and early nineteenth."

Well, it was good thinking to grow on. Old Grandfather and his kind were no useless strangers from the past when they led the mid-century rebellion against the common man and restored his quality to an epithet. And one may well scorn the denominators that reduce all men and their ways to terms readily thundered from the rostrum and sold in the marketplace but so simple that they are stumbling false. One may seek a richer way by the subtler values of diversity, where the extreme lies farther but equally precipitous. Yet the anchor values, at least some, still hold.

But the minds of another planet—totally alien from man. With alien values that proceed from unutterably alien bases. What genuine meeting of Martian and man minds could ever be, with no mutual values for a beginning? What understanding beyond the simplicity of a plus b equals c? It would take generations of mutual tolerance and effort rare on Earth among men themselves. And tolerance and effort to understand, they themselves were Earth values.

Dane was dismayed and depressed. His grand scheme of communication with the Martians collapsed to guessing at nonsense riddles. The clearest of human values was inevitably as obscure on Mars as explanation of the meaning of the Old Soldiers' march on Decoration Day, 1912. Where would you begin?

A tremendous arcing bolt leaped skyward and over the far curve of the world. For an hour the fires flashed wildly, the single discharges melding into an incoherent pyrotechnic that ringed the eastern sky like cannon fire in a great night battle.

Airman Humphries broke his silence. He had never seen the fires "so bad."

"What do you really think it really is, sir? I mean what's causing it? Lightning wouldn't come up out of the ground, would it?"

"It might," Dane told him. "If something on the ground could generate a large positive charge in one area and a large negative charge in another. In that case something like lightning might discharge between them. The charges would have to be tremendous, though."

Humphries followed his gaze to the radar photo plane table. Its opaque glossy surface boiled with light. "You don't think it's lightning, do you?"

Dane put down the annoyance at being forced on the defensive. The boy was asking for help. More nearly comfort. It really was a thing to amaze, how little concern had been apparent over the immobility of the spacecraft. Perhaps a general repugnance to admit a fear that would itself admit a possibility that the expedition might never get off the planet.

"No, I don't suppose we ought to say it's lightning, in the sense of Earth lightning," he said, conscious of the delay of his reply. "Although it's obvious it's a form of static electricity." He chose the words carefully. "It is very probable that the lichen plants generate charges during the heat of the day that build up by early night, before the cold numbs them. You can see local arcing in the form of the big networks in local patches. Then the local buildup must rise high enough to discharge to some other local network several miles away. Our pressure suits must either repel the charges or ground them some way." He thought of Tesla effects. "We have certainly felt no electrical effect out among the plants."

He swung around on the silence.

Humphries stared at the face of the plane table. "Come here," he whispered. "Quick!"

With two strides Dane was beside him. Messages again. He recognized some of the signs, but from the number of large and new ones something new was being attempted. "The camera!" he said sharply.

"You forgot the camera." He seized its overhead suspension and swung it down to bear on the receiving glass.

"It sent a picture!" Humphries' voice was shaky. "It sent a picture of that guy Houck that got killed out in the lichens."

"Nonsense," Dane said brusquely. He locked the camera in the rack and started its motor. "These signs are simple line-and-dot symbols. How would you send a man's picture into a radarscope?"

"I saw it. Plain as life!" Humphries insisted. With his hands he measured off two thirds the area of the screen. "It was his face. Plain as day and dead-looking."

Dane said, "I won't say you didn't see it." He waited for the boy to control himself. "Visual phenomena are still not too well understood. It's been proved possible that we actually see a great many things we just think we see." That one really floundered. "I mean our eyes and our nerves can fool us."

"I know what I saw." Humphries rebelled, face-strained. "When I saw the foot and the legs and the lichens around the body I thought I was just seeing things that looked like them. But the face was plain. Jesus, it was looking right at me! Right there! You'd of seen it too if you'd been looking. You couldn't miss it. It took up pretty near the whole screen."

"Okay," Dane told him. "So you saw it. Relax and tell me about it."

"I just did tell you about it."

"I mean how long did the pictures stay on the screen? What did they look like? Were there any other signs or symbols with them? What did you see first?"

Humphries looked at him blankly.

"Calm down, fellow. Take it easy. Let's take it one at a time. What did you see first?" Dane repeated.

Humphries tried to think. "The feet. The feet were first. Feet and legs. In a suit. But before that there were some of the other signs like we've been receiving."

"Okay. Then what?"

"They came awful fast. Just on and off. Then something else. I think the shoulders in the lichens came on twice, though. Then the face. Plain as day."

"This face?" Dane asked him. "Think back. Was it in outline? Like you draw a face with a pencil? Or solid, more like a photograph?"

Humphries shook his head. "I didn't have no time to think about that sort of thing. It just plain scared me half out of my pants, seeing this dead guy's face looking up at me."

"Think again," Dane pushed him. "You saw it. Plain as day, you said." He grabbed up a pencil and sketched a rough outline of a human face. "Was it just lines like this? Or was it filled in like a photograph?"

Humphries nodded.

"Which? Which one, man? You mean it looked like a photograph instead of like a line drawing?"

Humphries nodded again. "It looked like a real picture coming over the television, only not so plain. Plain enough to tell who it was all right, though."

"Couldn't have been your own reflection, by any chance?"

Humphries' mouth straightened. "Look, fellow, I'm reporting what I saw to Lieutenant Yudin. I know a reflection when I see one. Take it or leave it, whatever you want. I make my report to my officers. Not to you."

CHAPTER NINETEEN

The messages from "outside" had become the big and serious confrontation, dwarfing even the trouble with the drive.

Airman Humphries had been right enough about the pictures. At 1447 hours the next afternoon the Martian, as Dane sometimes thought of the sender of the signals because of its continual references to itself as the "One," began suddenly to transmit a varied stream of the photograph-like pictures that Humphries had described. Interspersed among the established number symbols were pictures of Houck, of men in pressure suits, of lichens growing in various patterns, including the plant peninsula running out to a very passable portrayal of the spacecraft. And then came the disturbing fragments of scenes from within the spacecraft.

"How do they know what the inside of the Far Venture looks like?" Noel fretted. "How could they get inside to spy on us. Maybe you were right about them being microscopic."

"They are not inevitably hostile," Dane told him.

That, Noel came back, was yet to be determined. In the meantime it was evident they were very close. It would be folly to regard them otherwise than as potentially hostile and dangerous.

The pictures resembled what the photographic men called reticulated negatives, illumined from below. They lacked all fine detail, but the identity of the images was nevertheless unmistakable, the outlines realistically sure and the shadows and highlights contrast but showing some tonal value. Most of the "shots" from within the Far Venture offered no apparent relevancy to their association with each other. There was one of a ladder, another of a man climbing a ladder. There was one of a man lying on a cot, another of the empty cot. Some showed men climbing into, or out of, the airlock.

Dane had some memory from school that the ancient Egyptian hieroglyphs had originally been conventionalized pictures representing what they actually depicted but that later they had come to stand for certain syllables of sound, so that words could be written by means of them, and had lost reference to the objects they originally depicted. The Martian language quite conceivably was not a language of sounds. It could perhaps be a language of visuals of some kind, in which, for example, an object was named by a composite of visual "syllables" in the manlier of the later use of the Egyptian hieroglyphs.

Among the yet uncoded picture sequences that Dane thought were ideogrammatic, two at least, if his inference was correct, were not assuring.

The oft-repeated sequence of the death picture of Houck among the lichens and one of a pressure suit standing up could very well say, *Living men will die,* or more directly, *Death to the invader.* More disturbing inference might easily be drawn from the juxtaposition of generative components of the drive with clumps of lichens. Considering the corrosive quality of the lichen plant, maybe in some way even an instrument of power or productive of a weapon for the Martians—acid war—this sequence might be intended to say, *We have destroyed your means of escape.*

Noel was right, of course. The Martians would be dangerous at the least hostile move of the otherworld invaders. What they might regard as a hostile act was unimaginable. To a worm the tenderest songbird would be a horrendous, devouring monster, cruel and implacable.

"They are probably very much afraid of us." Dane said to him. "To them our physical appearance must be revolting, if not terrifying. Our size may be enormous. Inadvertently we may have harmed or even killed some of them. We've got to convince them of our good will, but how to do it when we don't even have any good guesses about what kind of life they are?"

For three days the Martians continued to transmit—and ignore all replies. The one-way communications were spasmodic, coming in at various hours of the afternoon or early night but never for longer than a few minutes at a time. The careful teaching procedure of earlier transmissions remained, but there the Martians stopped. Apparently they were indifferent to any sign of understanding from their pupils.

"It's a peculiar business," he told Major Noel at supper. "They teach us a way to talk to them, but they pay no attention to anything we send out. It begins to look as though all the curiosity is ours. Why aren't they as curious about us as we are about them? An encyclopedia of questions waiting to be answered. Earth comes to Mars. What are we like? Where are we from? Yet they try to teach us how to talk to them and then ignore us."

The sharp-twisted features lit up. "Maybe the bastards are exclusive. Maybe they're just getting ready to give us our orders. All we will have to do is say, 'Understand and will comply.'" He pushed the bottle of calvados closer to Dane's elbow. "We'll have to get it over to them that we don't want to play rough but that we can if we have to. And plenty."

Dane said, "It would be a great pity. A confession of the inadequacy of intelligence."

Noel measured himself out a nightcap. "It's too bad. But what else can we expect? I suppose a guy like you would know about the big flying-saucer scares two or three generations ago. Everybody in those days just naturally took it for granted that if there were really beings coming to Earth from another world, they would be dangerous and hostile." He tossed off his brandy and stood up. "I'm for the bunk. It's a long day in this big can."

It made Dane think of his managing editor. He would have had a field day with the flying saucers. From a continuing story like that the legend Telford Ames would have extracted a million dollars' worth of rich red sustenance for the common man and ramrodded the arteries and the lesser vessels of Amalgamated Press full of it to the bursting, down to the farthest, most insignificant capillary. Sitting precisely and with the mien of a Boston banker behind his big desk and surrounded by hushed umber paneling and insistent department chiefs, he would suddenly sweep aside the spatter of daily planning, theretofore silently contemplated, and poke the spatulate finger that somehow had got attached to his stringy, desiccated, Vermont-Yankee frame into the middle of the soft-spoken words, "That's your news with a big N. There's your feature for the common man. Now give it to me from there."

Ames was a champion interpreter of the human interest. Nobody said "no" to that. He had his record to prove it. At twenty-five he had made history and was credited with the loss of Congress by a great political party as the result of the nationwide attention won by his whistle-stop polemic sustained in a series of daily articles for a month before the polls. "Mr. Common Voter Makes a Campaign Speech" he had entitled them, creating a shadow candidate and not so subtly associating him with the opposition party. Among newsmen, from metro cub to county weekly pressroom, the legend of "The Thirty Days" was as well known as the story of George Washington's hatchet. After the name-calling had died away, there were three press services instead of five, and Amalgamated's paneled executive offices had a fresh news executive. Before he was twenty-eight Ames stepped nimbly over eight other department heads and moved from the side-hall office into the big corner room vacated the day before by The Boss, who had just failed to convince The Publisher, even after ten years of rather successful steering of Amalgamated, that he understood the news tastes of the common man well enough to be kept on as its managing editor.

Well, Ames had brought Amalgamated more major beats and cash-ringing features than Dane had written stories for it, but his parting counsel made him squirm to suppose, say, Noel listening in on it. "Dane," he had led off, "I had to go to the White House to get you on the Far Venture. Over your old friend Colonel Cragg's dead body. He's back down to size all right now, but he was very positively averse to you under any circumstances. He put it rather too strongly for us, so that it reflected on Amalgamated. We couldn't tolerate that. Not by a damn sight. We were able to put it up to them rather successfully that if only one journalist could be included in the party, then as an impartial representative of all the news interests he undoubtedly must be from Amalgamated. Whence else? Naturally we could not submit to coercion in our choice among our own men. We must appoint to the task which-ever one we ourselves considered our most suitable representative. It was a neat piece of work, and your colonel may be rash but he is no fool. He still deeply resents your war dispatches about him, and I must say I don't blame him, although from our point of view they were good. They were news with a capital N. Properly good. A hero is just a very ordinary sort of fellow caught up in events he triumphs over. Very good thematic stuff, but Cragg still doesn't care for it. Good reader identification for the common man. Damn good. Every man a daydream hero to himself, if the circumstances could just somehow be right for him. Brought you to my attention."

He had poked the spatulate finger at Dane. "Now here's the story for Amalgamated. Our subscriber editors will want the science copy, just as much as all the other members of the pool. That's your official reason for going along. Just the same, I don't want you to forget it's not your primary job for Amalgamated. Our Amalgamated readers want to bleed over the flight of the Far Venture, not study a lot of professor data that might be collected. Sure, they are interested in the climate and the terrain. They want to hear about the biological forms on Mars. They even have some curiosity about the weather there and maybe the chemistry of the atmosphere. A few photographs and graphs and charts with captions will take care of all that."

He jabbed the paragraphing finger again. "What our readers really want to do, though, is bleed over a man standing on another world and knowing his wife and kids are a hundred million miles away. They want to know how he sleeps nights and how he eats his meals in the daytime on Mars. They want to know that the bravest of the crew was not ashamed to be afraid, because he was sustained by the spirit. Wave the flag, man, and don't forget the church for the old-timers."

Still, it was a good wage and a great adventure. Behind Ames lay the white roofs of Houston, and far off from the window a thousand feet in the air were the purplish flatlands of the Gulf plain out beyond the limits of the metropolis. The man stemmed from the decayed cities of the eastern seaboard, like the crawling, wallowing freighters cargoing cheap wares from the stagnant Northeast. His old-fashioned sentimentalism and cheap feminism were out of old New York, two generations gone, but the great Texas city dominated by his skyscraper dominated the ebb and flow of the nation no more than Ames the news interests of 215,000,000 Americans. Okay. The pitch had been remunerative for a century. It was part of the price for going. Dane listened, smiling some at the way he was caught up a little himself by the man. In spite of himself.

"They want to know what the men look forward to doing first after they get back to Earth. Go to the fights? Go out on a picnic with the kids? Marry the girl friend? Buy a home with the bonus money for down payment? You want to tell our readers how it feels to climb out into the planetary cold and walk around in an air-conditioned pressure suit. But most of all they want to bleed over the daily life of one of the crew. Give them a young, clean-cut American boy brought up by his mother's teachings. Show them Mars through his eyes and how his upbringing helps him. I want every mother in America to bleed for the mothers with boys on the Far Venture. And every wife to suffer with the wives suffering at home. There's a woman behind every man on that space ship. There's your news with a capital N. I want every woman in America to feel down deep inside what it is to give a man to the Far Venture and sacrifice so much to meet this challenge to the spirit of man triumphing over unbelievable odds. Now give it to me from there. All the way."

Not one precious paragraph had he yet set down to glorify the brave little nation builders whose travail brings forth strong men-children. But the chore lay in wait. Fifty thousand words of it. A hundred thousand driveling words of it. If the return to Earth was accomplished. Daily installments. Exclusive. An Amalgamated Exclusive: "Men on Mars." Only the fact that radio to Earth was out had saved him so far.

Work three years for Amalgamated and success. Endure for three years and success guaranteed. Please the great Ames and be anointed pimp for the bravely suppressed snivelings of fifty million frumps. He went into the toilet and relieved himself. In the spotless mirror over the lavatory the face that looked back was sharply outlined, the jaw line unblurred and reasonably uncompromising. He smote his belly. Not too much physical softness. It was in the mind, agreeing to connive and scheme like an ad man for the attention of idiot dreamers.

He splashed his face with the flat, manufactured water and dampened his close-cut hair, knowing he wasn't going to do it. Even saying it aloud to the gurgle of the drain. For whoever came and found it, he was going to write about how long and unheroic it was to die shut in a can—even unafraid once it had become inevitable—just as it was for an infantry soldier of a defeated army in one of the old wars, dying near the end in a confused woods from unaimed fire, after years of shrewd personal dealings with tanks and automatic weapons and probing patrols. It was no different on Mars. Not by a damn sight.

In the morning he woke to a bad taste from the brandy and a reluctance to get out of the bed. In the act of throwing back the sheet he remembered. He smiled caustically at the bottle of calvados he had brought with him for a last one-for-the-road.

Even so, he felt good. Considering the situation of the spacecraft, it was unlikely that Amalgamated would soon, if ever, know that he had resigned, but he could feel better about it.

CHAPTER TWENTY

Ernie Heileman was in the main-deck mess hall, his long legs jackknifed around the corner of one of the tables and his wide blond mustache bowed in devotion over a plate of scrambled eggs.

He grinned and kicked a chair around for Dane. "Since I am unable to pronounce 'eggs' in French, you will have to read the menu for yourself, my boy. The ham is not bad. As a matter of fact you may bring me another slice. Not to speak of a piece of lightly buttered toast and a fresh cup of coffee."

"It's fortunate that I happened to wander in during my morning stroll along the boulevard," Dane said. "Otherwise you might well have starved. Then we'd have had the impossible job of untangling you from that chair. Are you sitting in it or lying down on it?"

"Most persons are oafish in the early morning," Heileman sighed. "While you're at it, make that two slices of toast. I must build up my strength. Lightly buttered, mind you."

Dane loaded a tray at the serving window and took it back to the offered chair. Heileman attacked his fresh slice of ham. After a few mouthfuls he said, "It's getting pretty thick, isn't it?" He knifed precisely around the annular bone. "I've got a feeling of something closing in on us. Like waiting for a knock on the door, after you've broken a window and run home. The inevitability that something pretty terrible has to happen and there's nothing to do but wait for it. What do you think, John? What do you really think?"

It was discomforting to see Heileman disturbed, out of character. "There isn't much else to think except that some kind of intelligent somethings are looking us over very carefully," Dane repeated himself. "Maybe like specimens on display. Who knows? What did we do ourselves in the early days of exploration of Earth? Explorers brought back specimens as a matter of course. Curiosity and profit were more important than any consideration of the welfare of the specimens themselves."

Heileman looked carefully around the yellow and blue-trimmed premises of the plate-walled messroom. "I've got to admit I didn't think it would be like this. Immobile here. God knows what around us. Even the damned vegetation eating through metal bulkheads. We carry enough armament to defeat a small army, but what the hell good is it against something we can't even imagine? Where could they be? We surveyed the entire surface of the planet before we landed. We couldn't have missed any kind of civilization at all. We'd have been certain to see something of it, no matter how scattered and dispersed it was."

Dane didn't want to talk about it. "Unless the Martians are very small. Say on the order of a sixteenth of an inch tall. They could hide sizable towns under the lichen forests."

"You think they could be like some kind of an insect, John? Wertz was telling me last night about what you told Yudin. He said it was your idea they might even be submicroscopic. But how would a minute creature like that build a transmitter capable of sending the signals we have been getting? It's not mechanically possible."

"That we don't know. Or anything else, for that matter," Dane told him. He spoke with finality and got up to go. He just didn't want to talk about it. Not with Heileman, from whom he was accustomed to have light banter. It drew the menace in, all around and waiting, to have Heileman this way. Nonsense, he thought. He's scared just like the rest of us. And why not? It was peculiar that he should feel so about it. Just because it was Heileman.

"What's your hurry?" Heileman said. "Time for your train?" He managed one of his grins. "Let's you and me take a little stroll this fine summer's morn. We can put on a nicely pressed pressure suit and saunter over to Judah's mine. Maybe he's dug up Captain Kidd's treasure and we'll force him to share it. This is a heist," he flatted menacingly. "Fill up this bag with doubloons afore we turn off your air conditioner. Instanter."

It would be something to do. Judah was now down about ninety feet in his study of the planet's crust. Not that anything spectacular had been unearthed, but it would he interesting to see. "How do you get doubloons here? You couldn't very well unearth them. Do you unmars them?" he ventured.

"Nothing is forgiven," Heileman said sternly. "Never come home again. Meantime we leave in an hour for the doubloons. By the way," he added, "one is supposed to get permission to leave the ship these days. You'll have to get Noel's okay."

Major Noel was doubtful. He swiveled his chair around to face Dane and then swiveled back square against the command desk. He reached for the daily log and thumbed back a page. He picked up a sheaf of papers and flipped through the top half dozen sheets. Finally he grunted his dissatisfaction with purposeless risk-taking. If nothing else, it interfered with orderly operations. "Actually we don't know if there is any risk," he admitted. "We've been sending more than a few men out for scouting or for scientific purposes. Just for the sake of curiosity, it doesn't seem wise to take a chance on our people. We've already lost five men. Maybe two more. Beemis and Jackson are still unconscious and getting weaker."

"You don't want to forget that I'm the accredited correspondent on this little junket," Dane told him. "My business requires firsthand knowledge of whatever we find here."

Noel went on nosing through his stack of papers. He thought it should be just as newsworthy to go down and talk with Beloit and Vining instead. They were very near the end of a complete overhaul of the drive. "We may be able to try a take-off in two or three days."

He didn't sound very optimistic about it, Dane thought. "Why? They found anything?"

Noel shook his head. "Vining thinks we're trapped in some sort of magnetic zone, or maybe a force storm, that's upsetting the reactions. He's got the idea now that it could be only a temporary phenomenon.

Sort of comes and goes. Anyway, they're assembling the reactors and generators, and we're going to try again. Even if we blow ourselves out of existence, we don't have any choice. The radiation is still below what we've been calling the critical level, but that's mainly guesswork, based on cosmic-ray penetration data. We don't even know what this local stuff is. Maybe it's cumulative in some way we don't understand. Anyway, we're not going to take it an hour longer than we have to. Colonel Cragg laid the law down on that last night."

"Cragg!" Dane exclaimed. "I might as well be back on Earth for all you let me know what's going on! When did he take over? I thought he was still half in drowsy land."

"The commander's condition has been improving steadily since yesterday morning," Noel said sententiously. "However he has not been able to take over yet."

"Look," Dane said. "Put me down for a trip to the mine this morning, but first I want to talk to Colonel Cragg. If he's able."

Noel smiled sardonically. "He's able all right. In fact he's already made quite a point that he wants you to see him 'at your convenience.' This morning, that is."

Dane said, "That's one way to put it, I suppose."

"Yes," Noel agreed, "it is."

The nurse on duty sat meticulously straight at his small desk. When he put his paperback book down, Dane saw it was *Romany Rye*. In collarless white duck jacket and pants the young man looked only partly dressed.

He spoke up briskly, like a clerk tending store. "May I help you?"

Dane told him he could. And how he could.

The young man picked up his book. "No visitors. Maybe tomorrow. Colonel Cragg is still on the quiet list."

Dane explained that he was not exactly a visitor.

The young man put his book back down. "What's your first name and middle initial, Mr. Dane?" He fished a small card out of the desk and wrote the information upon it, noting also the time from his watch and setting it down. Then he wrote, "States purpose of visit to comply with patient's invitation." He thought a moment and lined out the last two words, writing above them, "Commander's (as patient) order." Still not satisfied, he struck out this substitution and wrote, "patient's (the Commander) order, as staled by Mr. Dane, for Mr. Dane to report to him before 1200."

Dane said, "You ought to put 'apostrophes' on the word 'Commander.'"

The young man considered the card. He shook his head doubtfully. "The appositive should agree in case with the word 'patient's,' but it wouldn't look right to make it. I think we ought to leave it the way it is."

Dane said, "You may be right. After all, it is your record card. I withdraw the suggestion. Now where do I go?"

The young man closed his book on his pencil to save his place. "Just have a seat here and I'll see if Colonel Cragg is awake." He disappeared around the angle in the corridor.

Dane looked at the book, memories stirring of George Borrow's gypsies and of his own sophomore year. Odd choice for a library destined to visit the surface of Mars. Maybe not so odd, he decided, thinking he would like to read *Romany Rye* again when young mister cross-the-t's returned it to the shelves.

The young man in white came back and reported that Dane could go in, if he would just please follow him. This, Dane was pleased to do, until they came to a guard standing at a door. Evidently Noel was taking no chances.

The head of the bed had been cranked up to a forty-five-degree angle, but weakness darkened the colonel's eyes against his blanched face and weighted his head back against its supporting pillow.

"They tell me not to talk," he said. His harsh, strong voice had lost some of its bass timbre. "But there's nothing wrong with my ears. I want the complete story on the messages we've been getting. They tell me you're the star performer on them. I want to know firsthand from you what you've done and exactly how you did it." He pointed at a sheaf of papers on the bedside table. "I've been over the reports. Now I want to hear it from you. I want to hear you answer two questions. One, what makes you so sure these signals are coming from outside the Far Venture? Second, if they are, how are you sure they are not of human origin?"

Down but not out, and no nonsense. The technique of command. Or more like it, the habit. How certain of himself and demanding did the man have to be to satisfy his neurosis for the throne! Dane seated himself deliberately in the unoffered chair. "I see, Colonel, that your recovery has progressed so far that you can be your normal self. Attack. Always push. Shove the other man off balance. Keep him on the defensive. Make him mad. Do you suspect me of concealing something from my reports?"

Cragg gazed at him sourly, his check scar reddening. "Never mind that. Haven't you stopped yet to think that some person or persons on board this spacecraft might have an interest in convincing us of the existence of Martians?"

"No," Dane said. "It would appear to me to be a complicated and useless effort. There's no way or means for anyone to do it. Even if there were, there wouldn't be any point. I hardly think we have any jokers of that caliber along."

"Tong Asia Pact," Cragg snapped. "Use your head."

The silence extended. Finally Dane said, "It doesn't figure. It's too farfetched. We wouldn't scare that easily. The United States would eventually send more spacecraft. Even if this one doesn't return. All the more likely to send them then."

"Suppose we reported that Mars not only was a barren, useless planet but also was inhabited by some kind of hostile, highly intelligent beings. The government might not send another expedition for years. Meantime, while we're on the sidelines, Tong Asia solves the secret of the drive and takes over here."

"Why?" Dane demanded. "What would they want with it? Assuming that a scheme like that would work, what would they want here?"

The colonel's hands clinched into fists. "There was a time in the past when you pretended to be more informed. When you didn't know anything at all, you still could nose into it and put together a half-baked story for the headlines."

Dane said, "It's ancient history now. Why don't you let it alone?"

The scar flamed. "What do you know about a command decision, with a hundred factors to bring down to the right answer, and none of them clear? You think they were clear in the middle of the night, with the reports contradicting each other and half of them raw data and the imponderables stacked up in your mind and knowing you had to do something right now and the crews standing by ready to be committed and maybe God help a few million people and maybe your country's existence if you weren't right? Exactly right?"

Dane said, "The facts had to be made known. What we were getting at—"

Cragg sneered. "What you were getting at was a sensation. To peddle your newspapers. At the critical moment Colonel Cragg made a wrong move and then lucked into a win because he had misjudged the enemy's timing and the arc of his main thrust. Pretty easy for you to figure it out. A military genius like you. Six months later with all the intelligence spread out in front of you for as long as you wanted it and a dozen second-guessing, so-called experts prompting you, you write it up like a student's staff exercise. Okay, smart man. Doctor Wiseman! Now we've got the makings of another ball on hand. And you don't even see all the figures in the problem! What's Tong Asia got to do with it, he wants to know!"

Dane thought of the long midnight at Sahara Air Force Base, with the rocket forces deployed over a thousand miles of sand, alert for the take-off. Speaking of luck, Amalgamated Press had had some good fortune itself to have a man there at the hour of decision, when the word was transmitted that Tong Asia was about to strike. A few hours earlier he had dined with Colonel Anson Cragg, commander of the 3rd Rocket Wing, a good beginning for an assignment to write up the new electro-radiant weather telemeasures installed on the Sahara plateau and in the Atlas Range. It had been apparent that Cragg was amiably willing to assist the mighty Amalgamated. But before bedtime Dane was sweating to put together a story of the alert from the broken sentences that were flung to him outside the operations rooms and the blacked windows of the blazing staff offices. Then it was dawn and Colonel Cragg was back from Lower Space, Hemisphere South, with the news of a great victory.

"But," Senator Hodge had persisted at the investigation, "you were returning to your bases when you picked up the Asian attack, which we now know came out of altitude orbit and was earth-tracking a thousand miles above the Indian Ocean ready to go into orbital attack against the United States squarely athwart your alert zone. Don't you agree that certain newspapers are right when they say it was only the flukiest of good luck that you came near them at all, after miscalculating their maneuver? At speeds on the order of three to five miles a second, Colonel, one doesn't expect or often get a second chance after the attack goes into glide phase, I am informed by competent testimony. Nor do we expect our commanders to make mistakes, however brilliantly redeemed, at the possible cost of Houston or Chicago or St. Louis, quite possibly all three and maybe more."

So the opposition wire and its five thousand editors chose to make him a martyr and a hero. A persecuted victor. It was good copy, and a good play against Amalgamated. But Cragg did not get his star. After three years he had not yet got it.

"So we're five years ahead of Tong Asia with the drive," Cragg went on. "They can't get anything of any size off Earth. You think maybe they're not going to do their damnedest to infiltrate this expedition? Two or three five-million-dollar bribes? Chicken feed to know what's up here. You're so good at figuring things out. Give that one a thought. No matter how we screen them, we've got to consider the possibility they've got a man on board. Maybe planted for this years ago."

Dane said, "Colonel, you should try writing a killer-thriller." In spite of himself he ran them through his mind. Spivak, the Central European? Vining, fanatic of mechanism? Too obviously obvious? Yudin—weak?

Wertz—selfish? It would not have to be the least likely. It didn't have to be someone beyond suspicion, like Heileman.

"For example," Cragg said, "why was Pembroke so anxious to get out on the surface? Why did he sneak out again against orders when he was supposed to be confined to bed?"

"Now wait a minute!" Dane jumped up.

"You've been friendly with him for years, haven't you?"

Dane said, "If there is any crime against a man that's vicious and contemptibly cowardly, it's slandering his loyalty on a damn supposition!"

"I recall that you had some very pressing business yourself out on the surface after Pembroke didn't come back."

Dane gave him a succinct four-letter word.

Cragg fell back on his pillow with a sigh. "Dane, you are an able man. In your way. But if you're on the level, you've got a lot to learn. I don't really much suspect you, but I do suspect Pembroke very much. If I'm right, he had a partner. Obviously, since he is dead. Maybe you, but I don't much think so. For one thing, I don't think you've got the guts."

Dane said, "Think what you like about me. I can take care of myself if you get rough. But Dr. Pembroke is a famous American and he's dead now. You're not going to yipe at his heels and slander his name."

"Power of the press, and all that? You get this straight. I'm going to do exactly what I think is best. I was suspicious of Pembroke from the first. Evidently he tumbled to it, when I had his stuff gone through while he was out on the surface. So he puts a knife in me."

Cragg! An intelligent man! In a position of high authority! "This is one that won't get far," Dane threw at him.

"Maybe we can agree on this much," Cragg said. "I think it's pretty likely the source of the messages is human. You think they come from Martians. We both can agree that it's imperative for us to discover their true source before we take off. If you want to prove your point, you've got to make visible contact. Get your Martians out in sight. If they exist, we want pictures. We've got to reconnaissance their civilization. Especially their capability for hostilities. I want to see these Martians. In the meantime here's something you can do about your friend Pembroke's mysterious actions."

He waited a moment. "This is confidential. Okay?"

Dane hesitated. "Just until we get back to Earth. I reserve nothing that bears on Dr. Pembroke, if any charges are made there against him."

Cragg nodded. "No one knows this but Major Beloit and Major Noel and myself. Dr. Pembroke didn't have a pistol on him when he got in the elevator. Somebody stopped the car and shot him and left the pistol to make it look like suicide."

Cragg spread a downturned palm over the quiet. "So, either he had some confederate who maybe decided his usefulness was over, especially if he would be caught for knifing me, or he had an enemy. He had enough of an enemy to kill. That wouldn't be too likely, if he wasn't anything but what he was supposed to be."

"Tong Asia again, I suppose you mean," Dane said bitterly.

"It adds up. At least it adds up to a good enough working suspicion for me. You got any better ideas?"

"Why do you tell me this?" Dane demanded. "Why tell me? A civilian and a newspaper civilian, and to add to the unusualness of telling me, one of your prime suspects?

"I'll tell you why you told me this," Dane rode on at him. "You've got Tong Asia on the brain. In another week you'll have Tong Asia agents under every bunk. You've really decided I'm it. In fact you hope I am. So tell me you only suspect me as a matter of principle and you think if you tell me this you'll drive me out in the open."

"Congratulations, mastermind," Cragg sneered. "Now put your razor-sharp intellect to work on this." His face flushed. "According to your lights, I am a blunderer. You did your best to ruin my career, and you damn near did it."

"I'm afraid you weren't that important to Amalgamated. Not as an individual," Dane said. "It was the national safety we had in mind. Preventing any more blunders. At least by you."

"Have it your way. I don't expect much from reporters. I do expect more from myself. Even if I made fifty mistakes, I've yet to dishonor the uniform by lying. When Pembroke came in off the surface just before he was killed, he was told to leave his pressure suit and all his gear in the airlock. He did, and it stayed there until the next day. And there his own pistol was found. The pistol that shot him was a spare from the stores. Now the man was stripped down to his shorts when he got into a suit of coveralls he didn't own. He couldn't have had the pistol on him when he got on that elevator."

The old rasp of authority came clear. "Now I want to give you an order. You will obey it. Keep your mouth shut and your eyes open. If the messages are Tong Asia, our man will be especially anxious to sell you. He'll want you to make a big headline play out of hostile Martians after we get back. Everything unroutine, you report to me. If you hold anything back, I'll fry your hide so brown when we get back that it'll take two Amalgamateds to butter you up again. That's not all. There's a technical charge against you in the official log. You want to clear yourself, the best way is to make like a detective. A good one. If you're on the level, you ought to want to prove it. And that's all."

"No," Dane said, "that's not quite all! Someone is out to get you." He pulled open the door. "I wonder why?"

CHAPTER TWENTY-ONE

It was the brightest morning they had had on the planet. In spite of his gear Dane stepped out away from the ladder with a springtime feeling of buoyancy. Even in a pressure suit it was good to be outside the metallic chrysalis of the spacecraft. He admitted that the ponderous, armored Heileman lowering his gangling self down the hatch ladder didn't look much like an emerging butterfly.

Dane was content to stand a moment and look out over the landscape undulating to the horizon like a sand-blown prairie. The coloring was not unlike the weathered red of the welt of sore soil across the southern United States, softer under the muted sunshine that fell to Mars. Pushed and respread by the gentle winds of the planet, the coarser dust and the sand of the surface had been sorted into a host of small crescent dunes, and the floor of the desert that bore them was intricately figured with arabesque leavings of powdery spindrift. The uninvited diversity of the three-phase power line was alien and inimical to the reticent curves and simple features of the scene it tore apart. The black wires snaking over the sand out to the raw heap of spoil at Dr. Judah's excavation and, even more alien and inimical, the immense geometry of the spacecraft itself, these were the frightening things here, Dane thought, not the limitless aloneness he otherwise beheld.

"You like to buy a few choice acres?" Heileman broke in. "Tax-free. No pets, no children, no nosy neighbors, no lawns to mow, no traffic, no nothing. Wonderful place to retire and write that book. Don't even have to raise chickens or sweat out a garden."

Dane turned down the volume in his earphones. "To him who communes with nature even the braying of a distant jackass is melodious, but not when amplified into his eardrums. I suppose it is useless for me to point out to you that there is a certain beauty about this place."

"Well, hardly useless," Heileman said. "The remark gives a flavor to your character that we might term generally as odd. More specifically we would call it nuts."

It was something like three hundred yards to Dr. Judah's "mine." A pair of pressure-suited figures sat alone on chunks of stone halfway down the sloping up of the trench-like scar gouged out of the red soil by tetryl explosive. The scoop shovel was upended near the dragline motor and cable winch, which was shut down.

"Looks like a strike has been called," Heileman said. "Us stockholders want to know what's going on here."

Dane saw one of the seated men turn his head. Then they both stood and looked up out of the pit. "We've quit digging here," Dr. Judah's voice came into the phones. "Nothing but igneous rock for twenty feet. Not very promising."

Heileman picked up a fragment of the stone. "Primordial lava," he observed. "This whole region is probably the impact plain of a big Imbrium-type planetesimal. The dark lava indicates that. High ferrous oxide and sulfide content."

"However you explain its origin," Dr. Judah said, "there is obviously little use to excavate it further. It's undoubtedly several miles thick."

"On the order of fifteen to twenty kilometers at least," Heileman agreed. "If you want to go by the estimates on the lunar explosion pits, like Mare Imbrium."

One doesn't accustom oneself to conversing normally with another man fifty yards away and in plain sight, Dane decided. He started down the drag incline of the pit, picking a way carefully over the rubble. He wanted to stand on the bottom and look at the Mars stuff all around, undisturbed for at least four billion years, the kind of a date that was expressed offhand as 4 times 10^9 years ago.

It was, after all, little different from a hole in the ground dug out in Texas, except, as Judah quickly pointed out, for the absence of alluvial gravel. There was the thick layer of sand, maybe five to ten feet, then heavy, hard clay-like stuff, as thick again, then a layer of heavy stone, the bedrock, all deeply tinged with the browns and dark red of the iron color.

Dane glanced into the mask of the second figure. It was Silverman, the civil engineer. The man responded with a grunt in the interphone and turned away.

At the bottom of the pit Dane found a right-sized chunk of the living rock and stowed it into his pouch. Luck granting, it would someday rest polished on his desk, yielded out of the vast original processes of planet formation to be sought in its eternal bed and placed, by the ingenuity of man, heavy on papers concerned with the ephemeral news flow of trivia.

"Migod, a souvenir hunter. Even in this Godforsaken place, he wants something to remember it by." Silverman said, acid in the rasping phones.

"It's a shame we won't be able to move to other locations," Dr. Judah said. "I had counted on a great many locations." His helmet bobbed. He was the sort one found far back in the recesses of university departments, with thick spectacles and a green eyeshade, nodding his head over a fresh specimen for the museum. Yet in some fashion fame had come to him, so that now, one of the chosen, he stood on the surface of Mars, still eager for specimens.

Silverman came up close, thrusting his stare through Dane's mask. "I've got something I want you to get through your fancy head, fellow," he said abruptly. "I served with the colonel in the Third during the war, and he asked me himself to come along on this goddamn flight. For my money he's a damn fine man and a damn fine commander. I don't like what your goddamn papers tried to do to him, and I don't like you. I kept my mouth shut because the colonel wanted it that way when we found out you weaseled your way on board."

Dane said, "Hold it! What's eating you?" The man had been taciturn, given to keeping to himself, aloof in the confines of the Far Venture, but this sudden animosity was unpredictable from anything that had gone before.

Silverman said, "I'll hold you, all right." He lifted up a geologist's short pick. "I got no reason not to crack your helmet this minute and your damn head along with it. We're not going anyplace any more."

"Hey!" Heileman shouted. "You nuts?"

The pick twitched higher. He was going to strike. Dane threw himself against him, inside the arc of the weapon, seizing the arm and bending it up and out. The man went mad, twisting and dragging Dane down on the rubble with him.

A rip, a cracked joint in the pressure suit flashing before him. Dane desperately threw his weight on the thickset body, feeling it fight to break his hold with powerful upheavings, managing to pin both arms down with holds on the wide wrists in spite of the awkward gauntlets and the encasings of Silverman's heavy forearms.

One flailing blow on the helmet and he was gone. A quick hiss of escaping pressure and he would be exploded for keeps.

Suddenly the upthrusting body went limp. Dane lay on it a moment warily, until he realized that Silverman's suit must have ruptured. He got on his knees, appalled at the bewildering uselessness of the man's death, but when he looked into the facemask he saw the eyes staring back malevolently. He stood clear with a great relief.

"Whatinhell's come over you two?" he heard Heileman saying. It had happened so quickly that neither he nor Judah had moved.

Silverman's voice cut in. He said it conversationally. Almost reflectively. "Maybe you stuck that knife in the colonel and maybe you didn't. Personally I think you did. But if anything happens to him again, you'll be the one that gets it. I'll kill you before the day is over. I promise you faithfully. You'll be the one that pays for it." He got up, cast around for his pick, and set off for the Far Venture.

"He's mad," Dr. Judah said. "God help us all!"

Dane burned with a quick heat. It would be a good thing to run the man down and have it out. His fists longed to strike and his fingers to choke. When he noticed the others regarding him silently, he cursed them and the Far Venture and everyone in it for fools and lunatics. "Including me," he added grimly. He began the climb up the rubble-strewn ramp.

After a few minutes of plodding Heileman began to talk. "A good many billions of years ago—"

They were doing what is known as handling him with care, regarding him, too, as a "case." The thought angered him; then it concerned him that it had angered him. It should have been funny.

There was the disease. If the Martians wished it, they had only to wait and the invaders would destroy themselves. It was the confinement sickness. The isolation neurosis. Claustrophobic dementia, with a whole planet underfoot. They were getting stir-crazy. All of them. Like Heileman, he thought, pressing down on the sore idea, discoursing of the utmost secrets behind the forbidden veil. Foolishly saying the unknowable, as if it were soothing verse. Once-upon-a-time stuff.

Heileman said, "For Mars it all started with the Solar dust cloud which contracted until the sunbody defined itself and fretted itself into high carbon fire. At the same time the gas and the dust flattened into a disk and coagulated with wet snow-solids into the protoplanets. The protoplanets accumulated the rest of the drifting dust and the large and the small planetesimals that also had coagulated. Then a time of high temperatures burnt away the bases and the opacity, and radiation cooled the surfaces and we had Earth and Mars. And the floods of water washed away from mountains of the planestesimals' impact and smoothed the surface with the new dust. Then Mars, a war god without iron in his heart, pushed up no folded mountains and waited for us through the eons, scarcely disturbed by hill or valley, bedded down with primitive dust and eventually sleeping with lichen parasites. Then we come. Loaded with psycho-instability and ill will even for each other. It's a downright anticlimax."

Dr. Judah said, "In a non purposive process nothing is significant...whether our dust falls to the right or the left of the dust that is already here."

Heileman said, "How did you like my sermon, Mars style, boy?"

Dane said, "As the ancients used to put it—bologna." He felt better. Dignity restored? He smiled.

Heileman said, "How could you neglect your literature courses so? The principal word of the twentieth century! Baloney, my boy. It's pronounced baloney."

The day was very clear. Although the sun was a dwarf half his familiar size, he beamed a friendly orange in the deep blue, bonding the white ball and sawed-off cone of the spacecraft with a tint of the fire glow he poured down upon the red oxide sands shimmering under heat waves. The brighter stars also hung in the chill sky, unidentified without their weaker cohorts, disturbingly unwanted. One they had all learned to recognize, the Mars Pole Star. But not Polaris, playing child's game with the comforting Big Dipper. A star called Deneb, a name that fitted no American tongue. Deneb, formerly of the constellation Cygnus, now chosen by the axis of this red, white, and blue world to be its constant. To mark its pole for these eyes that had come to see.

An alert burst into the earphones. All personnel return to spacecraft immediately. Three times it pre-empted the diaphragms. Then Dane heard the out-parties state their positions and acknowledge compliance, the specimen collectors, the teams scouting the lichen boundary. Something was urgent.

CHAPTER TWENTY-TWO

Thus it began.

"Standing order," Noel told him. "No civilians outside during signal reception."

"But this order called in all personnel," Dane persisted.

"Special order of the commander. As soon as the signal was reported to him, he extended the order to all personnel."

The signal had projected a recognizable map on the photo plane table, a sort of outline aerial view of the terrain immediately around the spacecraft. With the Far Venture almost in the center, it depicted the surroundings over a radius of about eight or nine miles, judging by the position of the boundary of the lichen forest, which ran halfway between the greatly out-of-scale image of the spacecraft and the edge of the map. It was still coming in.

"Look here." Noel pointed at it. "How many of these white dots do you count?"

Dane leaned over the image. "Six."

Noel took a charting protractor and a rule. Measuring off the positions of the six dots, he jotted down figures on a pad. "If we estimate distances according to the straight-line distance to the lichen boundary, we can approximate their co-ordinates." He jabbed at the intercom.

"Major Noel to Lieutenant McDonald." The acknowledgment squawked. "Give me the positions last reported by all out-parties."

When he had McDonald's co-ordinates down, he threw his pad on the table. "See for yourself."

The correspondence of the two sets of co-ordinates was close.

Dane nodded meaningfully in the direction of the guard on duty.

"Step down to 3-high and wait until I call you," Noel ordered.

Dane said, "You think the colonel's right now? You think we've got spies now? Or do you think we've got Martians?"

Noel's dark brows contracted. "The Old Man tell you too?" He nodded. "It might figure."

"Look," Dane said, "any Tong Asia agents here, we brought them. Supposing they could figure out a way to send the signals without being zeroed in. Even if we assume that very big if, they couldn't have sent this signal."

Noel nodded again. "If they were sending from outside, they couldn't know the positions of all the parties. That what you mean?"

"Right. And if they were sending from inside someway, even if that were possible, could they know? How could they? Not all the positions are fixed in advance before the parties set out, are they?"

Noel shook his head. "Only to a general area. I don't know myself until they report."

"We've got Martians, Noel," Dane told him. "Highly intelligent ones. They've got us spotted. Someway. Every move."

"Where are they?" Noel demanded. "Why don't they show? What's the idea of this hide-and-go-seek business?" He went over to the observation ports. "What's out there but empty sand and low-class vegetation? Where are the minds? They can't be far away. But whereinhell are they?" He came back and took up some photocopies. "A symbol message came first. You make anything out of it?"

Dane reached for the prints. The symbols he had seen many times. But some of the pairs and triads were reversed.

"Well, you read it or can't you?"

"Part of it maybe," Dane told him. "It says, if it makes any sense at all, it says, *Men are other-many. Martians are one.* Wait a minute," he said. "Maybe the reverse order means interrogation. If we put a question mark after that first one, it could ask a question: *Men are other-many?* Maybe it means, *How many men are here?* Then the next one wants to tell us there is only one kind of Martian. The rest of it could be a warning to stay in the spacecraft. Literally it says something like, *No men out spacecraft.*"

"Maybe our parties are getting close onto them," Noel said. "They don't want us exploring around. We might stumble onto something."

"Maybe they just don't like us here period," Dane said.

"This thing is not good. I've really got to go along with you now. Martians. It's almost inevitable they are hostile."

Dane shook his head. "Invasion from space is a pretty frightening business in any man's world. They've also got to find out about our capabilities and our intent. Whether we intend to harm them or not. It would be a great tragedy if we can't convince them we are beings that understand good will."

"What if they don't understand it themselves?"

"We've got to try," Dane told him. "If we fail, then the flight of the Far Venture is a colossal failure. Man, we're face to face with the first intelligent beings Earthmen have ever encountered. The conquest of space, if you want to call it that, oughtn't to be allowed to start out with war and death and destruction. We have higher ideals than that. We just have to make them understood. Someway."

Noel said, "I hear you talking. Maybe I'm no idealist by your standards, but first of all I want to see them. I want to know what we have to deal with. That's what I've got to know before anything else."

Slowly, with invisible movement, the six clots crept across the signal map, converging on the spacecraft. Dane stood by with Noel while one by one the out-parties came up and entered, and the dots that tracked them vanished one by one, until all personnel were inside and the Martian map stood clear.

Dane said, "Now I'm going to answer their question. If it was a question. We've got to make them understand we're friendly."

He began to send the message he had converted to the Martian number code, making and breaking the radar-beam circuit as he had done dozens of times without response since the earliest contact. The long inarticulate generations, he thought, striving to express the forming subtleties of their spirit and finding only broad, dull words on their tongue. Awkwardly he spelled out, *We are many men. From not-Mars. Add men to Martians equals good. What are Martians?*

Hopefully he looked at the photo plane table, but the map-like reception remained undisturbed. He went back to the switch and began his message again. *We are many men. Add men to Martians equals good.*

The map signal began to clear from the opaque glass. While they watched, pictogram symbols came on.

"They're answering!" Dane exclaimed. "At last they're going to answer us!"

He spelled it out, translating the symbols at sight. *"Martians are one. One is good. Not-one is bad. Many men equals bad."*

"Sounds like a dictator," Noel commented.

A flash of light briefly dominated the observation deck. A simultaneous crackling blast like diminutive thunder smote them. They stared at each other.

"Thunder and lightning?" Noel exclaimed. "Impossible!"

The flashes and the diminished thunderclaps increased in tempo, flaring at the ports like a barrage of old-time artillery in a historical motion picture.

"The spark fires!" Dane shouted above the cracking crescendo. "They're attacking us with the spark fires!"

Through the ports they saw arcing bolts dart heavily from the distant lichen beds upon the spacecraft.

"First daytime storm yet," Noel yelled. "We're right in the middle of it."

"It's an attack," Dane shouted again. "They're trying to burn us up with their electrical discharges."

Noel's face twisted up. He shook his head. "Electrical storm of some kind. Our metal is drawing it." He jabbed a finger at the intercom. "That thing's useless in all this. But our metal meteor shield will ground it okay. Nothing to worry about."

He could be right, Dane thought for a moment. But it was too pat. The message. An avowal of enmity itself. Then immediately the concentration of discharges on them. No, it was more than probable that the Martians had decided to destroy them. Fearful things from another world. Not to be trusted. But after the extended and laborious effort to establish a crude exchange of communication, what could have led them to a sudden decision? If it was the message he had sent, they knew everything in it already. Unless it was the one about adding men to Martians. Maybe that meant something different to them than he had meant by it.

The eye-splitting fires now leaped so rapidly upon them that the sand plain danced crazily under the staccato flashes. From horizon to horizon, up and down the long swing of the lichen beds, the bolts converged against the metallic toadstool hunched up antenna-like on the sands to receive them. It was impossible not to listen for the sounds of dissolution, for creak and groan of straining plates and beams.

Major Noel shouted below for a messenger, and the buzzers called the Air Force crew to emergency stations. Dane visualized the men hurrying to their posts in the channels and working recesses of the intricate, enormous mechanism. Then Noel was motioning him to go below. He shook his head.

The spark fire mounted steadily into a vast, flickering concourse, surging wildly over the full sunshine of the Martian noon. They awaited the unknown climax. There was nothing else to do. The circular, domed chamber in the nose of the Far Venture, like the interior of a metallic igloo, inspired no confidence of sustaining the spectacular assault mounted against it, for all its welded and rivet-headed seams. Its multi-wired electronic probing devices menacingly threatened the entry of the currents drenching the exterior sheathing and coursing down through it into the ground.

Dane and Noel and the crewmen now on station with them scanned the terrain under the unreal light. Perhaps their expectations shaped inevitably to Earth ways, but under cover of the eerie barrage some fantastic army might deploy and be closing in on them.

Dane sensed his mind running away down long dark alleys. If they came, how would they come? In what manner? Worst of all, in what shape? Monstrously large, grown huge in response to the low gravitational force of Mars? Sliding out of underground burrow colonies and slithering rapidly from beyond the horizon? Armed with undreamed-of devices? Or minute, insect-like beings from far off in the lichens, impelling themselves to the kill in unrealizable vehicles? Implacably hostile, insensate to any worth erected by humans? Their basic "Good" and "Evil" applied by fantastically divergent postulates from those of human man? His recent projection of the Martian mind seemed naively anthropomorphic, introspectively inspired, a mirror image of his own kind's universe of discourse. What valid reality could he have possibly read from the few small conceptual coins that had been tendered them by the simple, halting language of a picayune of pictograms?

For forty-two minutes the attack endured. Then suddenly it ceased. As abruptly as if a switch had been pulled. Sun-born light came back to Mars, and a pervasive quiet drowned the heavy staccato of giant firecrackers. All over the Far Venture movement was suspended while the assembly forbore to draw breath. Outside, the sands of Mars were as empty as through all the hours since the landing. There were no legions of monstrous beings.

They had come through. For the moment at least their defenses had held.

"Look!" Noel exclaimed.

A few pictogram symbols stood forth on the plane table. Dane read them aloud. *"Men move?"*

Noel said, "They're not too bright if they expect us to answer that. We sit tight and let them come to find out if we're still alive. We'll have a few surprises for them." He went to the phone. "I want all firing stations continuously manned. Double watch on all lookout points. And send two more men up here." He hung up sharply. "If they want to play rough when they show, we'll put some real heat on them. Then we'll discuss things with them some more. Maybe they'll talk another kind of turkey."

"No," Dane objected. "We don't want to hurt any of them, except as a last resort."

Noel lifted the hatch. "It's up to Colonel Cragg for the final decision. But they've showed their hand."

CHAPTER TWENTY-THREE

Dane stood for a while over the photo plane table, but the incoming signal showed no change. From time to time he went to gaze briefly out over the red terrain. Between the line of the lichen beds with the finger thrust forward at the Far Venture and the line of flat sand hills that completed the surrounding horizon lay nothing but the gentle drifts of the desert.

At 1217 hours the signal went off. Dane watched closely, but the opaque glass bore only the scanning of the near environs. At 1245 he commented to the command post on the state of his appetite. At 1300 Lieutenant Yudin's round face rose out of the hatch.

He said, "I've got word for you from Colonel Cragg. Orders, that is."

Dane spoke shortly. "Did Colonel Cragg enjoy his lunch?"

Yudin contemplated him with surprise. "I don't know. How come you give a damn?"

"I don't," Dane told him. "I'm willing to assume he did. I haven't had mine yet. You're an hour late. Supposing I enjoy mine first. Then Cragg can order me all he wants."

Yudin was pained. "Dane, you're a smart fellow. Why don't you act smart? So you don't like the man. So he's a hard man for anyone to like.

Right now he couldn't care less about you and your newspapers. That guy's got the decisions to make. Right down to the final yes or no that can make him or break him, and maybe save us or lose all our lives. Sure he's a cinch for a star if he keeps saying the right word. If we ever get back to where they hand out stars. Right now he's got the sweat. I can't say I like him too well either, but then I don't know him—really. No one ever really knows the commander. You always got to remember he sits in a damn hot and lonely seat."

Dane viewed the lieutenant with new interest. Misfitting uniform, comic-opera face, voice that suggested anything but leadership, not before had he revealed the consciousness of worth that characterized his fellows. Now he was actually insulted that anyone could suggest his commander's word was less than law. Dane thought a little wistfully of the absence of this hedgehog loyalty from his own life patterns, like the Amalgamated Press.

"Okay, Yudin," he said. "You talked me into it. Even if I starve, let's have it."

"It's only an order," Yudin said. "If you'd listened, you'd already be in the mess hall." He fished out a folded sheet.

Dane read, "Dr. John Dane. Under no circumstances will you send any messages to the Martians without my prior approval. Colonel Anson Cragg, USAF, Commanding Far Venture."

"The deal is this," Yudin volunteered. "We expect to have the drive ready for a trial take-off tomorrow. We play possum until we're fully operative. Then we resume contact with the Martians."

"Well, at least he admits we've got Martians. That's something."

At 1330 Dane left the messroom, pleased with his bellyful of German-grilled knockwurst, baked beans, and home-fried potatoes. Now he had the story of the electrical attack to write up for his thickening sheaf of untransmitted dispatches. He decided to go back up to the observation-deck typewriter.

On 3-high the fire-control center stood full alert. Dane looked in through the glassite panel at the eight men manning its electronic finders and gunsights. They swung in their seats, each half encircled by banks of dials and switches, the flowing scopes and lighted red alert buttons casting up their faces in the darkened cubicles. In the middle of the shadows the fire-control officer sat at his big radar plane table, waiting for the commander to whisper release into his phone for ordnance ranging from caliber .50 machine guns to fire rockets and nuclear missiles powerful enough to blast across a metropolis. Against what? Maybe the weapons might as well be addressed to the Martian sands, and their charges blasted into the dust and rocks themselves. Dane climbed on up the ladders. As soon as they escaped from the radio-choking Martian fields, Ames and his news-hungry Earth would cry worse for a bellyful of copy than he had for his knockwurst and beans.

At 1450 Lieutenant Yudin interrupted his clacking concentration. "Come here and take a look at this, will you?"

Airman Humphries had his finger pressed against the opaque surface of the radar photo plane table. Dane followed it to the image of the lichen peninsula.

"It looks longer to me," Humphries said.

Dane got out last night's scope pictures. He put a pair of dividers on a print taken at 0400 and measured off the peninsula. When he laid the dividers against the scale, he whistled. "It's grown about 500 yards closer today."

Humphries' jaw lengthened seriously. "It's done it since noon. I'd of noticed it when I came on duty."

Dane said, "That would be mighty fast growing." He thought of the explosive generation of the lichens inside the spacecraft. "It doesn't make too much of a projection on the table face. Maybe you just didn't notice it."

"I always notice that strip," Humphries insisted. "I always look at it. When I came on duty, it wasn't past that." He poked a pencil at one of the engraved grid lines. "That's for sure."

"You'd better report it," Dane told Yudin. He sharpened a grease pencil to a fine point and drew it across the opaque glass athwart the tip of the peninsula.

Major Noel came up at once. He studied the image on the oscilloscope. Then he took up the dividers and repeated Dane's measurement of the 0400 photograph. He called the cartographer for a chart of the region drawn up from the aerial photographs taken of the landing site before the Far Venture had settled down on the sand. When he was satisfied with his data, he carefully plotted the new extension of the growth.

Dane watched him sketch in the line connecting the plotted positions. It was no mere, prosaic pencil line that grew on the paper to show official concern. The precise marking on the chart brought it close, like the sweep of an invading army overlaid on an operations map.

"Keep a man on it," Noel told Yudin. "It hasn't extended any in the last fifteen minutes, but it may take another spurt. I want to know immediately about any detectable growth."

Yudin nodded at Humphries. After Noel had got through the hatch, he said, "Here. Like this." He took the dividers and set them to span from the tip of the peninsula to the first grid line behind it. "Now you can check it exactly."

No observable extension occurred until 1547. Dane was staring through glasses at the dirty line of the main lichen beds against the reddish flat. Humphries' startled shout was like a blow. One he had been waiting for. He turned slowly and went over to the table, breathing deeply and thinking that wearing the gravity boots was like limping, a tired man's limp.

"It's moving," Humphries gasped. "It's moving so fast you can see it move."

Minutely but perceptibly the luminous line crept forward from the point of the dividers he held to mark its tip.

Yudin went to the phone and spoke into the mouthpiece. He broke the connection and dialed another number. "Yudin calling Major Noel," he repeated. After a moment he said, "Sir, Yudin. It's creeping closer. Yes, sir. About one hundred yards." He listened a minute and put up the instrument.

"He already knew it," he said. "They've been watching the monitors at fire control or command. It was enough to show up there." He seemed disappointed. Even affronted. As if his big table had been slighted.

Rapidly now, the fingery apparition on the face of the oscilloscope lengthened toward the Far Venture, obviously pointing out to it even though it was yet three and a half miles away.

The loudspeaker sounded the alert. Major Noel's voice came on. "I am about to fire a small nuclear missile at the tip of the lichen peninsula. Range 6100 yards. There is no danger for us except from flash. All ports will now be covered. Repeat. *All* ports will now be covered and will remain covered until the all-clear is announced."

Humphries exhaled. "He's going to blow hell out of it!" He twisted the control switch for the panels, and the metal lids grated shut over the observation ports.

The speaker said, "Stand by for firing. Three minutes till firing."

Dane visualized the thing streaking on the course over which fire control would guide it to the precise destination. A short comet tail of blue fire would trail it. It would arch high and fall to the searing, blinding fission that would dispatch and disperse the target decreed for it by its master's invisible finger.

Three minutes was a long time. Dane stood woodenly as the sweep second hand slipped around the dial of the switchboard clock. For a nuclear missile, even a small one, 6100 yards range was close for comfort. Maybe they had decided to fire it now before the range shortened, though the object wasn't plain. The explosion should scorch and sear off the entire tip of the lichen peninsula, but hadn't it occurred to them that the lichen beds could sprout another peninsula? Especially if the present one was really the result of attraction by the metal of the Far Venture?

"Now!" Humphries shouted.

They stared at the photo plane table. The missile would move slowly enough. No need for hurry and supersonic speed here on Mars. It would pass circumspectly above the sands, its nose following its invisible pre-ordered path.

But when it did come to its detonation, there was only a wink of light on the plane table to announce it. Then as the reception image of the cloud spread deliberately, the burn area showed clearly on the glass.

"All clear!" the loudspeaker said. "All clear."

Humphries' face worked. "That'll give them something to think of!" He thrust suddenly at the port-cover switches, shoving at them.

The familiar explosion cloud hung in the Martian upper sky, spreading like surly contamination away from its funnel stem. Dane went close to the glassite port that faced the thing. He stood there for a long time, vague and wordless in mind, letting the feeling of ill-being vegetate, without fixation, without effort, gradually relaxing against it.

When the tension had ebbed, the troubled thought slowly emerged. Across the many millions of miles they had come, to be met with the old pattern of violence and to offer it up in return. The high skill of Earth expressed for a new world in the form of a nuclear bomb. Even against insensate plants the sign of limitless destruction.

CHAPTER TWENTY-FOUR

It began with darting filaments of lichen. They sprang out from the blasted end of the peninsula in radial tracery, fanning a net over the quarter-mile blotch of the burn. Dane strained his eyes at the scope. The net was filling in. In a minute it was a knob head on the stem of the peninsula. Filaments spurted ahead of the knob, spreading wider and inclining toward the spacecraft. In five minutes they had grown into mile-long streamers. Then, as suddenly as it had commenced, the phenomenon ceased.

"Dr. Dane to command post," the speaker blared.

Dane hurried down the ladders. Before he swung off on 1-high deck he could hear argument, Wertz's hoarse voice obscuring others.

The small command bay was crowded. Its door was open and men were overflowing into the passage. Major Noel sat at the command desk, idly snapping the key of the intercom. He nodded to Dane. "The gentleman of the press. We were discussing the lichens. Some of these other gentlemen are worried about the defense of the vehicle." He was practically affable.

Wertz broke in again. "I've been trying to tell him the things are too dangerous to risk getting any closer to us. In the first place, it was a big mistake to use the fission bomb on them. Now we've got to get over there and burn off their growing ends." He looked at his friend. "Even Cruzate here goes along with that. We all agree on that."

Dane recognized the appeal for a recruit. He saw Forrest, the bacteriologist, and Wade, the zoologist, nod. The archaeologist Steffany kept his opinion to himself.

"It was a mistake to use fission on them," Wertz repeated. "The radiation must have stimulated hell out of them. You're not up against a growth like a plant. A better word for it would be a 'formation.' These things may resemble Earth lichens, but in one way they're different as hell. They're biochemical in the most literal sense of the word. They're not plants. They're biochemicals. With the accent on the chemical aspect of their existence. We saw the evidence right here in the Far Venture. What happened here proved it. They form themselves chemically, like crystals in a saturated solution. The fission radiation maybe stimulated new plants to form like hell."

"What we've got to think about, at least what I have got to think about," Noel said, "is the balance between any danger from the lichens and our resources to combat them. I've got to assume that if they keep on advancing I'll have to keep them away from any contact with the Far Venture's hull. Now when I think about that, I've got to think about how much fire fuel I have in hand to expend—maybe a total of a eight or nine hours. I can't defend a perimeter of three miles' radius with that. Supposing we burn off the advance now, and then they come on again from a dozen other starts? I intend to hold a perimeter of about a hundred yards to a hundred and fifty in radius. I can hold that all the way around. We just wait until we can see the whites of their eyes, that's all."

Dane said, "There's always the thought that actually we may completely misunderstand why the lichens are thrusting out at us. Just to hazard a wild guess, they might be a vehicle by which the Martians are approaching us. Maybe, for example, the Martians are parasitic upon them. Maybe they live within the plants, like bacteria in a blood stream."

"Nothing wrong with your imagination," Forrest spoke up. "But there really is something screwy about the whole life setup on this minus-two-dollar-an-acre ball of real estate. I don't think we've given enough weight to it, except to be mighty puzzled by it. That's the total absence of any sign or semblance of life on this planet and certainly in this area except these damn lichens. It just doesn't add up. I'll admit the lichen is a low form, but it's a lot higher than many other forms of life. Bacteria, for instance. Why aren't there any native bacteria observable here? With a big part of the surface covered with vegetation, there certainly should be a wide variety of unicellular organisms. What I'm getting at is how do these lichens have an apparent monopoly, as far as we know, on the life principle here?"

"Except for our mysteriously hidden Martians," Dane reminded him.

"There is fossil evidence of the existence of blue-green algae and unicellular fungi on Earth two billion years ago," Wade said.

"Exactly," Forrest answered the zoologist. "How do you doubt such forms existed on Mars? How about the algae-like components of the lichen plants here? Captured sometime surely from someplace by the fungus component. Did all the other one-celled organisms commit suicide? Why can't we find any trace of evolutionary development? What I'm getting to is did the lichens come along later and somehow destroy every other form of life on the planet?"

"Oxygen," Steffany asked, "how about the lack of oxygen? Wouldn't that prevent any other form of life except something like the lichens with special apparatus for making their own?"

"There are anaerobic bacteria in the soil of Earth," Forrest told him. "They exist in the absence of free oxygen. Why not here? No," he went on, "I hardly can escape a conclusion that in some way all the forms of life that we might reasonably expect have been suppressed except the lichens."

"How about Dane's Martians?" Steffany put in.

"Obviously they have survived too," Forrest said. "Maybe the lichens fit someway into their economy or plan of existence. That's just it. How about the Martians? I wouldn't want to say no to the idea that maybe they know all about these lichens and their peculiar growing actions. And maybe a lot more. It's damned funny we can't find any trace of bacterial life here. There's nothing in the environment to forbid it. It suggests manipulation."

Noel said, "Well, one thing we do know, we've got lichens if we haven't got anything else. From what we know of them, we don't want them in contact with the Far Venture. We can't risk it. Any plan we make has got to be based on that. We start out with that."

Wertz nodded. "That's right for sure. We already know that they can attack timageel in their aggravated state. It could very well be that in their forming state—growing state if you want to call it that—they are especially acid producing. Maybe the older formations that have been standing for a while are weaker. That could explain our walking through them in pressure suits. But it is precisely their growing peaks that the peninsula is addressing to us. Obviously if it reaches the spacecraft, it will impinge newly forming lichens against the timageel shell."

"Major Beloit and Mr. Vining have set noon tomorrow as the earliest we can possibly attempt a take-off," Noel said. "The lichens now stand at a range of only forty-two hundred yards. Since the bomb strike, their advance has been a good two thousand yards. That took only five minutes. At that rate it's possible for them to be on us in ten minutes. Even if they have exhausted their spurt and return to the rate of growth we observed earlier this afternoon, then they are still capable of a hundred yards in a few minutes. Say six hundred yards an hour. That's too close for comfort, even if the night cold stops them dead. Seven hours would bring them here. Seven growing hours. Say four or five left before the cold gets them today. Any way you figure it, they're capable of getting to us before noon tomorrow, if not a whole lot sooner."

Dane felt a hand on his shoulder. It was the flight surgeon. Captain King murmured a "Pardon me" and pushed his little round belly past to get close to Noel and whisper in his ear.

Noel gazed at him with expressionless face. "I looked in on the infirmary myself at 1530," he said. "They were all right then."

Captain King bent over his ear again.

Noel jerked aside. "Speak out. These men are in this too."

King straightened up out of his pose. "As you wish, sir," King said, all in a stiff mouthful. "I was just going to say that I had been expecting them both to regain consciousness within a few hours. Both their respirations were good. Hearts steady. Color improving rapidly."

"I read your reports regularly," Noel interrupted him.

King glanced nervously at the circle of faces. "It's this." His voice dropped almost to a whisper again. "No one went in there. The nurse was on duty. He says he didn't move from the front desk since he went around with you. He's been sitting there reading ever since, until he went in to fill in the charts a few minutes ago and found them. Nobody could have gotten in there without him knowing it!"

"If it's not a military secret," Dane broke in, "what's this all about?"

Noel stared at him a moment. "Beemis and Jackson are dead," he said slowly. "Both of them. Killed dead," he added. He stood up in the middle of the quick gabble. "I've got to go."

"What do you mean, 'killed dead'?" Dane demanded.

Noel swung back at him. "They were murdered."

"They were murdered in their beds," King said. "Both of them. Unconscious in their beds."

"Come on, Major, make sense!" Wertz edged in sharply. "How could they be murdered? What makes you say were murdered? They've been out ever since Dane dragged them in from the lichen beds. They just died, that's all."

"You think somebody with his mouth stuffed full of red sand and it rammed up his nose just died!" King said fiercely. "You think red Mars sand just drifted into the infirmary and suffocated them? Just like that!"

It fell among them.

"But why!" Cruzate popped into the sudden no-talking. "Who wants to do this thing?"

"That's what I intend to find out," Noel said strongly. "Somebody wanted to shut them up. Now we won't ever know what Pembroke did or found out on the planet." He glared at Captain King. "Somebody else must have been reading your reports. Somebody didn't want them to regain consciousness."

"But nobody could have got in the infirmary without being seen," King protested. "The nurse was sitting at the door all the time!"

"I'm going up to talk to that gentleman now," Noel said. "He's covering up. He left his post. Either that or he's covering up for somebody else."

Forrest laughed nervously. "Why would a murderer use sand? Why would he use sand from outside? From Mars? There are lots of easier ways to kill a man. Especially if he's already unconscious." Behind his thick, tinted lenses his wide-spaced eyes darted to and fro, dancing from Noel to King and back again. He slapped the palm of his white hand against the back of its mate, flattening the thin black growth.

"It's frightening!" he exploded. "I don't like it. It must mean they're inside the spacecraft somehow. We don't see them but they're in here. That's why the man didn't see anybody!"

Major Noel observed him briefly. Then he grabbed his arm and shook him. "You better go lie down and take it easy. Meantime you can take my word it was somebody more substantial than invisible Martians. How do you think that sand got in there?" he shouted out. "You think microscopic Martians like Dane yammers about can carry in man-sized handfuls of red sand and ram them into a couple of guys' throats?" He snapped his head like a swimmer emerging from a dive. "Sometimes I wonder about you guys. Always good for a brainstorm."

Captain King was staring at Forrest. "I was working in my office," he said hoarsely. "I was there all the time. I could see the front desk out my door. Like he said, Takonik was sitting there reading a book. He never moved. If he had left, I would have seen him! But something got in!"

Noel wheeled on him. "Didn't you forget the fact that we had an alert at 1551? Didn't you forget all about the nuclear missile we fired at 1603?"

King wet his lips. "No. I didn't forget."

"Didn't you leave your office while all that was going on? Don't you think something might have happened then?"

King shook his head. "I stayed at my desk. I was there all through the alert. After it too."

"So you calmly stayed at your desk! While we track an N-bomb and explode it. You're not curious? You don't want to see what happens?" Noel's disbelief was rank. "You pick that kind of a time to shuffle papers on your desk?"

"I was writing a message to my wife." King's face reddened.

"You what!" Noel blared.

"A letter. I was writing to my wife. I didn't know what might happen, so I was writing a letter. In case something happened to us and another expedition came and found us maybe. Then maybe she would know."

Dane felt acute discomfort for the man's embarrassment. This was what the news hucksters called great human-interest stuff. If he were worth his salt to Amalgamated Press, he would now ask the man what his wife "would know."

Noel asked it for him.

King squirmed. "I wanted her to know I was thinking about her. That is, if anything happened and anybody ever found us again," he added apologetically.

Noel spread his hands. "You think with you in that state of mind that Takonik couldn't slip away from his post for a few minutes or maybe let someone go in without you even noticing it?"

King wiped his face with his palm. "I had an eye on him all the time. I know he didn't leave."

"Now look," Noel said sharply, "you mean you sat there and scribbled a note to your wife and watched that man too? All the time?"

"I was glad he was there," King said. "I was scared, and I was glad he was there where I could see someone."

"He could still let someone in, couldn't he?"

"I don't think so."

"You don't think so! But you don't know so?"

"I couldn't see the main corridor and the door, if you mean that."

"That's exactly what I do mean. All you saw was Takonik sitting at the desk."

"He's a good boy," King insisted. "I don't think he would lie to me."

"You don't know. All you know is you found those men dead. Murdered."

"He found them. He told me. Why should he lie about it? Not with it murder."

Noel said, "That's exactly what I'm going to find out. Somebody obviously went in there and kept those men from talking. I'm going to find out why and who. If Takonik didn't leave, then he knows who. Probably why."

Dane said, "Tong Asia enters the plot again."

"You got any better ideas?" Noel retorted. "Or do you want to vote for a Martian sandman too?"

"That makes six men we've lost. Six out of 125," Heileman said. "Every now and then we lose a man. You understand what actually kills each one of them, but you wouldn't ever have expected it. Something just happens. Every now and then another guy gets it. When you least expect it and for some cause you never could have foreseen or prevented. First it was Houck. Dane and Wertz find him dead and flat on his back in the lichens. How or why, nobody can guess. Then Dr. Pembroke gets off his bat and shoots himself. Then the lichens go crazy in Wertz's lab and Spear and Gonzales get it. Who could have thought of that? Yet they get it. Now Beemis and Jackson. That makes six of us. None of them dead in any way you might have expected, like a Martian snake biting one of us. If there had been any snakes, I mean. Still, at least you would understand something like a snake possibly living here. Or an accident of some kind here with the equipment. Or an infection by some unknown disease here. But nothing like that! Nothing simple like that! It's so irrational that I damn near got to think maybe something is going on with this Tong Asia business like Noel said. Without something damn funny going on, none of these guys getting killed makes any sense at all, except maybe the ones that got caught in the lichen explosion."

Dane couldn't deny him that. Some primary pieces were missing from the board that would have to be found before the jigsaw shaped up. If the Tong had managed to get a man on the roster of the Far Venture, it still didn't make sense. He would profit more by silent observation and report to his masters when he returned to Earth. Unless the Tong had already reached Mars, and in some obscure way the attacks served their purpose in keeping their landings secret. But that was technologically impossible. The Tong lacked the nuclear drive. Even if the working principles of the drive were common knowledge, there was still the intricate know-how of establishing the critical balances to give the thrust. Like lining up a hundred computers for one frenzied calculation, he thought as he swarmed through the hatch into the observation chamber.

He looked out at the sterile plains of Mars and the elongated shadow of the spacecraft pacing off toward the east over the red desert like a problem in geometry. Would they ever see Earth again? If they did, would men ever come again to Mars? That much was not in doubt. Whether the Far Venture returned or not, men would come again and again, in larger and larger numbers, until the secrets of the planet lay bare.

But departure was impossible without knowing. Where were they? What were they? In what form of being did they exist? What were their knowledges? Their aspirations? To depart the planet without coming face to face with the Martians, even for escape from possible death, denied the reason for coming to Mars in the first place.

In a few minutes possibly the last night on Mars would begin. No communication with the Martians had yet been achieved later than an hour or two after sunset. None before ten in the morning. Opportunity was fleeting fast. Dane went to the switch key. He began to send in the number code.

Men not know Martians, he managed in the roughhewn symbol language. *Martians exist? Men know not. Men know two plus two equals four. Men know Martians not equal zero. What Martians equal?*

He repeated that much twice and then sent, *Martians come spacecraft. Know is good. Martians come spacecraft. Martians equal what? Martians come spacecraft. Men know. Good. Good.*

He saw the photo plane table flicker with the beginning of a reply. Exulting, he watched it finally settle into the familiar symbols. He read: *Martians are one. One is good. Men and Martians are many. Many is bad. Men die. Men are not. Martians are one. One is good. Martians come spacecraft. Men die. Spacecraft die. Men and spacecraft not exist. Equals good. Martians are one. One is good.*

It was like a chant at the jungle's edge. From the flicker of cold light against the opal glass hate burned unmistakably through the halting tirade. Dane leaped for the switch key. Bigod, they had to understand. They had to come in peace and be received in peace.

Simultaneously with his clutch over the knob a clamor of metal burst around him. He fought it stupidly, before he realized the alarm gong overhead was clanging in his ear. The noise stopped abruptly, and he heard Major Noel's impersonal authority on the speaker. "Battle stations. All crew to battle stations."

Dane ran to the ports. "You see anything?"

Humphries shook his head. "Huh-uh."

If anything moved under the fading light it was too small or too distant to be visible.

Through the open hatch rose a hubbub of excited voices, hurrying footsteps, and whine of motors—the jolting staccato of the guns clearing. "They sure as hell spotted something," Humphries sang out. "Take a look on the table. I gotta stay here at my post."

Of course. The plane table.

The opal glass was dead! A thought stung. It's been knocked out. The Martians have blinded us. He jerked at the switch key. It was off.

Lieutenant Yudin thrust his head through the hatch. "What's up? I was asleep," he added.

"I don't know," Dane answered him. "Unless…"

The intercom squawked again. Then it said, "Stand by at all stations. Lichens are advancing rapidly. Point of closest approach is 112 degrees. Repeat, 112 degrees. Range 2600 yards. Repeat, 2600 yards."

Dane whistled. "That's fourteen hundred yards closer." But he couldn't have killed the plane tables more than ten minutes by the messages, he thought guiltily.

On the plane table the line of the lichen peninsula ran straight across the sand plain toward the spacecraft, a finger of light that crawled purposively across the grid lines.

Dane put the dividers on it. "It's making a hundred yards a minute. A good hundred yards! You ought to be able to see it through the port by now," he called to Humphries.

Humphries turned to Lieutenant Yudin. "No, sir. It's too dark now."

The last slice of the small sun floated over the low hills in the west, wrapping itself in smallish yellow blaze. They strained to see through the thick glassite ports, but the light was almost gone. To the east the land had disappeared under starless night. The rotating guard beacon strained weakly at the twilight.

In five minutes the lichens had marched another measured six hundred yards. The range had closed to two thousand yards.

"They're going out!" Humphries exclaimed. "They're taking out the flamethrowers."

Dane counted eleven pressure-suited figures on the sand below, looking down at them past the bulge of the spherical hull. They seemed to stand almost under the shelter of the curving sides. All but one had the cylinders of the self-oxidizing flame ejectors strapped behind their shoulders. Two one-man flame-throwing tanks darted from under the spacecraft, their armor red with the dust they kicked up in motionless clouds. Then the little party spread apart and deployed in a bowed line facing the oncoming lichens.

Abruptly Dane left the port and yanked at the exit hatch. "See you later," he said.

CHAPTER TWENTY-FIVE

The airlock guard observed him indifferently. Dane came the rest of the way down the ladder with his pressure suit and helmet. When the man saw him start hooking in the radio equipment, his mouth line straightened.

"Not allowed to go outside," he Georgia-drawled. "Nobody supposed to."

"I am," Dane told him. "I represent the almighty press. Amalgamated, that is."

"Nobody allowed outside," the guard reiterated. He shifted easily on his feet and peered out the port. "Fire party out there right now, besides."

Dane pushed a leg into the heavy, articulated casing. "I am on my master's business. The public must be told. See all, hear all, tell all, know nothing. That's us. Molders of public opinion. Have to be Johnny-on-the-spot, and all that."

"Mebbe so," the man grunted. "You have to do your looking from here, though." He brightened a little. "Unless you got a pass. You gotta pass?"

"That's a wonderful idea," Dane said. "Why don't you call the command post and tell them John Dane wants to go out with the fire party on press duty?"

He got a headshake. "They want you out there, they let you know."

Dane got the suit over his shoulders. "I'm supposed to be a newspaperman. A reporter. Supposed to be right there when anything happens, so we can put it in the paper when we get back." He held up his head camera. "See? I have to take special pictures. Go ahead and ask them," he added. "They're going to say okay."

The guard allowed he didn't care, one way or the other, but he picked up the phone and spoke briefly. "Yeah," he said, "it's Dr. Dane." Out of the corner of his mouth he said, "They're checkin' with Major Noel. He's outside." After a minute he said, "Yeah. I'll tell him."

He hung up. "Sergeant Peeney says the major says okay, but you gotta stay behind the fire party. That's so you don't get hurt," he threw in. "Case they light up the flame throwers."

"You're a pal," Dane assured him. "How about helping me with this gear?"

He stepped down into the red sand. Mars, he thought. This is the planet Mars. He became freshly aware of the huge night. Laden with what the old storytellers called menace. Maybe even now the Martians were fulfilling their promise to come to the spacecraft. From somewhere out in the dark. From beyond the rim of the lighted landing site, where the brilliantly illumined circle tapered off into the solid dark that was periodically dealt a shallow wound by the beacon.

Once a minute the broad blade of the light swept around. A man should be visible in the observation-deck telescope at a thousand yards. The radar should pick him up at ten thousand. Only they were not looking for men.

Major Noel's voice spoke into the ear set. "Come over here, Dane. Get behind me. Number two. The lichens are coming up fast. They're at five hundred yards now."

The men with the flamethrowers had stretched their skirmish line to fifty-yard intervals all around the Far Venture. Behind them waited the squat flame tanks. Suddenly Noel barked a command. One of the tanks wheeled abruptly and churned the dust to station beyond the southern arc of the perimeter. The other remained in place, facing the east.

"You want some pictures," Noel's voice rasped, "get ready. We're going to burn hell out of them!"

A timbre of elation sang in the cry. Dane pressed the shutter release button on his belt, snap-shooting the wide-legged stance Noel had taken against the east, the luminescent numeral 2 large on his back tank. He got one of two good ones of the waiting picket line of outlandishly garbed men before a jumble of excitement rattled against his eardrums. Everyone was shouting into microphones at once.

Dane stared at the lichen clump that popped up a couple of hundred yards out in the light. A supplementary searchlight came on from the spacecraft and sought it out. More lights came on and shifted about, showing up one…two…three…four…then more and more clumps standing along a broad front where only one had sprung into view an instant before.

Noel crackled orders on the command frequency. Dane saw the flame bearers shift to meet the approach, like an elongated football scrimmage line.

The stuff pulsed forward in livid spurts, giving the appearance of impinging like bushy darts laterally across the sand. It was suddenly very close. So close that Dane saw the new plants erupt from the sand in front of the stands of plants that had themselves burst into existence in the van a second or two before.

He remembered once writing that a man caught in choking suspense can think or talk only in trite patterns and phrases. No epic speeches, like the epic heroes spout. Generally he says something like "God damn it," and afterward he can't remember that he thought anything except that things were not different as they should have been. To face great peril and have your surroundings look just about the same as always denies the rightness of things. It is inappropriate, Dane had written, for a man to endure the slow crisis of approaching death, then to escape in the nick of time and describe his feelings later with so puny a simile as "It was like a bad dream." Now he had just caught himself thinking, *It's like a nightmare*. One of those where you want to run pell-mell away and are rooted where you stand, while the menace stalks you, aware of you, closing in to take you.

He heard Noel say, "Light your pieces."

Down the line and around the flanks spurts of bluish, chemical flame stabbed out shortly from the nozzles.

"What's he waiting for!" Dane cried out.

Noel still stood broad-legged…immovable…bestriding his few inches of sand. Like the Colossus sadly dwindled in size, Dane thought.

"Let 'em have it!" he ordered at last.

The lichens were barely fifty feet from the perimeter line when the heavy spurt of flame arched from the tank out across the sand and hosed back and forth. Four smaller flame thrusts stabbed at the flanks.

A miasma of oily smoke boiled thickly from the scorched plants, clinging to the ground and billowing under the dripping flame. It drifted slowly, coming in on the men holding the nozzles to hang a dense curtain over the fire tips and their targets. Then it piled in so close that it swallowed the fire lances in its creeping front.

"Cut your fires back," Noel commanded.

The flame thrusts sucked back to their nozzles. The sortie stood intent while the searchlights played across the face of the smoke fog. Dane felt an impatience to brush off the confining helmet to see better.

Noel's voice came on again. Quietly now. "I'm going into the smoke for a look. Seckinger, you advance your tank with me ten feet at my left. Hold your fire down unless I give the word."

Seckinger, Airman First Class, said, "Yes, sir." Dane visualized his square face set behind the port of the sealed tank. He was a quiet, chunky young man. His square shoulders suggested the blue, double-breasted sea coats his ancestors must have worn on the voyages he had told about. He was a good choice for a wingman.

Seckinger moved the tank up close, and Noel started forward. Before they got to the wall ahead, a cry came from the right flank. "They're coming through the smoke over here. They're coming through the smoke!" the man repeated.

Dane saw Noel turn ponderously. The tank halted at his upraised arm. Then his command came sharply. The other tank darted left in the dream scene, and the blue fire spurted ahead of its nose. A searchlight twisted from the towering bulk of the Far Venture and picked up the new attack.

Remembering his business to get pictures, Dane moved down the line. A great flash of light dazzled him. A roar of noise tore at him. He froze, stunned under another flash that scared his eyes, followed quickly by a third. "Spark-fire bolts!" he shouted into his microphone. "It's a spark-fire storm!"

The tank belched its stream of fire in an undeviating line. One of its supporting flame bearers lay on the sand, his own fire jet spurting into the dust at right angles to his body. The bolts were aimed at them! Dane turned quickly, stumbling off balance in the clumsy gear.

"Noel!" he shouted. "The bolts! They struck one of the men!"

No time for answer. Lightning streaked out of the east and slammed the tank by Noel. Little bans of orange fire bounced briefly on its metal. Noel lay on the ground.

Something moved against his legs. Dane stood still, breathing hard. His helmet air tasted light and dry, like the stale atmosphere of a long-closed building. He looked down, knowing what he would see.

The lichens had sprung up all around him. Knee-deep.

The airmen shot out their small streams of fire, burning swaths back to the Far Venture, now aground in a sea of lichens. As the heavy smoke drifted from some of the burned areas, Dane saw with quick apprehension the lichens pop up again from the scorched sand, swallowing the remnants of the burned-out plants. They devoured sand and charred plants alike, burying the scours left by the flames in their leaden green.

Both tanks stood motionless. Their tongues licked ahead, but they made no movement in traverse nor gave any other indication that the operators inside were still alive.

A bright bolt spat over the east and lashed down another flamethrower.

Dane drew a deep lungful of his stuffy air. For a quick moment he imagined he could smell an acridity. Lichen acids eating against his suit? Frantically he trampled the plants down around him, playing his electric torch on his armored legs. His breath sighed out relief. Suddenly he shouted into the microphone. "Turn off your flames and get inside. You're not doing any good. They're coming up again where they've been burned off."

His shouted words were drowned by the sharper tone of the Far Venture's command set. "Turn off all fire. Return to the spacecraft." The familiar voice named itself. "Colonel Cragg to Major Noel. Turn off all fires and return to the spacecraft. Immediately."

Another spark bolt snapped home. Dane counted the same number of men still standing. He wondered if the few bolts that had fallen so far were prelude to a storm like yesterday's. Maybe it was too late in the night for the bolts to build up in any profusion. The cold of the darkness must be rapidly deepening, if there was a real connection between the phenomenon of the dwindling spark fires and the oncoming night. Maybe whatever was directing the lightning weapon was short of ammunition.

It occurred to him to move himself. This was no time to linger. Not even for Amalgamated Press pictures.

He took a few steps, breasting the lichen stuff, wading it gingerly before he thought of Noel. If the bolt at the tank had not hit him directly, he could still be alive.

He turned back from the Far Venture, fuzzily amazed at the need to do it, and began plowing through the lichens toward the immobilized tank marked out for him in the smoke by its spouting flame. How much longer would it burn before its fuel was exhausted? He was not sure how the stuff burned anyway, except that some of its ingredients provided oxygen for combustion.

One of the Far Venture's lights came circling around and picked him up. "Dane," he heard Colonel Cragg's voice in the ear set. "You're going the wrong way, man. Turn around and follow the light. Just follow the light."

It was an odd thing to say. He turned a moment and waved his arm against the light. When he thought of his radio, he switched to the liaison frequency of the spacecraft. "I'm going after Major Noel." His heart began to pound at the declaration. Now there was no turning back.

"Come on inside. Right now," Colonel Cragg said.

Dane took up his wading through the stand of lichens. Toward the tank. The throbbing of his heart resolved itself into a surge of power. The fine thrill of discovery that he too was able to make himself to move.

"Noel will be picked up. It's been provided for," Colonel Cragg said.

Dane waved his arm again in the bright light and kept on wading. The lichen stuff was relatively widely spaced, sparse compared with the stands of the lichen forest.

The earphones crackled with Colonel Cragg's voice. "Good luck, fellow!"

Dane approached the tank uneasily. If Seckinger was still alive, maybe dazed, he might move about in his confinement and inadvertently swivel the nozzle and its streaking flame around. In which event John Dane's suit would quickly fry.

As if he had divined his thought, Colonel Cragg came on, "We can't raise Seckinger. Take a look at him, will you?" He switched off but came right on again. "Watch that flame nozzle. It's on 360-degree swivel."

"Roger, and thanks," Dane answered. Fine. Swiveled for 360-degree coverage. All the way around the circle, and dodge that if you can.

He came cautiously up to the side of the midget armor. He couldn't see Noel. The lichens were thick enough around the tank. After the metal, maybe. Better get the job done and get out of here fast. What the tank was made out of, he hadn't the foggiest idea. Maybe the same double-alloyed timageel as the hull of the spacecraft. Certainly not the softer metal of the interior partitions. He poured his light over the tank's lower plates, in the lichen shadow. He could see no corrosion even where he pushed aside stems in direct contact with the metal.

He straightened and shot his light into the side port. Its metal shutter was not closed over the glassite.

Seckinger hung forward against his shoulder harness. His eyes were open. At least the one eye Dane could see was open, as if he were staring at his instrument panel. Dane could detect no movement of breathing. He rapped sharply on the rim of the port.

Colonel Cragg came in.

Dane said, "I think he's dead."

"You think you can make it in with Major Noel?"

"I can try." Whatinhell did Cragg think he was here for if he didn't think he could carry seventy-five pounds?

"I'll send you out some help. Stand by. It will only take a few minutes."

"Stand by hell," Dane told him. "I'm getting out of this. I'll bring him in. No use risking anybody else."

To underscore his thinking about the spark bolts, a big one banged in. It must have struck the other tank. Its flame could have turned. It seemed to be pointing in a slightly different direction.

"See what I mean?" he demanded, arrogant that he was here and they were there, safe in the spacecraft.

The bolts were farther apart, but they were as sharp as ever. He guessed the next accumulation would be discharged against Seckinger's tank. Or John Dane. Time to move, boy, he told himself. Time to go home.

He moved to the right and came on Noel face down. Lichens swarmed thick around him.

"Watch your suit," Cragg admonished him.

He could pick Noel up easily enough, he knew. Probably carry him in his arms, with a few stops for rest. Might even get him over his shoulder. Also could very easily spring a joint in either Noel's suit or his own. For a quick end. He rolled Noel over carefully and pointed his light through his visor. The mouth was moving. Slowly with heavy breathing.

"He's alive!" he reported.

Now he had to make it.

With inspiration he remembered his Boy Scout tricks. He unhooked the shank of guard rope from his belt and cut a yard from it with his sheath knife. He lashed Noel's wrists together as carefully as he could, binding around the heavy cuffs above the intricately articulated handpieces. It was a feat to tie the knot, but he managed it, flinching at the thought of the tank. If they were shooting at the fire.

When he had the job done, he got Noel under the armpits and brought him up on his knees and then to his feet, facing him and holding him against his chest. Next he managed to turn himself enough to support Noel's chest against his back. He bent forward and pushed Noel's arms up and over his head and slipped the loop of his lashed wrists under his own chin. When he straightened up, the smaller man's feet swung clear in a kind of dangling piggyback. His own hands were left free to steady the weight and restrain Noel's bound arms from jamming up against his neckpiece and helmet. Just pull down on the tag ends of the rope around his wrists. Simple. He walked a few steps and decided that it was going to work. "Be Prepared!" he gloated.

"Nice work!" Colonel Cragg congratulated him.

"If you can get it," Dane said.

"Save your breath, fellow."

How did Colonel Cragg get in on this, anyway? he suddenly wondered.

It was hard to hold himself to a slow, level gait. He wanted to put distance between him and the metal of the tank in a hurry. Most of all he wanted to climb up the ladder and be inside the Far Venture. He made himself endure the slowest, most cautious movements and hunt around the denser lichen clumps.

Now it occurred to him that Noel was a heavy devil for his size. He was thankful for the smaller mass of Mars. The planet's surface gravity was 38 percent of Earth's. That meant a 150-pound man on Earth would weigh only 57 pounds on Mars. He doubted that Noel weighed 150 pounds. His load should not be 75 pounds, even with the equipment. He caught up short. He had forgotten to remove the weights on Noel's belt and shoulder harness. No wonder the guy was heavy. He had a good 150 pounds on his back, and then some.

All that weight could play hell with the pressure suits. They were rugged enough and made to withstand falls against hard surfaces, but still he ought to stop and get rid of all the weight he could. It was only being smart. Even if the putting down and picking up again were a dangerous strain, it was only smart to get rid of half his weight. He cursed gently and eased his burden down.

He cut away the four weights from Noel's belt and shoulders and finally the anklet weights.

Two bolts struck hard, so close together their flashes blended. Dane straightened up and looked around. The fire was gone from the other tank. He couldn't locate it. The flame of Seckinger's tank had swung around more than 90 degrees. A little more and it would have reached them.

Then he noticed that the line of fire was drifting, swinging closer. It was arcing slowly around. At them! He eyed the distance to the tank. The flame would easily reach where he stood over Noel. At its present angle he could see that clearly, shooting out the way it did, more than two hundred feet from its nozzle.

"Run for it, boy!" Colonel Cragg sounded off in his ears. "Save yourself! Run for it! That last bolt knocked it on traverse. Run!"

Fifteen or twenty yards would do it! "God damn you!" he raged. "If you hadn't forgotten the weights, we'd be out of range now!"

All the while he was busy. Automatically and desperately busy. Fighting for the calm to move smoothly, he pulled Noel up and eased him into position.

The earphones were ominously quiet. They're keeping their mouths shut, he thought. So they won't rattle me. He couldn't have even a minute left, no matter how slow the traverse. Already the relentless second hand of flame was passing three o'clock to his six o'clock. Sobbing for breath, he thrust his head up into the loop of Noel's arms and churned forward into an urgent shuffle.

No time for caution now. Decompression was the lesser of the evils. Stumble and fall, and it was over. He knew that, but still he did not curb his lunges against the lichens that thrust back against his legs.

He tried to look where he was placing his feet, at what the next step would bring to defeat or circumvent, but it was more than a human could do not to look back over his shoulder at the triggered fire.

It was lancing ahead of him, now practically at his side, so close that nothing but the insulated suit kept him from feeling its fierce heat. He was inside the peak of its range.

Doggedly he bent forward to the business of putting foot in front of foot. He had lost, but it was still going to be a good try!

They kept the searchlight directly on the path he trod. As long as he looked down, it could not blind him, and under its brilliance every detail of his footing stood clearly forth. Except for the tangling lichens. Except for the damned tangling lichens he would have made it.

Now he waited for the bite of the fire or the quick boiling death of decompression. The instant his suit leaked his air pressure, his blood would boil. How does it feel when your blood boils? How does it feel in the instant before consciousness blacks out forever? The next tick of the second hand on his watch might be the last. He would not feel the fire when it first licked at him. Its first bite would momentarily be repelled by his suit insulation until the flame wrapped him in and scorched him to a crisp, as the phrase went. Time for one more step maybe. In a detached sort of way he knew his legs were fighting, but he seemed just to be standing there, waiting for the streaking pain. He was annoyed by somebody trying to talk to him, rasping and shouting in his ears. He ought to turn down the volume. Turn it off altogether.

Then he realized that words had meaning. "Take it easy, boy. You've got it made. Take it easy!"

Dully he stopped and swung around. The fiery arm of the compass had already described its arc past where he stood. Already it pointed past! A great joy burst over him. "You made it, boy. You made it!" he gurgled, feeling the smile ripple his face.

"Nice going!" Colonel Cragg was saying, and words to that effect.

"Well," Dane said aloud, "I'll be goddamned!"

"So will I," Colonel Cragg agreed.

He had forgotten about the microphone, but he didn't mind forgetting a great many things. He was happy. Just goddamned happy. Right now that's what he was. Happy.

When he got his breath, he was entering in the shadow of the Far Venture. Well, that was to be expected. Seckinger's tank could not have been two hundred yards out. The lichens were now against the base of the spacecraft's tail cone where it stood upon the sand. A few more steps, and he came under the airlock. He eased Noel off on the cargo hoist that came down and climbed on himself. He did not know until later of the final spark bolt that came in and exploded Seckinger's tank.

He was tired and happy. That was all he knew or cared about. So the lichens were in contact with the Far Venture. Tomorrow was a new day, and tomorrow they took off for the blessed Earth.

CHAPTER TWENTY-SIX

It was Lieutenant McDonald, his hard, youngish face crinkled into a big grin. When they had got Dane out of his suit and hustled Noel off to the infirmary and the contaminated equipment had been properly disposed, he came riding down on the elevator into the airlock. He stuck out his hand and yelled, "What do you want to do? Win a medal? You think they add anything to the pay check?" He stood aside in mock politeness for Dane to get into the cage. "You scared the you-know-what out of all of us. What do you use for nerves? Piano wire?"

You couldn't help liking just plain animal admiration. McDonald bubbled with transparent sincerity. Dane felt himself grinning all over his face. "I—"

"You were just out for a walk? So you thought you'd just bring in this guy Noel? With that big squirt gun about to burn your tail off, you take your own sweet time about getting the guy up on your back. You drape him on you just so; then you walk right out around the end of a jolt of liquid fire like you had on asbestos drawers in hell. They can close the snack bar tonight. The whole damn crew from the commander down has just finished a good meal off their fingernails."

"If you think I wasn't in a hurry," Dane said, "you ought to see a centipede with a hotfoot."

The cage slackened and stopped. McDonald said, "Colonel Cragg wants to see you. My guess is he'll chew you out for not obeying orders and then kiss you for being a damn hero."

Dane looked out on 1-high corridor. "Wrong deck," he said. "Infirmary's on 2-high."

McDonald affected an air of disapproval. "You think they're going to keep that guy in bed with all this going on? He's at the command post in a wheel chair."

Cragg was nearly his old self. His color was back and his voice was strong. He sat ramrod-straight in the invalid chair. Dane would not have been surprised to see him in his blue uniform coveralls instead of pajamas.

He ignored Dane's comment that he was looking good. "I owe you the life of a fine officer." He stopped before he went on, as if he wanted to be careful of what he had to say. "I doubt that we would have been able to get to him in time before the tank blew up. Even if the flame went over him, that would have finished him off. Very likely. You know about Seckinger's tank?"

Dane nodded. "They told me while I was getting out of my gear. He was a good man."

"I lost five good men out there!" Cragg said harshly. "You know about the others too?"

"I didn't realize they were all dead," Dane said.

"We got the three men in who were on foot. They were all dead. They all got it direct. Noel was the only one who didn't get a direct hit."

"You said five. Who was the other one?"

Cragg stared at him coldly. "Three men were brought in dead and both tanks blew up. That's your five. It would have been six if it hadn't been for your timely action. The survivors had to come in and get the flamethrowers off before they could go back out. They couldn't have got back out to Noel as soon as you did, and you barely made it out with him. Likely I would have lost two more men."

He hitched impatiently at the cover on his knees. "As I say, you saved Major Noel, if he pulls through, and they say there's nothing wrong with him besides shock. Maybe he'll be up and around tomorrow. I haven't got much liking for you, but I've got to say there's nothing wrong with your courage. I couldn't have censored you if you had left Noel on the ground and got yourself the hell out when the tank flame started around at you. You didn't. It took guts to do what you did. I acknowledge that and commend your action and respect your courage. I regret that I cannot respect you. When it comes to your damned newspapers, you are as tricky and as reckless as ever!"

"Just a minute!" Dane interrupted. "I am not a member of your crew, even if I am temporarily under your command. My principal business on this flight is to represent the press. What I write is my own business. Past as well as present."

"Your business is not to meddle!" Cragg roared. "Are you aware that it is the opinion of some of the scientific party that the lichen growth might be controlled by intelligent beings who are using them to destroy us? Of course you are!"

Dane decided he had had enough, even if he would like to know what the man was driving at. "What I know or don't know makes very little difference," he snapped. "It happens to make a great deal of difference to me if somebody chooses to shout at me. Supposing I just say good night and go about my business." He spun around the mouth-open Sergeant Peeney.

"Sergeant!" Cragg barked. "Switch over to fire control and step outside. Close the door and stand by." He jerked back to Dane. "I've got some more to say. Quite a bit more. You will be kind enough to stay and listen."

"It doesn't look as if I have much choice," Dane said grimly.

"You are well aware that there is hostile intelligence on this planet. Pretty damned hostile, I'd say!"

Dane said, "I've been exchanging messages with Martians. We all know that."

"That's it exactly." He jerked the wheel chair around to square off at Dane. "That's it exactly. Yesterday you send a message, and all at once we are attacked by lightning bolts."

"You think I ought to anticipate that?" It was his manner. His damned arrogant manner. Dane fought his anger. The bunched soreness that was developing low in his back caught him with a sharp twinge at his sudden movement. "You figure everything out ahead of time yourself?" he asked unpleasantly. "Or maybe you expect somebody else to figure things out for you."

Cragg pulled the corners of his mouth down. "I expect you to obey my orders, and my orders were not to send any more messages after that. Do you obey orders? No. You take it on yourself to send messages again tonight. And what happens! In less than an hour we have five men dead from more lightning bolts."

"What I sent—" Dane began.

"I know what you sent," Cragg snarled. "What's the difference what you did send? The fact is you sent it and then all hell breaks loose. So we got we don't know what kind of Martians on our neck, and you stir them up while we're still stuck here on the sand without power for take-off and evasion. All to make some news for your damn papers." His lips went white. "All these men dead because a news punk's got to try to make news for his damn papers. You think I'm going to be easy on you? What do you think I'm going to do to you for getting five of my men killed!" He raised his head and roared. "Peeney! Think that over!" he added.

"I doubt if I'll have time," Dane told him hotly. "I'm going to be damn busy thinking you're completely nuts."

Cragg clamped his jaw down on that one. "Suit yourself. One thing you're going to do for sure. You're now going into confinement. Then you can do any kind of thinking you want to." He barked at Sergeant Peeney standing in the half-opened door. "Take this man to his quarters and post a guard over him." He swung the wheel chair around hard and slammed the papers from his lap at the command desk.

Peeney said, "You heard the colonel."

"If I didn't, I'd get a hearing aid." Dane laughed briefly at the shock on Peeney's face.

With the sergeant in tow he climbed up to 3-high. He slid his door panel shut and locked it, somewhat irrationally, against the guard he knew Peeney would post.

The bunk felt good. He was so tired he was sore. The muscles in his flanks were on the edge of quivering, and the pain came sharp in his back when he breathed in deeply in preparation for a long exhalation. Sighing a little less rashly, he plucked at the heavy belt and the binding coveralls and raised up enough to peel them off. Then he lay in the dark, but sleep would not come. Once or twice he swore out loud, but he kept coming back to the spark fires and the pattern of the long bolts and the network areas that were obviously some kind of energy centers where the long bolts were generated. The idea that formed was preposterous, but what else would accommodate all the known facts?

He thrashed at it until he was as weary of it as he was tired himself, but he couldn't make it go away. Finally he switched on the lights and went to his notebook. Write it all out. Set down the observed evidence and the happenings. Relate them to each other and total up all their bearings on the idea. The best way to clarify your thinking, Professor Acher had been fond of repeating. Even if he was too tired to figure it out, he could set it down. Maybe then he could go to sleep.

He wrote for two hours, regretting the portable lost in the wreckage of his former quarters. When he was finished, he square-stacked his sheets under the cone of the desk light to ready them for the ring binder. But instead of snapping them in the notebook, he shoved it away and fished an envelope out of his portfolio and sealed what he had written inside. Before he signed his name on the envelope, he took a soft blue pencil and struck out the TO AMALGAMATED PRESS, HOUSTON, TEXAS. Just below the strikeout he printed: TO COLONEL CRAGG (IN THE EVENT OF MY DEATH).

Things written down take on an existence and a new validity of their own, he thought. We write too many things down. He sat, thinking some more with the dimmed clarity of extreme fatigue about the night the first signals came from the Martians. Why had Dr. Pembroke gone out on the sands, mysteriously alone, to return to his own death? Again Dane tried to put down the nagging thought that the going out had been the deed of a crazed mind. What other reason than madness could have lifted a man from a hospital bed to wander out alone on a strange planet and return empty-handed? If mad enough for one such deed, then maybe why not mad enough for another? Such as putting a knife in Cragg on his way out for his mysterious sortie.

Dane came up short. Wide awake. Not Pembroke. Conclusively not him. The proof of that and of his own innocence as well had rested in his own hands all the while. Unrecognized, it had been his all the while.

He began to write again. Furiously. When he had it all down, he broke open his envelope and rescaled its content and his case for Dr. Pembroke inside a new cover. He pondered a minute and then addressed it to Major Noel, also in the event of the death of John Dane.

He was documented. In any event he was documented. He crawled on his bunk, thinking. If certainly not Pembroke, then who? Which was what he had said all the time. Only without any proof to make them listen. Finally he went to sleep.

CHAPTER TWENTY-SEVEN

The buzzer wasp-buzzed. Dane climbed up on one elbow and looked at the 0747 hours on his watch.

"No breakfast," he yelled, remembering very well the confinement practice of waking you up to feed you whether you wanted to eat or not. "I don't want any breakfast."

He let himself go backward on the pillow. At least he could sleep all he wanted to.

The buzzer came on again and stayed on. Muttering about fools who insisted on ordering life to their own time, he got out of bed and slid the door panel back from its latch.

Major Noel stood outside. "Greetings," he said cheerfully. "Just getting up?"

Dane said, "No. I just got back from a swim off the pier."

Noel grinned. "How about getting on some clothes? There's things to do."

Dane said, "I had the impression from your boss man that I was supposed to stay put until he changed his mind. You got new news about that?" He stood back and let Noel inside.

"It's changed. We're getting messages."

"This early!" How did it fit in?

Noel pre-empted the armchair. "Yeah. They don't make any sense. The Old Man wants you to take them over."

Dane followed his eyes to the envelope he had scaled the night before. He got out fresh undershorts and pulled on his coveralls.

"I got to thank you for pulling me in last night," Noel began again. "I hear you were kind of terrific."

Dane fumbled under the bunk for his gravity footgear. "How you feeling this morning?"

"Good as ever except for my shoulder muscles." Noel flexed his arms indolently. "That piggy-back ride they say you gave me must have stretched them a real stretch."

"If I'd had enough sense to shuck your weights, it might have helped."

"Hot damn about it! It took plenty of guts to deal the hand at all. Let alone remember to turn trumps."

Dane stood up and stamped his feet, clumsy with the weighted boots. "Forget it."

Noel twitched off his familiar shrug. "Anyway, I owe you one. A big one. Nothing changes that."

"How about time out to brush the teeth? I can't go far if I escape."

Lieutenant Yudin had photo record prints scattered over the chart table. "These are the best." He shuffled them a little. "Still scrambled, it looks like. The table's been dead for a long time."

It wasn't scrambling, Dane decided at once. It was more like a distortion of the code symbols, as if their shapes had been imperfectly transmitted. Their characteristics were bent and portions of them were suppressed.

"No can do?" Noel asked.

"I don't see anything yet," Dane admitted. "Maybe their transmitter is out of tune."

Noel said, "One thing is for sure. Don't you send out any messages yourself. The colonel gave strict orders about that." He stepped over the hatch. "Things are shaping up for take-off," he went on. "We're scheduled to go off at 1100 hours, but there's a chance we might be able to move it up to 1030."

"Major," Yudin spoke up, "what do you think?"

"What do I think about what?" Noel asked.

Yudin fumbled. He took off his glasses and rubbed his eyes. "About the take-off," he blurted. "Does it look to you like we'll make it? Get off the ground, I mean."

"It won't be a take-off if we don't," Noel said coldly. "I've got work to do. Stand by your equipment." He let himself down out of sight.

Yudin wiped his glasses with care. Dane felt the man's embarrassed fury. "How's things look outside?" he asked him conversationally.

Yudin put on the glasses. He felt around in a pocket and pulled out his curved pipe and tobacco pouch. Dane had gone to the ports before he answered. "They're all around us. The same as they were last night, as well as I can see." He made an effort to speak lightly. "How does it feel to be a hero?"

Dane laughed briefly. "I don't think running like hell makes a hero." He was going to have to kick this sort of thing around all day.

"Go ahead. Be modest. Isn't that the way you newspaper fellows always write it up? Modest hero bashfully denies he did anything but his duty?"

Dane swung around and looked at him.

Yudin shook his head. "Forget I said it, will you? That guy gets me sore. You got plenty of credit coming for what you did."

"Skip it," Dane said. "We're all on edge. Bound to be. Everybody in this teakettle is on edge. Why wouldn't they be?"

The Far Venture sat within the tip of a broad tongue of lichens at least three hundred yards wide and pushed a good hundred yards past the spacecraft to a round terminus on the western side. The vegetation didn't look fresh grown. It was brown-green and moribund, laced with streaks of fibrous gray, like plants that awaited a killing frost. Looking directly down on it, or at least as directly down as the rounded ball of the Far Venture would permit, Dane could see a suggestion of red, but the sweep of bare sand, friendly in contrast, was now far removed from the space-craft.

Dane fiddled with the record prints, dealing them out one by one. The early hour of the reception was a puzzle in itself. No previous messages had come in earlier than 1000 hours. The early transmittal didn't jibe at all with his theory. Unless, he thought suddenly, it came from far over the horizon!

That would fit. Perfectly! It could also explain the distortion. Now he couldn't doubt it! He had to be right!

He got on the telephone and called the command post for Major Noel. Major Noel was on 2-low, the main drive deck. The voice that answered there told him the major couldn't be interrupted. It promised that the major would call him back as soon as he could. No, it couldn't call him now, he was inside the generator block with Major Beloit.

His eagerness cooling a little, he thought of calling Colonel Cragg. Might as well forget that. Noel was the better bet for this story. At first, at least. Especially with little more than two hours' time left before the take-off trial.

He went over to the ports. It was already a bright day. Very little high-altitude haze. Yellow sunlight poured over the lichens, warming them. The ice crystals would have already melted in their intercellular spaces, photosynthesis would soon be in process and their metabolism flourishing—in short, they would be living and growing. Seeping acid.

"Lieutenant," he said, "if you ordered them, do you suppose they would bring us up some sandwiches and milk?"

Yudin looked up from the papers he incessantly scribbled on watch. "Yeah. Why not? Hungry?" He picked up the phone and called the mess. After he had hung up, he said, "Good idea. I could stand one myself."

"You must be writing a book," Dane said on impulse. Yudin was an uncommunicative sort, until you got him started. Then he could talk you out of all patience. So you didn't often start him.

Yudin looked startled. "Journal," he said. "Two sections. One technical; one personal. It passes the time and I might be glad to have it someday." He gathered up the penciled sheets and carefully folded them away in his pocket, as if he were afraid Dane might ask to read a sample.

After they had eaten their sandwiches, there didn't seem much use in more talk. Until the phone rang.

Yudin picked it up. He listened for a minute and said, "Jesus." He listened again and said, "Yessir." He let the phone drop on its cord. "The lichens are beginning to cover the spacecraft. We're going to take off at 1000. He wants to speak to you."

Dane glanced at the clock. It stood at 0937. "Noel?" He grabbed up the instrument.

Noel came on briskly, with a tone of confident command. "If you like, you are welcome at the command post during take-off. Journalist's press pass, so to speak."

"Lichens on the outside of the hull?" Dane demanded.

"About a third of the way up to the midline. Colonel Cragg just now advanced the take-off to 1000 on account of them. Check in at the command post about five minutes before, if you are coming down."

"I've got something important—"

"Can't it keep until we get in the air? I'm crowded for time, man."

It might as well keep, Dane admitted. Certainly no time for it now. "How about sending a message?" he tried.

Noel didn't hesitate. "No. Absolutely not." He rang off.

Dane quickly dialed the control operator. "I've got to speak to Colonel Cragg. Urgent."

The man was doubtful. After a moment he came back on and wanted to know what was the nature of the urgency.

"I'll tell the colonel," Dane insisted.

The operator was sorry, but the colonel could not be interrupted unless they knew what the message concerned.

"Tell them to tell him John Dane is certain he has discovered the Martians and wants to send a message before we leave. For confirmation. We've got to make as sure as we can before we leave."

"What's that? What did you say?" the operator demanded.

"I've got it," another voice said. "This is McDonald. You mean what you said or you gagging to get through to the colonel?"

Dane referred him to an apt place to go.

"From here?" McDonald laughed, not too brightly. "Hold on."

In a minute he was back. "The colonel just chewed me out for even giving him your message. He says no transmitting. Absolutely none. Now I've got to speak to Yudin."

"Okay, it'll have to wait." Dane handed the phone to Yudin, who listened a minute and hung up.

"The idea is that you're not to send any messages to Martians or anybody else," Yudin told him. "I'm not supposed to let you even get close to the switch." He frowned. "Say, whatever goes on with you, I don't know. You've been a good guy to me and damn nice. I hope you don't try anything. That is, if you've got anything in mind. I just had orders to shoot you if you do. I don't want to have to do that. Not to you."

Dane whistled. "That guy's really got Tong Asia on the brain!"

169

"Look!" Yudin exclaimed. He pointed dramatically at the photo plane table.

The message stood forth bold and clear, the symbols as steady as vibrating light could make them.

"One arrives at spacecraft," Dane read aloud. While they watched, it faded and the familiar symbols came on for *One is good.* These faded immediately. The next that came read, *Death to men.* Abruptly it disappeared, to be followed by the first symbols, *One arrives at spacecraft.*

Yudin rushed to the port. "Damned if I see anything!"

"Don't be too sure," Dane said. Though he was sure himself that he knew, he went to the glassite panels. Outside was nothing to be seen but the lichens and beyond them the red sand.

Yudin was checking his revolver.

"I don't think that will do you any good," Dane told him.

Yudin looked him in the eye. "It'll take more than words, whoever sent it," he said with a dignity not at all absurb. Dane thought with surprise that the man had become confident and sure of himself. "If it's Tong Asia, it's a bluff," Yudin went on. "If it's Martians, they're up against the first team. Whatever they are, they're going to get a going over they'll not forget in a hurry."

He gestured at the far ports. "You, my friend, will stand over there, back to me. You will keep your hands on the guardrail. You can look out—"

"What in hell's eating on you?" Dane demanded.

"Do what I'm telling you," Yudin said. "I'm sorry but I can't take any chances. Get over there with your back to me and don't let go of the rail. If you're clean, it won't do any harm. You can watch the take-off just the same." A burr came into his voice. "I mean it. As far as I'm concerned, you're a good guy, but you're under suspicion. If you turn around, I'll have to fire. If you're clean, just stand there and you won't get hurt. It won't do any harm, and I'll apologize later."

Dane continued to stare. "You?" he said. "So maybe you're Tong Asia. Colonel Cragg wasn't all wrong after all."

"I mean it, Dane," Yudin said. He flourished the pistol purposely. "Turn around now and you can complain all you want to later. Take it to Colonel Cragg, and I'll apologize all you want. Right now, turn around! Like I just told you."

Dane saw the little beads of sweat under his temples. He said, "Okay." He went to the east port and took hold of the handrail below it, as if the game were cops and robbers. Behind him, he heard Yudin call down the message.

The phone clicked into its hook. "They say take-off is under way," Yudin said.

"I'll be sorry about this," he went on, "but I'd be a lot sorrier if I didn't do it. Right or wrong, I haven't got much choice. You agree with that?"

Dane said, "I suppose so. From your point of view."

"You see," Yudin said, "I've always admired you in a way. You've got a lot on the ball and you've made a name for yourself in your business. I always liked to read your stuff. It's not half baked like most of the newspaper stuff when it comes to any kind of technology. You always write like you really know something, instead of picking up a few facts and some of the words in a couple of quick interviews."

Dane laughed. "You're the first admirer I've ever met at gun point. As a matter of fact I haven't had too many."

The alarm buzzers sounded three shorts, followed by two longs, then repeated. A dull roaring made itself known below.

Dane eased his grip on the handrail. He shifted his palms slightly, feeling their stickiness. Earth, he thought. Home. In a few minutes the red landscape with its hostile lichens would fall out from beneath them, and soon they would pass out into the void, with the great mystery only guessed at. He knew the fear of death was deep inside him, as it was in everyone, but...well, there was no use thinking about that.

Yudin said, "One more minute!"

Dane braced himself for the application of lift thrust while the seconds ticked away. There would come only a gentle trembling of the Far Venture and a barely perceptible floating of the deck on which he stood. Still he couldn't keep from bracing himself.

It was happening before he noticed it. The rocket tubes were whispering like piny wind. Now metal quivered underfoot, and the whisper changed to a sullen humming as the power stepped up. Dane recalled the full-throated change of key to a whistling, whining blast when the Far Venture had repelled the weight of Earth and risen into the night sky of Arizona. Ears tuned for the rising pitch, he stared out at the lichens, waiting for them to sink away below when the Far Venture shook itself free.

"Here we go!" Yudin shouted above the mounting rocket song.

It was immediately obvious that they were not going. A hush sliced through the spacecraft. All power had been cut off.

There was a full minute of the unnatural silence before the speakers came on. A voice boomed harshly. "Colonel Cragg to crew. The take-off has failed. We have not been able to mount enough thrust. Work is being resumed on the drive, and another attempt will be made after further adjustments. All crewmembers and all civilian party will be kept equally informed. Periodic announcements will be made. You will all know any developments as soon as they occur."

Yudin cursed mildly. "And that, my friend, is our death warrant. He doesn't know anything more to do. That's what he really means. Since there isn't any hope, he'll tell us everything but that one thing. That he hasn't any real hope we'll ever leave this goddamn planet."

"Look," Dane reminded him. "Let's you and I forget about this game we're playing and put up that popgun. I've got something to tell him that may make a big difference."

He turned around slowly. Yudin managed a sheepish grin. He shoved the pistol back in his holster. Then his face hardened. "Now that I think of it, you just might at that. By any chance Vining wouldn't be involved in it, would he? Maybe you know something about why the drive won't move us?"

"Don't be a damn fool," Dane told him. "I think maybe I do know something about what's the matter with it. But if I'm right, Vining didn't do anything to keep the drive from working. And neither did I."

"A few days ago there was a pretty big think that maybe you did."

Dane went over to the photo plane table. "You think I want to rot here any more than you do? Take a look at this," he added conversationally. He was not surprised.

The message stood forth again. *One arrives at spacecraft. Death to men.* He read it off. "I think I've got the answer to that too."

Yudin grabbed up the phone and spoke rapidly. After a moment he stopped and listened. When he had hung up, he looked quizzically at Dane. "He says your ideas are probably as good as anybody's. That was Colonel Cragg himself," he explained. "He wants you to come down." He went over to the chart table and sat down. "The Old Man must really be stumped."

"Command post?" Dane was already on his way.

"Yeah," Yudin said.

CHAPTER TWENTY-EIGHT

Cragg swung the wheel chair around sharply. "So now you're ready to talk."

"I'm pretty sure about the Martians," Dane said. "And I've got an idea that may work to get us away."

The hard eyes did not deviate. "So it's still Martians. We have Martians in the drive, you think?"

"I think," Dane said. "I think the messages we have been receiving are genuine, so I think we have Martians right here at the spacecraft. Just as they say they are. I also think they are preventing us from a take-off."

"Just a minute." Cragg rolled his wheel chair to the bench and toggled a switch. "I want to record this."

"Suit yourself," Dane said. "Maybe I'm wrong and maybe I'm right, but it won't cost you anything to try out my idea."

At least Lieutenant McDonald and Sergeant Peeney were all attention, their headsets cocked up off one ear. "For days now we've received messages. The evidence is inescapable that there is knowledgeable life on Mars. Unless we go back to your Tong Asia theory. Then what are the Martians? Where are they?"

"Reasonable questions," Cragg dug at him. "Now are we to understand that you're going to tell us?"

"I may be," Dane said. "We have discovered only one form of life. As far as we have been able to investigate, we have entered an antiseptic world. Nothing lives in it except lichens. Why?"

"An equally obvious question would be why don't you come to the point?"

"For the sake of making your recording complete, let's add one more preliminary. The reason is that one form of life is so completely dominant that it has been able to exterminate any other life."

"If you mean the lichens," Cragg said, "what about your Martians? How come they were able to live?"

"Now I come to my point," Dane answered. "My first point. The answer is, the lichens are the Martians."

For a minute they were still; then Colonel Cragg grunted. He looked with mock patience at Lieutenant McDonald. "Complete with equipment to broadcast television messages, I suppose. Lichens!" he burst out.

"Excuse me, sir," McDonald interrupted. He pushed his headset up from his other ear. "Captain Finerty reports that the burning party is ready to go out."

"Hold it!" Dane exclaimed. "If you please," he added, not wanting to add to the man's temper. "The lichens will kill them. Like last night. At least let me say what I've got to say."

McDonald looked at the colonel. Cragg chewed at his lip but he nodded.

This man is not stupid at all, Dane thought suddenly. He's not missing any bet. "Supposing," he said, "the lichens might not only be individual plants but could also be, each one of them, members of a colony of plants made up of a lot of lichens that function as a whole, as one big plant. As an entity, I mean. We have colony plants like that on Earth among the lowest forms. In a college botany course I took in algae and fungi we made drawings of them under the microscope. I've always remembered one in particular called Volvox. The name reminded me of the *vox humana* stop, and I've never liked pipe-organ music."

Cragg hitched around to another position in his confining chair. "You're doing one helluva lot of talking, as usual. Without showing me anything. How about let's skip the biographical details? They're not very fascinating. Then you can get down to the point. I suppose you're going toward one. How come I'm always telling you to get to the point? You ought to talk less and say more. That goes for your writing too," he added. "In plain English, how in hell could lichens be Martians and send messages over the radar? That's what you said. That's what we're waiting to hear about."

It wasn't any time to get sore. Even to point out that that monologue itself was quite a speech for a man who admired brevity. "Volvox," Dane said, "is a hollow microscopic globe made up of thousands of independent one-celled plants connected by strands of cytoplasm, so that the colony functions like a multicellular individual instead of a mere physical aggregate. It reproduces as an individual to form new colonies. Forms eggs inside the colony, so to speak. What if the lichen plants here on Mars are formed into colonies something on the same order, individual plants linking themselves together to form a super-individual? Then what if the colonies have evolved intelligence, so that each colony is like a brain, one brain? Then each individual lichen plant in the colony might be the equivalent of one brain cell, or a cluster of brain cells. Just like the neurons and clusters in our own brains."

"The spark fires!" Cragg exclaimed.

"Right," Dane said. "The spark fires could very well be the discharges of mental action, just like the electrical currents in our own brains, only on a very large and powerful scale. Assume that the lichen colonies cover a large area and are all brain, then the network patches of spark fire are mighty suggestive to me of neural patterns, with the big bolts to connect them in larger associations, just as in human conscious thought."

"Now I'm damned!" McDonald gulped. "If you'll excuse me, sir."

"You and I both, Lieutenant," Cragg told him.

"It has to be right," Dane said. "By two or three hours after sunset the lichens are cold frozen. The spark fires die down and disappear. In the morning the plants warm up, and metabolism gets under way, and we get messages, starting about ten o'clock. By then they're warm enough to think. You remember how the patterns of the fires built up around Dr. Pembroke's scout and how they focused on the spacecraft. How they are aware of us I don't know. Maybe by projecting electromagnetic radiation and receiving reflections that are cast back. Like we do with radar. Maybe that's the way they communicate with us. One thing for sure, they can concentrate their mental electricity, assuming I'm right, and project it beyond themselves. The way they did at us last night. It all adds up," he urged. "The messages say the Martians are coming. Then the lichens grow out and surround us. We haven't found any other life here. Maybe long ago they did away with all other life. Now they can't endure the thought of any life but their own. Maybe the very idea of another life horrifies them and shocks them. Maybe it frightens them. Like we would be frightened by, say, the ants mutating into an intelligence like our own, but with mores descended from the folkways of ants. It adds up. They have covered Mars themselves, in a moral solitude of identical life. Now we come. A different life. Therefore evil. So they will destroy us. If they can."

Cragg shook his head. "It sounds impossible, Dane. If you're right, then they grew themselves out to reach us. Possibly to corrode the hull. But that doesn't account for the failure of the drive to activate like it should."

"But it does account for it!" Dane said. "Remember the radiation we experienced the first days we were here? What if they are able to emanate that? You remember the radiation built up in the daytime and reached its peak late in the afternoon. Then fell away to almost nothing at night. That points to the lichens again. When they noctivate, nothing much happens. When they are awake, we get messages, radiation, and spark fires. What if that radiation was meant to kill us off? Maybe along with it the lichens can also exert an electromagnetic field, like Vining thinks has got us caught. Maybe they are purposively exerting a field that throws out the balances of the drive so we can't get away."

"That's a lot of maybes," Cragg said.

"How can you fight a vegetation that grows all over the planet?" Lieutenant McDonald burst out. "There must be billions of plants. They grow faster than you can watch them."

"Maybe we might," Dane told him. "There is one more thing. It puzzled me, so I thought I was all wrong. This morning we got messages at 0700 hours. How could the lichens send them? With the sun up only thirty or forty minutes they would still be frozen. I was sure I had everything all thought out last night. I even wrote it down. Then when the messages came in so early, they upset the whole idea. Until I thought of something else. That was the one that scared me, but maybe it also gives us a chance to get away."

He went over to the globe of Mars in the corner and set it spinning on its axis. "There are vast lichen forests all around the globe. The sun is always shining on them. Somewhere it will be daytime and they will be awake and fully alive. The early messages simply came from lichens where it was already later than ten o'clock in the morning."

"The colonies linked together," McDonald said.

Dane said, "Maybe. It's the only answer that explains the early messages."

McDonald said, "Jesus! I say again how do we fight something like that! If we could destroy the plants around here, the rest would simply grow more. There wouldn't be any way to kill them all off!"

"Unless we find a way to break their hold on the drive, we haven't got a chance," Dane said.

Colonel Cragg was studying the wall charts of the planet. "There are several million square miles of them. Impossible to blast them all."

Dane said, "I wasn't thinking that, but of course it's a possibility. What I was thinking was that if we could only apply enough force to the Martian colonies to shock them severely, their attention might be relaxed or diverted enough to cause them to lose control of our drive. Then we could take off before they recovered."

"You got that one figured out too?" Cragg wanted to know.

"Maybe this might work," Dane went on. "We know they're sensitive to our radar transmissions, because they can get the messages we send. What if we transmitted a series of high-energy waves? We might be able to upset their mental processes temporarily. Maybe an overpowering transmission from us might have the same effect on the lichen brains through their receiving organs, whatever they are, as tremendously loud noises do on man. Maybe we can shell-shock them. Or maybe it might jam their mental currents and weaken their field of force against our drive. Assuming Vining is right."

"You told anybody about this?" Cragg demanded.

Dane said, "Not yet."

"We'll try it out," Cragg said abruptly. "Get Major Beloit and Lieutenant Yudin in on this," he ordered McDonald. "I want all the power we can put into the big peripheral antenna. I want all radar equipment—all the spare stuff—assembled and power line laid in and everything ready to blast out the granddaddy of all jamming in an hour.

Whatever you do, I don't want any testing to get into the antenna. When you're ready, let me know."

He nodded at Dane. "If your Mr. Martians can be jammed, maybe like you think, we'll give them one hell of a shock."

He grabbed at the hand wheel of his chair and rolled around at McDonald again. "Tell Major Beloit that the drive is to be ready to try another take-off in the next hour. I don't want any disassembly or adjustments that make it inoperative. Not unless I personally approve them."

McDonald said, "Yessir."

"Sergeant Peeney," Cragg plowed on, "I want our primary scientists in the mess hall right away. I want an opinion out of our head think gents before we start something."

"What's the matter, you think they might retaliate?" Dane asked him. He hadn't thought of that. But how could they? If it worked.

Cragg looked surprised. "I always expect retaliation when I attack. If I'm attacked I try to devise a successful counterattack. Why should I expect less of my enemy? Even if he is a Martian and I don't know one damn thing about him."

CHAPTER TWENTY-NINE

Dane looked around at the animated faces. "That's it. It adds up."

He was using that trite little phrase a lot recently. "The lichens are the Martians," he repeated defiantly.

He stood a moment before their gabble. Then he looked at Colonel Cragg. "That's it," he said.

Cragg said, "Gentlemen! Time is short. Supposing we speak one at a time."

In the new quiet Silverman's remark penetrated harshly. "What I'd like to know, Anson, is whether it's Dane or the lichens that are supposed to have plant cells for brains."

Dane decided Cragg didn't look any too well pleased at the civil engineer's introduction of the first name. He said, "It fits the facts. What facts we have." As for the crack, he let it fall.

"Except how do they think?" Wade demanded. "You can't have thought without something physical to support it. What tissue can we point to in the lichen that might support a thought process?"

Wertz frowned at the zoologist. "That's not a hard one. Many plant tissues on Earth are sensitive to various energies or stimuli. A lot of so-called organic substances respond to stimuli, particularly electrical. Even the shrinkage or expansion of iron under a temperature change is a form of internal sensitivity, reflecting a sort of rudimentary awareness to external change. It all depends on how you look at it."

"But *non!*" Cruzate exclaimed. "There is not the presence of nervous tissue. They are insensate plants. These lichens."

"My friend Jose," Wertz said, "you have the reputation of a great descriptive botanist. Possibly the greatest of our day." He paused while Cruzate acknowledged the compliment with a nod that became a bow. "But someday you're going to have to get up and leave at least the nineteenth century. Next you'll be telling us they can't think because they have no soul. I'm sorry," he added to Cruzate's shocked eyebrows. "But it's true, nevertheless, that abstract nomenclature like 'nervous tissue' has very little to do with actuality. Terms live in the half-line of descriptive science.

"Seriously, gentlemen, we don't want to forget for a minute that Earth experience isn't necessarily significant here. Even on Earth I wouldn't want to say that it was impossible to have conscious thought without nervous tissue. I don't see any reason, for example, why sensation couldn't float on the temperature changes of matter, building itself into complexities that could in their turn influence infinitesimally the temperature of the matter stuff, a body of matter if you like, and eventually erect consciousness and ratiocination within it. You can think of a thousand ways for thought to get born in the realm of chemistry, none of them requiring anything like nervous tissue. What do you say to that, boys?" He patted the table three times, as if that made his sayings so.

Dane found himself staring at the yellowed lids over Dr. Judah's dimming pupils. He was suddenly completely convinced that he had been right. "Then each unit of the body stuff, a lichen plant for example, might record units of awareness and associate itself with other units in interchanging reactions of sensitivity."

"I'm inclined to agree with you," Dr. Forrest broke in. "The spark fires could be energy discharges of lichen complexes that have been imprinted with stimulus patterns."

"Wait a minute, Mr. Bacteriology," Cragg said. "Hold it. Let's see if you can say that so the poor folks can understand it."

Forrest grinned. "What I meant was that the lichen acids could react on the soil and generate energy. Then emanations from the energy might be altered by external objects or even events, like temperature or light changes. These alterations might in turn modify the stored-up energy in the plant, so that the plant would be conditioned like a nerve cell. Then if groups of plants formed into special aggregates and took on larger and more complex modification patterns, you could have a basis for reflex awareness, then memory, then association, and finally conscious association or ratiocination."

"It's as good a hypothesis as any," Wertz said.

"*Non!*" Cruzate cried out. "It is impudent!"

Forrest said, "Another hunch has been hunching me ever since Dane started talking. Maybe some evolutionary change long ago jarred the lichens into an anti-life pattern, even before conscious thought evolved in them. So that it actually became their nature to seek out and destroy anything that lives."

Heileman regarded the bacteriologist. "They would have to have a method."

"It sounds farfetched," Forrest admitted. "But supposing they have evolved this unidentified radiation we register and, like Dane says, they tried to kill us with it. Maybe it's an anti-life radiation, if you want to call it that."

"*We're* still alive," Wade objected. "How come it doesn't get us?"

"It's just a speculation." Forrest shrugged. "Could be we're not susceptible in small amounts. After all, we're from another planet. It's only reasonable that we should be different. Like for them maybe it's only natural to destroy us."

Colonel Cragg said, "Okay. Apparently most of you agree. For my money John Dane's made as good a guess as any and I'm going to act on it."

He rolled his chair away from the head of the table. "Dane," he said, "how about giving me a shove to the lift? I'm a damn poor pilot for this thing."

CHAPTER THIRTY

Cragg put down his headset. He nodded at Dane. "All set."

The minute hand stood at seven minutes before 1100 hours. Dane looked at Major Noel. He was watching Cragg with the intensity Dane had seen on the faces of the roulette players at Golden Beach. The memory of the Gulf Coast smote him, lazing under the cumulous puffs, bright white and high over the sand splashed with girl colors. A new life, he resolved. If we make it okay. A new girl and the rest of the long Gulf summer to look for pleasure. Maybe an hour or two a day to write up the journal and cull out his photographs. Maybe most days to forget Mars as anything but a stained speck in the southeast evening sky. It was impossible to think that the beach would never come for him again.

You hope! Dane almost said it aloud, seeing the vivid beach scene.

Cragg was giving Lieutenant McDonald his orders. Pour out the shock waves for ten minutes. Then they would try the take-off.

He turned to Noel. "You will go to fire control and remain there for emergency, all guns and weapons ready. Report when you're ready at your station." He snapped his chair around smartly. "Sergeant Peeney, sound the alert. Take-off will be at 1110 hours. All personnel will now remain secure at their stations."

All at once Dane felt that now or never was the time to say his piece.

"Can you wait just one minute?" he said quickly. "There's one more thing I ought to tell you and Noel both, while we're all here together. I've got positive proof that Dr. Pembroke couldn't have knifed Colonel Cragg. Absolute airtight proof."

Noel swung hack. "Yeah. That I'd like to hear. It'd have to be good and airtight."

Cragg said, "We'll get on with our present business, gentlemen, if you don't mind. Time enough later for that."

"We don't know what's going to happen here in the next few minutes," Dane said. "I've got it all written down and sealed in that envelope I told you about. It's among my papers addressed to Major Noel, to be delivered to him if anything happens to me. It ought to be told first, before we take any more chances. So more than one will know about it."

"Noel?" Cragg said. "Why Noel?"

Dane said, "Because if I'm right, you're certainly still on somebody's list. And I know without any doubt I'm right."

"You've got a lot of envelopes around, haven't you, son?"

"It's pretty simple, after it occurred to me," Dane said. "I should have thought of it a long time ago."

Cragg moved impatiently. "Skip the preliminaries. Let's get right down to it."

"It's just this," Dane said. "The assumption has been made all along that Dr. Pembroke left the infirmary when the nurse went to mess from 1730 to 1800."

"That's the only time the door was unguarded," Noel said.

"There had to be at least one other time, and a later one at that," Dane told them. "Because Dr. Pembroke was still in his bed at about 1830. Here's how I know. We started receiving the first Martian signals that night about 1815. Almost immediately I called Captain Spear and asked him to check to see if anyone was outside the Far Venture. A few minutes later Captain Spear reported everybody present and accounted for. If Dr. Pembroke hadn't been in bed where he was supposed to be, Spear would have found it out."

Cragg said, "Sergeant, check the log."

Peeney flipped the pages, selected one, and ran his finger down the margin. "Yes, sir," he reported. "It's here. Just before the entry about the first signals coming in."

"Read it."

"Yes, sir." Peeney frowned at the page and cleared his throat. "'Checked all personnel for presence inside the spacecraft,'" he read. "'Requested by Dr. Dane. Dr. Dane reported reason to believe one or more personnel outside contrary to order of the commander. Head count completed at 1831. All present.'"

"There you have it," Dane said. "The colonel was attacked immediately after 1800 when Captain Spear relieved him at the command post. Dr. Pembroke was not guilty. He couldn't possibly have been. He was still in his bed at 1830 or very shortly before."

Noel said, "Unless he slipped out and did his knife act and went back to bed and then slipped out again after the head count."

Dane said, "After 1800 the nurse was on duty. He couldn't have got back in. Once maybe, watching for his chance, he might have slipped out when the nurse was in the john or something. But not in and out like it was payday at the bank. Not on that tight schedule. That nurse's station is right at the entrance and he sits there all the time. You also want to remember that Dr. Pembroke was still unconscious at 1600, when Captain King made his afternoon examination. Huh-uh," Dane told them, "You've lost your candidate."

Noel said, "Where's that put you, Dane?"

Dane said, "Right back on the observation deck. At 1800 I was climbing the ladders to get there."

Cragg said, "That's enough for now. We get away from here, we'll have a full-dress investigation. I know one thing. I didn't put that knife in my own back."

"One other thing," Noel said. "Spear's roll call wasn't a hundred percent perfect. If he made it around 1830, he ought to have discovered the colonel didn't answer and sent somebody to see why."

"He wouldn't check on me," Cragg said in a tone of affront. "Besides, he had just relieved me at the command post at 1800. He knew I was in the spacecraft. Whatinhell do you think I'd be doing outside!"

Noel said, "It was just a thought."

"Let's get on with this jamming idea," Cragg ruled impatiently. "Sergeant, change the alert. Take-off will now be at 1115."

Peeney flipped the switches and addressed a low, slow voice to the microphone. Neither Cragg nor McDonald moved when a jumpy buzzer gouged at the hushed command post.

Peeney flipped another switch and listened.

"Major Noel at station, sir. All weapons are ready."

The tardy minutes counted down. Cragg sat his wheel chair with irreproachable calm. Dane thought of Grant on his log in the evening of Shiloh's first day. Sergeant Peeney stood at the signal board like an acrobat on edge for his routine. Lieutenant McDonald perched a hip on the chart table, swung a leg to and fro.

At last Cragg moved his eyes, sweeping over them, each one, and said, "Here we go. Have Lieutenant Yudin apply full power to the antennas."

Peeney pulled a key and spoke into his microphone. After a moment he said, "Full power on now, sir."

It was anticlimax. Something visible or at least audible should happen. Dane needed events. He knew the unseeable, silent power was surging outward from their human island, but there was no difference now between four men waiting in a sealed, assault-proof chamber and what there had been before Cragg had given the word for action.

While the seconds ticked off, they held their tight tableau. The commander being silent, the others were constrained to silence. Dane felt the oppressive weight of it, heavy on the man who sat contemplative and outwardly indifferent among them.

Then there was no more suspense. Cragg leaned forward and said, "Start the take-off."

Peeney chucked a key on the communications panel. McDonald stood briskly up from the chart table and spoke into a microphone, "Commence take-off."

Cragg said, "Ten percent power."

McDonald repeated it in his microphone.

One of the banked speakers came alive, sporting its red pilot light. "Ten percent power recorded."

Cragg said, "Work it up to twenty-five."

McDonald repeated the order into the microphone.

Cragg looked reflectively at Dane. "Fifty-five will do it."

"Twenty-five per cent," the speaker interrupted. The voice was excited.

Cragg shot Dane a triumphant look. "It looks like you hit it! That's the best we've reached yet." His voice took edge. "Push it up to fifty-five. Then give her sixty."

Dane wondered at the absence of drive noise, before he remembered that the command post was soundproof.

The deck lurched. Dane fell hard against the bulkhead. The floor was dancing, and he was falling and sliding against the other wall. No take-off, he thought dimly, shielding himself against the clattering cascade of things.

The chamber's box swung once drunkenly and righted itself. A voice said, "Are you all right, sir?"

McDonald was bending over the colonel. Dane saw the frost pinching Cragg's lips.

"I'd better call Captain King," McDonald urged.

Cragg caught his breath. "No!" he grunted. He waved the lieutenant back. "Check on the damage. I want to know what happened." His eyes sought Sergeant Peeney. "Get Major Beloit on the hand phone."

Dane righted the wheel chair. He got his hands under Cragg's armpits.

"I can make it," Cragg protested. He put his palms down against the floor and pushed himself up on his knees. "Maybe," he gasped.

"Here," Dane said. He steadied Cragg's arm and shoulder and got him back in the chair, seeing his lips go white again.

"Major Beloit, sir," Peeney said.

Cragg took the phone. "What happened?" he demanded.

He listened without interrupting. Finally he said, "Check it over." He put down the phone. "That was a close one. The drive generators were entering runaway fission when Beloit and Vining managed to stop them. Basic field ratio shot up all at once. Emergency control had no effect on it. It looks like they blew at least two rocket-tube heads. Well?" he acknowledged McDonald.

"Sir, there isn't any indicated damage to the hull or principal structural members. Only one casualty. One of the civilians thinks his arm is broken."

Cragg brightened. "We came out of that one pretty lucky. We almost went over on our side." He shook his head. "That would have been it. Anyway, it sure looks like we're on the right track. We nearly made it that time. We were up to thirty-seven percent when we went out of control. For a guess I'd say we damn near had your Martians."

Dane said, "You mean they almost got us. Maybe we shocked them a little, but they were still able to come out of it and upset the balances on the drive."

"Maybe next time they won't." Cragg pointed at the wall charts of the two hemispheres of Mars. "There are millions of square miles in the green areas. That could mean a good many thousands of your colony intelligences. Nations of them maybe, with common interests and objectives. Such as destroying us. Maybe they don't even know we are trying to leave. They could easily think our take-off radiation is an attack on their life. You don't know what they think."

Dane wondered briefly at what had become of Tong Asia.

"Maybe we don't have the power to jam enough of them," Cragg went on. "But we're going to try it again if the drive will still operate. This time we'll heat 'em up for an hour before we try our take-off."

McDonald was holding one of the phones to his ear. He slapped it back on its contact and said, "Sir, Dr. Spivak reports external radiation has gone up rapidly since the explosion. It's now at twenty-eight percent penetrations and still climbing. Dr. Spivak says it's nearing double our estimated critical point. Hull temperature is rising."

A particularly unattractive death, Dane thought. For all their timageel shell, almost impregnable to a diamond drill, for all their careful insulations, the infinitesimal bullets were tearing through their bodies, smashing their soft organs, enfeebling their brain cells. In a few minutes, perhaps no more than an hour, they would be inseminated with the seed of death. By another day the Far Venture would be tenanted by the walking dead.

Cragg said, "Get me Major Beloit. We'll attempt another takeoff in fifteen minutes. Have Yudin turn full power into the antennas immediately."

Dane broke in. "Colonel, I've been thinking."

Cragg said, "Later."

Dane kept on talking. "The messages we have received have always talked about the Martians as 'one.' In the singular. Always. Maybe it's just their idiom, but then again it might mean that there is only one Martian. What would you think," he pressed on, "if all the lichens of Mars formed one big single plant colony? One enormous unit of intelligence? So that the entire growth of lichens on the surface of Mars is like the cortex of one tremendous brain? That could explain the 'one' business. Maybe the whole planet is one single mind. The local lichens around us would be just a small part of it. Even those in this hemisphere would amount to only about half. Maybe we only jammed a small part of the whole thing!"

"A vital spot!" Cragg exclaimed. "You mean that if there is only one big intelligence, all we have to do is find a vital spot? So how do we find it?"

"Not a vital spot. I wasn't thinking of a vital spot. It's a possibility, but I don't see how we're going to broadcast enough force to jam a mental activity that spreads over a whole planet."

Cragg banged down his fist. "We'll not rot here for lack of trying!"

A buzzer sounded. Dane saw the red light wink on the communications panel. McDonald flicked the key and spoke into his mouthpiece. When he had finished, he turned a serious face to Cragg. "Sir, the foreign radiation has passed three times the critical point. Spivak says maybe we have underestimated the critical point but not so much that we can take a triple dose. He says the hull temperature is already over four degrees higher. After correction."

Cragg pushed himself to his feet. With effort plain he made the few steps to the wall charts. He took up a grease pencil and made X-marks over the green continents. When he put the pencil down, his black crosses stood at roughly even intervals over all the lichen forests of Mars.

He said, "McDonald, take the co-ordinates of those points. Approximate them. Tell fire control that I want major primary nuclear missiles laid simultaneously on every target point I marked. Tell Major Noel that I will expect him to be ready to fire number one inside of five minutes."

He nodded at Sergeant Peeney. "Get me Major Beloit on the horn. Then alert all stations for another take-off."

He grinned crookedly at Dane. "I'll give you enough radiation to shock hell out of something. We'll see how your Martian brain can take a fission headache."

Dane counted the marks on the charts. Twenty-eight. Two dozen and a quarter of atom missiles. It was a grand slam or nothing!

Cragg got back into his chair without the help he disdained. He took the hand phone and said, "Beloit, I want another trial on take-off immediately... That's what I said," he repeated. "Immediately. In fifteen minutes, that is... I don't give a damn about the tubes. She'll have to climb out of here on what we've got left."

He listened some more. "Vining, I don't give a damn about the runaway fission either... No, you're mistaken. You don't have any responsibility for you to refuse to take. I have the responsibility."

He handed the instrument back to Sergeant Peeney. "He's a little nervous, Vining is."

Dane said, "He's got company."

Cragg laughed, "Why not? This isn't what I'd call a Sunday afternoon drive, myself." He shrugged. "So she blows, she blows. One thing for certain, we don't sit here on our rears for your Martian to roast us without trying something."

CHAPTER THIRTY-ONE

Finally five minutes were gone, and yet no word from Noel. The devil's eggs were not so quickly hatched. Dane noticed that he was rubbing his eyes. The incalculable particles plunging in through solid timageel and beryllium fluff, through the charged negate shield. Had they already burned his more vulnerable tissues?

The dull metal of the confining bulkheads seemed to glow with the malignant radiation. Dane stared at it, unable to dismiss the metallic sheen as simple reflected light. Sweat ebbed from his shoulders and trickled down under his coveralls.

At 1131 the buzzer sounded and Noel's voice came through. "All missiles laid for firing." It was six minutes after Cragg had given him the word.

Cragg pointed at the hand phone. He lifted it from Peeney's reach with expressionless care. "Buzz drive," he said. When he had his connection, he said, "Beloit, you ready for take-off?"

Dane heard Beloit husking the diaphragm.

"Good," Cragg replied. "Stand by." He swung to McDonald. "What does fire control calculate the lag from firing time to detonation on targets?"

McDonald sent the question over the wire. "Minutes 14, seconds 19," he relayed the answer to Cragg.

"We won't take it that long," Cragg snapped. "Step it up to maximum lag of minutes 5."

McDonald hesitated. "Sir, they're over escape velocity now. Major Noel is already afraid the missiles won't control."

Cragg swore. "So they don't! Just make sure they strike somewhere in the target regions. Hurry it up, man!"

McDonald grabbed at the microphone, missed, and grabbed again, but he repeated the order steadily.

A speaker crackled. Noel's voice came on the emergency circuit. "Noel to Colonel Cragg. Colonel, it won't work. I am preparing to fire on original calculations."

"Shut that damn thing off," Cragg roared. "Give me that pad, Sergeant." He scribbled rapidly. "McDonald, deliver this order to Major Noel. He is relieved from duty. You take over down there. Hurry it up. Take it over and let's go."

McDonald sprang smoothly alive. With one motion he snatched the paper and thrust past Dane. Peeney jumped to the door and worked the seal-off handles.

Cragg said, "I didn't think he'd ever crack. The man's like a machine." He swiveled the wheel chair around and urged it to the control desk. Jabbing out a hand, he scooped up the microphone and manipulated the switch keys. "Put Major Noel on. This is Colonel Cragg."

Dane heard a choked oath. He whirled around at the door. Peeney had it open now. Wide. Major Noel stood framed in the opening. He pushed a snub-nosed Air Force revolver rigidly forward, his lips twisted in a tight grin.

"At your service, Colonel," he said. "Temporarily." He swung the muzzle at McDonald. "If you and the sergeant will be good enough to get back out of my way."

"What in the very hell are you trying to do?" Cragg shouted. "You're under arrest!"

Noel chuckled. "A slight correction, sir. You are under arrest. I have taken over the command." He stepped inside. "Here are my orders." He waved the pistol.

"I wouldn't try it," he cracked sharply at McDonald.

McDonald's hand relaxed.

Cragg's voice shook with anger. "Noel, you will put that weapon here on the table and go to your quarters. We're under severe radiation. It's your life as well as ours, if we don't get off the ground immediately."

Noel nudged the heavy door shut with his foot. He put his other hand behind him and pushed down the dogging that sealed it. "Now that we're alone I'll attend to the take-off. First there are a few preliminaries." He looked at Dane. "I'm sorry you had to be in here. I owe you a debt. Anyway, you think too much. Worst of all, you talk too much."

Cragg said earnestly, quietly, "Noel, if you don't put that weapon down immediately, I'll give the order to shoot you."

Noel's eyebrows twitched. "No," he said conversationally. "I'm going to kill you. All of you."

With small movement he diverted the barrel and fired. McDonald cried out. He drove hard back against the bench and slumped to the floor.

The muzzle came squarely around. "That's one," Noel remarked. "Peeney, you're as good a first sergeant as there is in the Air Force, but you're here and armed too, so I'm afraid you're next."

Peeney shouted loud. "Not so damned sure..."

Dane saw Noel's eyes move away. He dived quickly at him and felt his shoulder hit hard. They went down in a thrashing heap.

The small body was wiry. Stringy strong. Dane swarmed all over it violently, expecting the blast and the tearing slug. When Noel's shoulder jerked powerfully, he knew where the weapon was. He flung his hand along the escaping arm and got it by the wrist. He felt the arm wrench and heard someone say, "Okay, I've got his pistol."

Noel's quick upthrusting hands found his throat and the thumbs bit gagging in. Dane fumbled for a finger to snap, felt the body go limp.

"That'll fix him!" he heard Peeney shout.

Dane got up on his knees over Noel's crooked sprawl.

Peeney said, "I socked him with his own pistol."

Dane saw Cragg busy on the microphone. Who's like a machine? he thought.

Cragg cut on the bank of speakers. "Missiles three, four, and five away," a voice announced. Then again, "Missiles six and seven away."

Cragg twisted around. "They're averaging out the co-ordinates. Is the lieutenant dead?"

They looked at Peeney bending over McDonald.

He nodded. "God damn him!" he said slowly. "I didn't hit him hard enough!"

Cragg said, "He's coming out of it. Watch him and have him taken out of here."

The metallic voice droned on, announcing the flight of the missiles.

"McDonald was a fine young officer," Cragg said.

Peeney said, "Yes, sir, he was at that."

"One more now we'll have to leave here," Cragg went on. "Even if we get off, we'll have to commit him to the air over Mars." He suddenly flared at Dane. "So he died at the post of duty. That won't make much of a story for your newspapers. Maybe you can find room for it, if you ever get there yourself, to say that it's not a bad end to meet. Even for a very young man."

"I'm sorry about the lieutenant, sir," Dane said.

Cragg looked up again. "Yes," he said, "of course. I don't always mean to be taking things out on you. You undoubtedly saved our lives. At least for a while."

"It was quick work," Peeney said. "I'd never have gotten in a shot. He had me covered."

Dane said, "Forget it."

Cragg was no longer listening. Eye on the sweep hand of the big clock, he stretched out his hand for the microphone. "Beloit? Thirty seconds…fifteen seconds…five seconds…"

A bank of red buttons winked simultaneously on the board before him. The missiles had exploded.

"Now!" he cried into the microphone.

All over Mars, Dane thought, the mushrooms were evilly erupting, piling up into the alien-thin air.

Cragg steadily poured on power. When he gave the order to push past twenty-five per cent, Dane took a long breath.

"Take it on to fifty. Easy," Cragg said into the mouthpiece.

Noel was mumbling now, a drool of words breaking up his harsh breathing. Possible skull fracture, Dane thought. Peeney would hit hard.

"Fifty-five," Cragg ordered.

Dane felt the deck move. Ever so slightly, yet a move! But his eyes on the radar altimeter still read zero.

"Sixty!" Cragg ordered.

The altimeter needle trembled. Then it shook itself free from the zero peg. Steadily it moved around to five hundred feet.

"Seventy-five!" Cragg demanded.

This I will never forget, not one small detail of this. Dane knew that. Not Peeney hunched and staring at the dials that were scoring their life or their death. Not the little lump of muscle that knotted along Cragg's scarred jaw. Not McDonald on the floor, dead two minutes too soon for the hope of life. Not the harsh blue coming back from the timageel walls and ceiling. Most of all, not the way one man was willing them off the ground of Mars.

Now he could feel the weight of his body against his leg vessels. The accelerometer trembled aslant from its null.

"Hold it right there," Cragg ordered Beloit. "Steady on seventy-five."

The words were scarcely said when the Far Venture lurched. Cragg's chair rolled hard against the wall. She bucked again and seemed about to lay herself over.

A speaker flared. "Yudin to Colonel Cragg. A message is appearing on the table!"

The Far Venture staggered like a skiff in a heavy tide rip. Dane was unable to stand free or loose his hold on the handrail. He thought of the altimeter. The needle was moving counterclockwise. They were losing altitude.

A monitor speaker sputtered again. "Colonel Cragg! Beloit to Colonel Cragg. We're not gimbaling right. We're losing the balance. Suggest we attempt a landing."

The Far Venture was falling in a list of thirty-five degrees. It was impossible to move against it on the canted deck or even to get out of the gutter that had received them, men and bodies, between crazy floor and tilted bulkhead.

"The microphone!" Cragg shouted.

Dane didn't dare look at the altimeter. He inched hand over hand along the rail toward the dangling instrument.

"Beloit to Command! Beloit to Command! Unless you instruct, I will attempt a landing."

Dane got his hand on the microphone. Grateful for the long cord on the spring reel, he slid back and gave it over to Cragg.

Cragg snatched it to his lips. For one flashing moment Dane saw his brow furrow and his eyes turn to the instrument panel askew overhead. Then he saw the decision form, the marred face relax, turn impassive.

He spoke impersonally at his mouthpiece. "Beloit. I want full power. Blast us to the hell off of here."

With some kind of a loud crash the bulkhead came up and smote Dane. Then another crash and they were rolling over floors and walls, pelted and battered by the odds and ends of furniture and each other's bodies.

Dane heard Beloit come in again on the speaker. "Beloit to Colonel Cragg. She's leaving us. Index is 117 percent. She'll rip herself apart!"

Cragg was sprawled in the stools and topped by his own wheel chair. Triumphantly he held to his phone. "Cut it back till it reads one hundred. Peeney," he shouted around the mouthpiece, "get to the switches and put me on to fire control."

Except the danger in the drive room, their flight was smoother.

After all, Dane thought, runaway fission is nothing but a chain reaction out of control. Just like a bomb. If it gets away, we'll never know it. Never know what hits us. Ergo, never feel it. "Christ, I must be radiation nuts!" he said out loud.

"Fire all remaining missiles," Cragg ordered.

Now the Far Venture entered hurricane seas. She pitched and rolled until only men strapped in their places could pretend to function. Cradling his head and face inside his arm, Dane abandoned himself to the forces that were wrenching the big spacecraft asunder. How the smoothly firing drive, no matter in what fashion disturbed, could produce such gyrations, he could not imagine.

Vaguely later, he caught a glimpse of a multitude of winking reel buttons. "Bombs exploded!" he yelled.

Some placated sea god laid hand over the angry waters. Listing far over, the Far Venture hung quietly in whatever space embraced her.

Dane got to the photo plane monitor and switched it into the message circuit on observation deck antenna. A scramble of meaningless lines danced randomly, like a madman's game of jackstraws.

The Martian was jammed! At least for the moment it was incoherent.

"Colonel Cragg!" he cried. "Are you all right?"

"Get me out from under!" Cragg sang out, loud in the quiet.

They lifted McDonald's body off him.

Cragg stared at the blood on his hands. "I don't think it's me." He felt inside his torn robe. "I don't think so."

"Give it full speed and let's get away fast!" Dane urged. "The Martians' transmission is all fouled up. Maybe we have stunned it. Now's our chance."

They helped Cragg to his feet and supported him while he watched the spasmodically flashing lines in the oscilloscope. He nodded to Dane. "Looks like you hit it right on the head."

He threw a glance at the angle-of-flight indicator before he raised the phone he had never let go. "Beloit. Give me maximum acceleration as fast as possible. To hell with the damage," he retorted. "Just give me as much speed as you can as quickly as you can. I want to get out in space. Away out in space. We'll worry about course later."

With acceleration the floor became the floor again. Shapes assumed their normal form. The Far Venture was again the familiar world where men stood upright.

CHAPTER THIRTY-TWO

For an hour the spacecraft shot up from the planet. Cragg let the acceleration grow until the ride felt like an elevator going through the roof.

Once he grinned. "She's responding perfectly to control. Now we make space, and it's good-by to your Martian." Then he sat with his eyes fixed on the command banks while the minutes worked around the clock. The fell radiation had vanished, but the radiomen could not raise Earth.

Finally he spoke to Major Beloit. The automatic acceleration control took over, and they stood free of their boots and weights at apparent gravity Earth. Then he said to Dane, "Give me a push. Let's take a look."

They went down the lift to 2-low and opened a port. The variegated disk of Mars bulged its green and red shapes of false continents and seas out from the tail cone against the star-spangled blackness.

Cragg pushed out his silver case brusquely at Dane and lighted one of the black stogies for him. Dane marveled at the man's vitality. If the rough-and-tumble take-off had any physical effect on him, it had been tonic. Cragg put the lighter to his own stogie and breathed out the first cloud of the pungent smoke, his eyes looking over the flame at Dane. "I think we've carried it off. Unless your Martian mind has got a long reach when it snaps out of its razzle-dazzle."

Dane said, "It disturbs me. I can't feel good about it. I hate to think that we found intelligence on Mars and then maybe destroyed it. Or left it impaired. Maybe insane. It's a pity we couldn't make it understand us!"

"Maybe it did," Cragg said. "Though for its own purposes. Maybe it understood us well enough to know it didn't want anything we had to bring. Maybe it just didn't like the idea of change."

Dane said, "We've had quite a history of that on Earth. Either you agree with me or I'll smash you for your wickedness, which you have already proved by your disagreement with me."

Cragg looked his stogie over carefully, rotating it in his fingers, inspecting the entire wrapper leaf. "When I was a young man I used to worry a lot about the poor prospects of heresy. The thing that bothered me was that the very idea of change came inevitably from reflective thought, but then the man who reflected couldn't help choosing some of his reflections as the best ones to believe. The next thing he inevitably did was to believe the others were wrong to believe. From there he had only one more step to take to intolerance and a new orthodoxy."

He stopped to puff at his failing light. "So we weren't so far from home on Mars after all. Your Martian's self-worship of its oneness is not so different from what we call doctrine. We were the heretics on Mars by the very fact of our existence. Why are we surprised? I'm pretty far away from my line, making a speech like that," he broke off with a deprecatory grin.

Dane shook his head. "Colonel, you've been the source of a lot of surprises to me on the Far Venture. Never any more than now."

"You once labeled me a man of action. I'm pretty sure you didn't mean it to be any compliment. That what you mean?"

"I underestimated you."

Cragg shook his head. "I underestimated you more than plenty. A week ago I'd have bet a million you didn't have the foggiest idea why sometimes you've got to make a decision and act on it just like it was one hundred percent right. Even if you're not sure of anything else except that it's high time to do something, one way or the other. Now I've seen you act when you couldn't add up the score. Like the night you brought Noel in. And today. When you took him out again. You turned out to be quite a man of action yourself.

"What I was trying to say about that heresy business," he went on, "was that I found in the Air Force the simple and satisfying belief in translating objectives into action. If you think about it that way, maybe even the way a guy like you would look at it, a man can have a rational and deliberate belief in the necessity of action. You can believe along with us that action is a right end in itself and that in its larger aspects, in what we call strategy and tactics, it stems from reflection. But what put the icing on my cake for me, what I'm trying to get across, is that I found out, after some time, I admit, that the only fixed Air Force doctrine was the insistence on constant change. The high rating on surprise and divergence from anything that could be predicted. Under the uniform of discipline I found a society of heretics. I don't say it very well, but that's what I mean."

Dane said, "Well, maybe so. But while we're on the subject of action and decision, I want to tell you it'll take quite a bit of something to match the way you jerked the Far Venture off the ground of Mars by single-handed main strength and pure cussedness."

Cragg wheeled over to a phone. "We're going on course for Earth," he said to Dane. "You want to watch?"

Dane was pleasantly warmed by Cragg's embarrassment. He was going to end up liking the guy if he didn't watch out.

"You know," he said, "you've maybe put the pieces of this trip back together for me. We've all got to hump like hell to avoid a society that organizes us into something like the Martian mind. It's a lot harder than avoiding the twentieth-century-style totalitarian state. Maybe the real danger is not so much in majorities squelching the heretics but in the simple gravitation of ideals to mass averages of conduct and attainment. After all, the worst threat of the twentieth century wasn't the nuclear revolution but the population explosion and the taboos that encouraged it. We don't want any Martian society of the common man stifling the uncommon man. That's the story I want to take back, but it will gag every wire of Amalgamated."

"You'd better sugar-coat it a little," Cragg said dryly.

Hour after hour the Far Venture sped among the star-bright constellations along its straight-line collision course with Earth. Noel's Automatic Interspatial Navigation Control delicately noted the Doppler shifts in the spectra of its three-star fix under the onrushing speed of the spacecraft and threaded them through its computer, balancing against them the shifting angle of Earth, checking the perturbations of course by sun and planets, firming the constancy of acceleration, juggling and firing the gimbaling steering jets, ever seeking the mystic point in space toward which home rolled in its orbit at eighteen miles a second, its own speed slimmed to a trifle by the massive velocities accumulating to the Far Venture.

Mars rapidly fell away, shrinking until it disappeared behind the Far Venture's flaring tail. When they neared the 600,000-miles-out mark, they passed into radio communication with Earth. Colonel Cragg sent out the momentous message of success. Thousands of words of reports began feeding into the coding and transmitting machines, and Dane plunged into the writing of bulletins and dispatches for official release on Earth by the Air Force. Not too heavily slashed, he hoped, by security review.

A few minutes after first radio contact Colonel Cragg posted a message of commendation from the White House, personal from the President of the United States. Dane could imagine the milling pressrooms at Amalgamated. Ames would have taken over personally. No doubt about that. Already television and radio bulletins and the banners of extras had spread the opening lines of the greatest news story of all time. Dane icily penciled the head on his copy paper. The inevitable head. LIFE ON MARS! You could bet on that one. With it the unique Earth, stubbornly held by millions as the only possible abode of life, was gone forever. And with the news of intelligent life, also went the stubbornly insisted uniqueness of man. If here, on a second planet, then there on millions of planets orbiting everywhere amid the countless trillions of suns. In the near galaxies and the far galaxies. In myriad forms. The miracle of life was reduced to the commonplace and the expected. Likewise the miracle of man. Not alone, in solitary majesty, did he exist, but as neighbor to a billion sensate fantasies beyond his feeble mannish imagination. How would he take to such new gospel?

On the second clay, early, they passed the quarter-way point and had attained a speed of over 575 miles per second. Earth was bright, dominant among the stars off the right nose. The spectacular sun sealed out on the left rear shot its prominences visibly higher on the observoscope, crimson tongues licking at its black panoply. In the afternoon Dane had word that Major Noel wanted to talk to him.

The room was stripped down to the built-in bed. The nurse brought Dane a light plastic stool. The insignia missing from the blue coveralls hadn't changed Noel's appearance. To Dane his mixed-up dark face looked the same as ever. His voice was normal, like his manner, when he said hello.

"How are you feeling?" Dane couldn't think of anything else to say.

Noel darted his eyes about for a moment, then got up and closed the door the nurse had left ajar. At once it reopened, and the nurse stuck his head in.

"Shut the door, man," Noel snapped in his familiar manner of command.

The nurse looked at Dane. Dane nodded, and the door drew quietly shut.

"I want to talk to you," Noel announced.

"You know I'm a newspaper type," Dane said.

"That's why I picked you. There'll be a lot of crap printed over this and I want to make one thing plain to you. If I can do it. I'm no goddamn traitor."

Dane said nothing.

"I want you to believe me. You've been along with us. You know why I want you to believe that. I don't want that on my name." He picked at the blue coveralls. "Or on this. I don't want it even mentioned on this."

Dane decided there was nothing to say to that either.

"I've committed a sin," Noel said. "It's an obsolete word, but the act is not obsolete."

It was going to be an uncomfortable session. "I don't get you," Dane said. He couldn't think of anything else to say.

"I've committed a crime too. Murder. But I'm no goddamn traitor. Murder I can pay for. The sin I can't ever pay for. Call this a confession if you like. In the old meaning of the word."

"Look," Dane said, "like I told you, I'm a newspaper guy. Don't tell me anything. You're going to need a lawyer before you do any talking."

For a minute he thought he had lost the man. The tight little face squeezed into its wrinkles. The eyes suddenly reminded him of acorns. Why that? he wondered. You couldn't write a thing like that. Every damn reader would think howinhell can eyes look like acorns? But they did.

Noel grabbed up a stogie that looked exactly like the ones Cragg preferred.

"God damn him, he sends me these. So God damn him, I'll smoke them. At least I'll break even for once with the bastard. I put a knife in him and he sends me a box of cigars. For good services rendered-up to now. I know how the guy thinks. What do I get if I hit the jackpot! He whips me even with his back turned. I couldn't even kill the sonofabitch with a wide-open invitation. That old woman King thinks I'm a nut; so Colonel Cragg thinks I'm a nut and puts me in the hospital and sends me cigars. I want you to put that straight too. I'm a nut all right, but not the way King thinks. If he thinks. I've got to add up my own score. No hospital, no prison, no damn box of cigars is going to help a damn bit."

Noel hitched closer on the edge of his bed. "That's why I called you in. You're right in my book. I also owe you a big one, even if I do wish to hell you'd left me out there. But you had to drag me in. So now you owe me too. I'm your baby, boy."

Here it comes, Dane thought. "What do you expect?" he said.

"It's a sin. The worst one of all. My goddamn vanity. *Vanitas vanitatem,* crieth the preacher. For once he was right. The unseemly vanity of vanity. It's the sin of command. First you think it's you. Then you think it ought to be you. Then you think it's got to be you. I wanted the power, okay. Then I coveted the name. Not okay. So I tried to kill him for his name. Commander of the Far Venture. First flight to Mars. My spectrum beacon or he wouldn't even have been here. I would have brought the spacecraft home just as well as Colonel Cragg. Christ, what a cockeyed idea. The guy's got it. He's got it. He was born with it. That's why I put the knife in him. He's got it and I don't have it. And he and I both know it."

"Pembroke?" Dane interrupted him. He was embarrassed. Men like Noel shouldn't break down.

"How do you think he got out of the spacecraft? Sure the lock works automatically. He leaves the outside trap open, the next push on the inside entrance button, it closes before the upper hatch can be opened. I saw him go. I let him go. You think all that goes on and I don't know? He thinks he's after Beemis and Jackson. He's on the goof. So I help him. He's a good murderer. But he comes back. Somehow he comes back. Pembroke was just a cover-up. I can pay for that. The law provides a payment for that."

"Beemis and Jackson?" Dane wanted to know.

Noel shook his head. "I don't know. It was a good idea at the time. Foul it up for Cragg. Work him into it. Make him look bad. Call it whatever you want to call it. I can pay for Beemis and Jackson too. But the sin. How do I pay for that! I might just as well have been a goddamn traitor. I betrayed the uniform, you dope! Not to Tong Asia. Here!" he pounded his heart. "Here I betrayed it! For the damn lousy sake of vanity!"

He got up and opened the door. "That's it. Think about it yourself a little, before you write about me."

Ames, Dane thought down the passageway. Ames! The vanity of despising Ames! Because he was good, what he was good at was worthless, even if millions found it good. A negative vanity to match the more forthright one of Noel.

Captain King was in the flight surgeon's office. He shook his head. "He's caught now. It's a defense mechanism. It won't play in tune with the facts. Besides, it's characteristic."

Dane said, "I don't know. Maybe yes."

"Dane, it's typical. For days he would go along level, and he doesn't like what he's thinking. Then blip, he goes haywire for a while. Once he goes too far haywire. Then he's got a load to carry, and that doesn't help him any. Probably he's had a latent paranoia for a long time. Aggravated maybe by the situation. That rap he had on the head once wouldn't help it any. Brain's a funny thing. Hurt it—who knows how it heals? Confinement in the spacecraft. Worry. Responsibility. Looking back, you can see he was different after he took over. Then Cragg comes back. He's depressed again. But it's always been there. Probably from adolescence." He shrugged a *quod erat demonstrandum.*

Dane said, "No, I don't go along with that at all. Noel's probably as sane as you or me or any of us. We all straddle the rail. We covet our neighbor's ox and his wife too, maybe. One man takes one more drink and there's hell to pay. One way or another. Maybe he doesn't get caught. But he has to pay for hell just the same. The rest of us just keep on lusting. Noel's sound as a dollar on that one. It's not the punishment that's worrying him. He cracked his own idol. His own idea of himself. It wasn't the overt act. It's the idea that led to it that's eating him."

"You think I trifle on my wife?" King huffed.

Dane said, "Do you? How should I know what you want?"

At thirty-seven hours out the Far Venture sped near the midpoint. The power was cut, and with all personnel strapped in place, the delicate job of firing the steering jets to nudge the Far Venture into a half turn on her transverse axis was undertaken and successfully completed. Now with her nose again addressed to far-off Mars, she plunged tail-first toward the meeting with Earth, fifty-five million miles away. The drive was brought on, and deceleration began. Slowly the speed dropped off, and Earth, the green star that blazed brighter than all others, disappeared in front of the onward rushing tail cone.

On the third day they were so near that a segment view of familiar shapes and continents hung past the edge of the rocket housing. In a few hours they would be landing.

As he watched from the lower ports, Dane saw the cloud-flecked coast line of the Mexican Gulf swing up out of the distortion of the arcing globe, rising out of the rim fog and the vapor masses that circled the visible partisphere and merged into the halo of ambient air, clear-cut against the black of space. In only the inner elements could Dane make out the homely outlines of his childhood maps, but there, clearly, was the coast of Texas and opposite it the long thumb of Florida pointing at a Cuba veiled by the cloud pocks of the Caribbean.

The United States of America! Dull tints after dazzling Mars, a commingling of brownish-yellowish-greenish nondescript hue, but touched with a glory carried unforgotten and brought with them home.

Yes, as Colonel Cragg had pronounced, the reconnaissance had succeeded. Much of what they had gone for had been done. They had answered the riddle of the ages. Now men would go again, and elsewhere, being bred not only to vision but to action. Men would not rest content with bare knowledge that there are other minds than man's, that mankind does not dwell in solitude amid the insensate matter whence it sprang.

The persistent edge of depression fell from him. Only their own far venture had, in its larger meaning, failed. Perhaps other venturings would sometimes, somehow, overcome the universal hostility to the unknown, and man would communicate peacefully in yet unnamed worlds with the wide-apparent phenomenon of mind. Meantime much of a kindred and more important achievement remained for him on his native Earth.

THE END

If you've enjoyed this book, you will not want to miss these terrific titles…

ARMCHAIR SCI-FI, FANTASY, & HORROR DOUBLE NOVELS, $12.95 each

D-1 **THE GALAXY RAIDERS** by William P. McGivern
SPACE STATION #1 by Frank Belknap Long

D-2 **THE PROGRAMMED PEOPLE** by Jack Sharkey
SLAVES OF THE CRYSTAL BRAIN by William Carter Sawtelle

D-3 **YOU'RE ALL ALONE** by Fritz Leiber
THE LIQUID MAN by Bernard C. Gilford

D-4 **CITADEL OF THE STAR LORDS** by Edmund Hamilton
VOYAGE TO ETERNITY by Milton Lesser

D-5 **IRON MEN OF VENUS** by Don Wilcox
THE MAN WITH ABSOLUTE MOTION by Noel Loomis

D-6 **WHO SOWS THE WIND…** by Rog Phillips
THE PUZZLE PLANET by Robert A. W. Lowndes

D-7 **PLANET OF DREAD** by Murray Leinster
TWICE UPON A TIME by Charles L. Fontenay

D-8 **THE TERROR OUT OF SPACE** by Dwight V. Swain
QUEST OF THE GOLDEN APE by Ivar Jorgensen and Adam Chase

D-9 **SECRET OF MARRACOTT DEEP** by Henry Slesar
PAWN OF THE BLACK FLEET by Mark Clifton.

D-10 **BEYOND THE RINGS OF SATURN** by Robert Moore Williams
A MAN OBSESSED by Alan E. Nourse

ARMCHAIR SCIENCE FICTION CLASSICS, $12.95 each

C-1 **THE GREEN MAN**
by Harold M. Sherman

C-2 **A TRACE OF MEMORY**
By Keith Laumer

C-3 **INTO PLUTONIAN DEPTHS**
by Stanton A. Coblentz

ARMCHAIR MASTERS OF SCIENCE FICTION SERIES, $16.95 each

M-1 **MASTERS OF SCIENCE FICTION, Vol. One**
Bryce Walton—"Dark of the Moon" and other tales

M-2 **MASTERS OF SCIENCE FICTION, Vol. Two**
Jerome Bixby—"One Way Street" and other tales

If you've enjoyed this book, you will not want to miss these terrific titles…

ARMCHAIR SCI-FI & HORROR DOUBLE NOVELS, $12.95 each

D-71   **THE DEEP END** by Gregory Luce
        TO WATCH BY NIGHT by Robert Moore Williams

D-72   **SWORDSMAN OF LOST TERRA** by Poul Anderson
        PLANET OF GHOSTS by David V. Reed

D-73   **MOON OF BATTLE** by J. J. Allerton
        THE MUTANT WEAPON by Murray Leinster

D-74   **OLD SPACEMEN NEVER DIE!** John Jakes
        RETURN TO EARTH by Bryan Berry

D-75   **THE THING FROM UNDERNEATH** by Milton Lesser
        OPERATION INTERSTELLAR by George O. Smith

D-76   **THE BURNING WORLD** by Algis Budrys
        FOREVER IS TOO LONG by Chester S. Geier

D-77   **THE COSMIC JUNKMAN** by Rog Phillips
        THE ULTIMATE WEAPON by John W. Campbell

D-78   **THE TIES OF EARTH** by James H. Schmitz
        CUE FOR QUIET by Thomas L. Sherred

D-79   **SECRET OF THE MARTIANS** by Paul W. Fairman
        THE VARIABLE MAN by Philip K. Dick

D-80   **THE GREEN GIRL** by Jack Williamson
        THE ROBOT PERIL by Don Wilcox

ARMCHAIR SCIENCE FICTION CLASSICS, $12.95 each

C-25   **THE STAR KINGS**
        by Edmond Hamilton

C-26   **NOT IN SOLITUDE**
        by Kenneth Gantz

C-32   **PROMETHEUS II**
        by S. J. Byrne

ARMCHAIR SCIENCE FICTION & HORROR GEMS SERIES, $12.95 each

G-7   **SCIENCE FICTION GEMS, Vol. Seven**
        Jack Sharkey and others

G-8   **HORROR GEMS, Vol. Eight**
        Seabury Quinn and others

www.ingramcontent.com/pod-product-compliance
Lightning Source LLC
Chambersburg PA
CBHW030326180626

46810CB00003B/1241